naive, and deeply satisfying. I devoured it. This is one that's going to stay with me for a long time."

—Sarah Gailey, author of *Magic for Liars*

"A deeply satisfying and darkly funny feminist fairy tale . . . The plot snaps along as quickly as a good joke, and beneath the whimsy, there's an underlying sympathy and sincerity that enables Kingfisher to handle tricky issues like domestic violence with great compassion and care. At its heart a story of good people doing their best to make the unjust world a fairer place, this marvelous romp will delight Kingfisher's fans and fairy tale lovers alike."

—*Publishers Weekly* (starred review)

"Somehow, Kingfisher writes stories that put you at your ease and make you want to crawl out of your skin at the same time. I loved the way this horrified me—and, in the end, gave me hope. Marra's journey is a memorable and entertaining one filled with bone dogs, demon chickens, godmothers, and conversations with the dead."

—Kevin Hearne, *New York Times* bestselling author of the Iron Druid Chronicles

"Charming and macabre—often both at the same time—*Nettle & Bone* has bite, proper jokes, effortlessly good storytelling, and a really wonderful tomb labyrinth. I finished it and had to go read three more of T. Kingfisher's books because I was sad it was over. *Nettle & Bone* is so good! I loved it."

—A. K. Larkwood, author of *The Unspoken Name*

"This book is so exciting, deeply wise, sad, brutal, and compassionate all at once. And beautifully written, with a plot as cunning as fine embroidery. I can tell that this is a story that will linger with me. I hope it does. When I finished I could hardly bear to tear myself away from this eerie, vivid world, with its struggling, flawed, wonderful characters. I will miss Bonedog in particular."

—Catriona Ward, author of *The Last House on Needless Street*

NETTLE
&
BONE

T. Kingfisher

Tor Publishing Group
New York

NETTLE & BONE

Endpaper art by Ursula Vernon

A Tor Book
Published by Tom Doherty Associates/Tor Publishing Group
120 Broadway
New York, NY 10271

www.tor-forge.com

The Library of Congress has cataloged the hardcover edition as follows:

Names: Kingfisher, T., author.
Title: Nettle & Bone / T. Kingfisher.
Other titles: Nettle and Bone
Description: First Edition. | New York : Tor/Tom Doherty Associates Book, 2021. |
Identifiers: LCCN 2021041767 (print) | LCCN 2021041768 (ebook) |
ISBN 9781250244048 (hardcover) | ISBN 9781250244031 (ebook)
Classification: LCC PS3611.I597 N48 2021 (print) |
LCC PS3611.I597 (ebook) | DDC 813/.6—dc23
LC record available at https://lccn.loc.gov/2021041767
LC ebook record available at https://lccn.loc.gov/2021041768

ISBN 978-1-250-24400-0 (trade paperback)

Our books may be purchased in bulk for promotional, educational, or business use. Please contact your local bookseller or the Macmillan Corporate and Premium Sales Department at 1-800-221-7945, extension 5442, or by email at MacmillanSpecialMarkets@macmillan.com.

First Tor Paperback Edition: 2023

Printed in the United States of America

0 9 8 7

dedicated to Strong Independent Chicken,
a bird in a million

NETTLE
&
BONE

Chapter 1

The trees were full of crows and the woods were full of madmen. The pit was full of bones and her hands were full of wires.

Her fingers bled where the wire ends cut her. The earliest cuts were no longer bleeding, but the edges had gone red and hot, with angry streaks running backward over her skin. The tips of her fingers were becoming puffy and less nimble.

Marra was aware that this was not a good thing, but the odds of living long enough for infection to kill her were so small that she could not feel much concern.

She picked up a bone, a long, thin one, from the legs, and wrapped the ends with wire. It fit alongside another long bone—not from the same animal, but close enough—and she bound them together and fit them into the framework she was creating.

The charnel pit was full, but she did not need to dig too deeply. She could track the progression of starvation backward through the layers. They had eaten deer and they had eaten cattle. When the cattle ran out and the deer were gone, they ate the horses, and when the horses were gone, they ate the dogs.

When the dogs were gone, they ate each other.

It was the dogs she wanted. Perhaps she might have built a man out of bones, but she had no great love of men any longer.

Dogs, though . . . dogs were always true.

"He made harp pegs of her fingers fair," Marra sang softly, tunelessly, under her breath. "And strung the bones with her golden hair . . ."

The crows called to each other from the trees in solemn voices. She wondered about the harper in the song, and what he had thought when he was building the harp of a dead woman's bones. He was probably the only person in the world who would understand what she was doing.

Assuming he even existed in the first place. And if he did, what kind of life do you lead where you find yourself building a harp out of corpses?

For that matter, what kind of life do you lead where you find yourself building a dog out of bones?

Many of the bones had been cracked open for marrow. If she could find two that went together, she could bind them back to wholeness, but often the breaks were jagged. She had to splint them together with the wires, leaving bloody fingerprints across the surface of the bones.

That was fine. That was part of the magic.

Besides, when the great hero Mordecai slew the poisoned worm, did he complain about his fingers hurting? No, of course not.

At least, not where anyone could hear him and write it down.

"The only song the harp would play," she crooned, "was O! The dreadful wind and rain . . ."

She was fully aware of how wild she sounded. Part of her recoiled from it. Another, larger part said that she was kneeling on the edge of a pit full of bones, in a land so bloated with horrors that her feet sank into the earth as if she were walking on the surface of a gigantic blister. A little wildness would not be out of place at all.

The skulls were easy. She had found a fine, broad one, with powerful jaws and soulful eye sockets. She could have had dozens, but she could only use one.

It hurt her in a way that she had not expected. The joy of finding one was crushed easily under the sorrow of so many that would go unused.

I could sit here for the rest of my life, with my hands full of wire, building dogs out of bone. And then the crows will eat me and I will fall into the pit and we shall all be bones together . . .

A sob caught in her throat and she had to stop. She fumbled in her pack for her waterskin and took a sip.

The bone dog was half-completed. She had the skull and the beautiful sweep of vertebrae, two legs and the long, elegant ribs. There would be at least a dozen dogs in this one, truly—but the skull was the important thing.

Marra caressed the hollow orbits, delicately winged in wire. Everyone said that the heart was where the soul lived, but she no longer believed it. She was building from the skull downward. She had discarded several bones already because they did not seem to fit with the skull. The long, impossibly fine ankles of gazehounds would not serve to carry her skull forward. She needed something stronger and more solid, boarhounds or elkhounds, something with *weight*.

There was a jump rope rhyme about a bone dog, wasn't there? Where had she heard it? Not in the palace, certainly. Princesses did not jump rope. It must have been later, in the village near the convent. How did it go? *Bone dog, stone dog . . .*

The crows called a warning.

She looked up. The crows yammered in the trees to her left. Something was coming, blundering through the trees.

She pulled the hood of her cloak up over her head and slid partway down into the pit, cradling the dog skeleton to her chest.

Her cloak was made of owlcloth tatters and spun-nettle cord. The magic was imperfect, but it was the best she had been able to make in the time that she had been given.

From dawn to dusk and back again, with an awl made of thorns— yes, I'd like to see anyone do better. Even the dust-wife said that I had done well, and she hands out praise like water in a dry land.

The cloak of tatters left long gaps bare, but she had found that this did not matter. It broke up her outline so that people looked through her. If they found some of the bands of light and shadow lay a little strangely, they never stayed long enough to puzzle out why.

People were remarkably willing to dismiss their own sight. Marra thought perhaps that the world was so strange and vision so flawed that you soon realized that anything and everything could be a trick of the light.

The man came out of the trees. She heard him muttering but could not make out the words. She only knew it was a man because his voice was so deep, and even that was guesswork.

Most of the people of the blistered land were harmless. They had eaten the wrong flesh and been punished for it. Some saw things that were not there. Some of them could not walk and their fellows helped them. Two had shared a fire with her, some nights ago, although she was careful not to eat their food, even though they offered.

It was a cruel spirit that would punish starving people for what they had been forced to eat, but the spirits had never pretended to be kind.

Her companions at the fire had warned her, though. "Be careful," said one. "Be quick, quick, quiet. There's a few to watch for. They were bad before and they're worse now."

"Bad," said the second one. His breathing was very labored and he had to stop between each word. She could tell that it frustrated him, trying to speak between the pauses. "Not . . . right. All . . . of us . . . now"—he shook his head ruefully—"but them . . . *angry.*"

"It doesn't do any good to be angry," said the first one. "But they won't listen. Ate too much. Got to like the taste." She cracked a laugh, too high, looking down at her hands. "We stopped as soon as there was something else, but they kept eating it."

The second one shook his head. "No," he said. "More . . . than that. Always . . . angry. Born."

"Some are born that way," Marra agreed, nodding to him. She knew too well.

Some of those people are men. Some of those men are princes. Yes, I know. It is a different kind of anger. Something darker and more deliberate.

He looked relieved that she had understood. "Yes. Angrier . . . now. Much."

All three of them sat in silence around the fire. She stretched her hands toward the flames and exhaled slowly.

"Mostly they kill us," said the first one abruptly. "We can't always run. Things get confused—" She sketched a gesture in the air above her eyes that Marra could not begin to understand, although her companion nodded when he saw it. "We're easy to catch if it's like that. But if they see you, they'll try for you, too."

The fire crackled. This land was very damp, and she was grateful for the heat, and yet— "Aren't you worried that they'll see the fire?"

The woman shook her head. "They hate it," she said. "It's the punishment. The more they eat, the more they fear it—they do not cook the flesh, you see . . ." She rubbed her face, obviously distressed.

"Safer," said the man. "But . . . can't burn . . . all the time."

They leaned against one another. She bent her head down against his shoulder and he reached his arm across his body to hold her close.

A few days ago, Marra would have wondered why they did not leave this terrible land. She no longer did. They might not be sane, as the outside world understood it, but they were not fools. If they felt that they were safer here than they were outside it, it was not her place to tell them otherwise.

If I had to explain to everyone I met what had happened to me, have them judge me for what I'd had to do—no, I might think a land with a few roving cannibals was a small price to pay, myself. At least here, everyone understands what's happened, and they are as kind to each other as they can be.

As a girl, she would not have understood that, but Marra was not the girl that she had been. She was thirty years old, and all that was left of that girl now were the bones.

For a moment she had envied them, two people punished through no fault of their own, because they had each other.

Now, as she sat in the pit of bones, the skeleton cradled against her chest twitched.

"Shhhh . . ." whispered Marra into the skull's openings. "Shhhhh . . ."

Bone dog, stone dog . . . black dog, white dog . . .

She heard the footsteps as he approached. Had he seen her?

If he had, then he, too, dismissed it as a trick of the light. The footfalls skirted the edge of the pit, and the sound of breathing faded away.

"Probably harmless," she murmured to the skull. Even if he were not, she would be a difficult target.

The other, gentler folk in here were uniquely vulnerable. If you had learned not to trust your own senses, you might wait too long to run from an enemy.

Marra was no longer as sure of her own perceptions as she had once been, but the edges of her mind were only slightly frayed, not blasted open by furious spirits.

When the footsteps had been gone for many minutes and the crows had settled, she sat up again. Fog lined the edges of the wood, hanging in low swirls over the meadow. The crows cawed together like a disjointed heartbeat. Nothing else moved.

She bent back over the bone dog again, fingers moving on the wires, hoping to finish her task before darkness fell.

* * *

The bone dog came alive at dusk. It was not quite completed, but it was close. She was bent over the left front paw when the skull's jaws yawned open and it stretched as if waking from a long slumber.

"Hush," she told it. "I'm nearly done—"

It sat up. Its mouth opened and the ghost of a wet tongue touched her face like fog.

She scratched the skull where the base of the ears would be. Her nails made a soft scraping sound on the pale surface.

The bone dog wagged its tail, its pelvis, and most of its spine with delight.

"Sit still," she told it, picking up the front paw. "Sit, and let me finish."

It sat politely. The hollow eye sockets gazed up at her. Her heart contracted painfully.

The love of a bone dog, she thought, bending her head down over the paw again. *All that I am worth these days.*

Then again, few humans were truly worth the love of a living dog. Some gifts you could never deserve.

She had to wrap each tiny foot bone in a single twist of wire and bind it to the others, then wrap the entire paw several times, to keep it stable. It should not have held together, and yet it did.

The cloak had gone together the same way. Nettle cords and tattered cloth should have fallen apart, and yet it was far more solid than it looked.

The dog's claws were ridiculously large without flesh to cloak them. She wrapped each one as if it were an amulet and joined them to the basket of thin wires.

"Bone dog, stone dog," she whispered. She could see the children in her head, three little girls, chanting to each other. *Bone dog, stone dog . . . black dog, white dog . . . live dog, dead dog . . . yellow dog, run!*

At *run*, the little girl in the middle of the rope had jumped out and begun to run back and forth through the swinging rope, the only sound her feet and the slap of the rope in the dust. When she finally tripped up, the two girls on the ends had dropped the rope and they had all begun giggling together.

The bone dog rested his muzzle on her forearm. He had neither ears nor eyebrows, and yet she could practically feel the look he was giving her, tragic and hopeful as dogs often were.

"There," she said, finally. Her knife was dulled from cutting wire and it took her several tries to hack the last bit apart. She tucked the sharp end underneath the joint where it would not catch on anything. "There you are. I hope that's enough."

The bone dog put its paw down and tested it. It stood for a moment, then turned and sprinted into the fog.

Marra's fist clenched against her stomach. *No! It ran—I should have tied it. I should have thought it might run—*

The clatter of its paws faded into the whiteness.

I suppose it had another master somewhere, before it died. Perhaps it's gone to find them.

Her hands ached. Her heart ached. Poor foolish dog. Its first death had not been enough to teach it that not all masters were worthy.

Marra had learned that too late herself.

She looked into the pit of bones. Her fingers throbbed—not in the horrible stinging way they had when she pieced together the nettle cloak, but deeper, in time to her heartbeat. There was redness working its way up her hands. One long line was already snaking through her wrist.

She could not bear the thought of sitting down and sculpting another dog.

She dropped her head into her aching hands. Three tasks the dust-wife had given her. Sew a cloak of owlcloth and nettles, build a dog of cursed bones, and catch moonlight in a jar of clay. She'd failed on the second one, before she'd even had a chance to start the third.

Three tasks, and then the dust-wife would give her the tools to kill a prince.

"Typical," she said into her hands. "Typical. Of course I'd manage the impossible thing, then not think that sometimes dogs run off." For all she knew, the bone dog had caught the wisp of a scent and now it would end up a hundred miles away, chasing bone rabbits or bone foxes or bone deer.

She laughed into her swollen hands, misery twisting around, as it so often did, into weary humor. *Well. Isn't that just the way?*

This is what I get for expecting bones to be loyal, just because I brought them back and wired them up. What does a dog know about resurrection?

"I should have brought it a bone," she said, dropping her hands, and the crows in the trees took up the sound of her laughter.

Well.

If the dust-wife had failed her—or if she had failed the dust-wife—then she would make her own way. She'd had a godmother at her christening who had given her a single gift and smoothed her path not at all. Perhaps there was a debt owing there.

She turned and began to make her way, step by dragging step, out of the blistered land.

Chapter 2

Marra had grown up sullen, the sort of child who is always standing in exactly the wrong place so that adults tell her to get out of the way. She was not slow, exactly, but she seemed younger than her age, and very little interested her for long.

She had two sisters, and she was the youngest. She loved her oldest sister, Damia, very much. Damia was six years older, which seemed a lifetime. She was tall and poised and very pale, a child of Marra's father's first wife.

The middle sister, Kania, was only two years older than Marra. They shared a mother but no goodwill.

"I hate you," said twelve-year-old Kania, through gritted teeth, to ten-year-old Marra. "I hate you and I hope you *die*."

Marra carried the knowledge that her sister hated her snugged up under her ribs. It did not touch her heart, but it seemed to fill her lungs, and sometimes when she tried to take a deep breath, it caught on her sister's words and left her breathless.

She did not talk to anyone about it. There was no point. Her father was not unkind, but he was mostly absent, even if he was physically present. At best he would have patted her awkwardly on the back and sent her to the kitchen for a treat, as if she were very small. And her mother, the queen, would have said, "Don't be absurd, your sister loves you," in a distracted voice, opening the latest dispatch from her spymasters, making the political decisions to keep the kingdom from falling into ruin.

When Prince Vorling was betrothed to Damia, the household rejoiced. Marra's family ruled a small city-state with the misfortune to house the only deep harbor along the coast of two rival kingdoms.

Both those kingdoms wanted that harbor, and either one could have rolled over the city and taken it with hardly a moment's effort. Marra's mother had kept them balancing between two knives for a long time.

But now Prince Vorling, of the Northern Kingdom, would marry Damia and thus cement an alliance between them. If the Southern Kingdom tried to take the harbor, the Northern Kingdom would defend it. Damia's first son would sit someday upon the Northern throne, and her second (if she had one) would rule the harbor city.

It was, perhaps, a trifle odd to expend a firstborn son on so small a thing as the Harbor Kingdom, but it was said that the royal family of the North had grown thin blooded and had married too many close cousins over the centuries. They were protected by powerful magic, but magic could not fix blood, so the kings looked to marry outside their borders. By sealing the Harbor Kingdom and its shipping port to them by marriage, the Northern Kingdom enriched their blood and their coffers at a single stroke.

"At last," said Marra's father. "At last, we will be safe." Her mother nodded. Now the Southern Kingdom would not dare to attack them, and the Northern Kingdom would no longer need to.

It was only Marra who cried. "But I don't want you to go!" she sobbed, clinging to Damia's waist. "You're going *away*!"

Damia laughed. "It will be all right," she said. "I'll come visit. Or you'll come visit me."

"But you won't be *here*!"

"Stop it," said her mother, thin lipped, pulling her daughter away from her stepdaughter. "Don't be selfish, Marra."

"Marra's just bitter because she doesn't have a prince," said Kania, taunting.

The unfairness of this made Marra cry harder. She was twelve and she knew that she was too old to throw a tantrum, but she felt one coming on anyway.

The nurse was fetched to take her away, and that meant that Marra did not see Damia leave, with all the pomp and ceremony of a bride going to her bridegroom's kingdom.

She was watching five months later, though, when Damia's body was brought home in state.

There was a black wagon pulled by six black horses, flanked by riders dressed in mourning bands. There were three black carriages before and after the wagon, the curtains drawn. Their horses, too, were black. They had black bridles and black saddles and black barding.

It struck Marra, watching, as an extravagance of grief. Someone wanted the world to know how sad he could afford to be.

"A fall," said the whispers. "The prince is heartbroken. They say she was carrying his child."

Marra shook her head. It was not possible. The world could not be so poorly ordered that Damia could be allowed to die.

She did not cry, because she did not believe that Damia was dead.

It seemed very strange that everyone else did believe it. They ran back and forth, sometimes weeping, more often planning the details of the funeral.

Marra crept into the chapel that night. If she could prove that the body lying there was not Damia, then all the foolishness of funerals could be set aside.

The shrouded figure smelled strongly of camphor. There was a death mask atop the shroud. It was Damia, her face composed.

Marra stared at the figure for a little while and thought that it had been several days since they had heard of Damia's death. They had been cool days, but not cold. The camphor could not quite chase out the scent of decay.

If she tried to push aside the death mask and tear off the shroud, she would see a rotting corpse. Who knew what it would look like?

I was thinking like a little child, she thought angrily. *Thinking that I would be able to tell if it was Damia. It could be anyone under there at all.*

Even her.

She crept away and left the shroud undisturbed.

The funeral was lavish but rushed. The riders that the prince had sent were better dressed than Marra's mother and father. Marra resented her parents for being shabby and resented the prince for making it obvious.

They lowered the body into the ground. It could have been Damia. It could have been anyone. Marra's father wept, and Marra's mother stared straight ahead, her knuckles white where they gripped her cane.

Days followed, one after another, chasing each other into weeks. Marra came to believe that it had been Damia, mostly because everyone else seemed to believe it, but by then it seemed too late to mourn, and anyway, how could such a thing be possible?

She tried, once, to say something to Kania.

"Of course she's dead," said her sister shortly. "She's been dead for months."

"Has she?" asked Marra. "I mean—she has. But . . . dead! Really? Does it make any sense to you?"

Kania stared at her. "Don't be ridiculous," she said. "It doesn't have to make sense. People just die, that's all."

"I guess," said Marra. She sat down on the edge of the bed. "I mean . . . everybody says she is."

"They wouldn't lie about it," said Kania. "Marrying the prince meant that we were going to be safe. If Damia's dead, then the prince will marry someone else and we'll be in danger again."

Marra said nothing. She had not thought of that, either.

I must start to think like a grown-up. Kania is doing it better than I am.

The two years between them seemed suddenly vast, full of things that Marra knew but had never thought about.

Kania sighed. She reached over and hugged Marra with one arm. "I miss her, too," she said.

Marra accepted the hug, though she knew her sister hated her. Hate, like love, was apparently complicated.

* * *

The edge of the blistered land was before her. Marra looked at it for nearly a minute, thinking.

It was strange how clear the edge was. It looked like the shadow cast by a cloud. This bit here was dark and that bit was bright. It took a moment or two for wind blowing from one side to reach the other.

She could hear the crows calling back and forth. The ones on the outside sounded like normal crows—*Awk! Awk! Awk!*

The ones over her head sounded like *Gah-ha-hawk! Gah-ha-hawk!*

She wondered if the outside crows hated the crows of the blistered land the way that the villagers outside hated the people inside. They had warned her against going inside.

"They'll kill you soon as look at you," one man had said, leaning against the fence. A second man—his friend or his brother, Marra wasn't sure—nodded in time. "It's creeping," the second man said. "Gets a little bigger every year."

The first one nodded. "There's trees that used to be on this side that are on that side now." He spat. "Full of cannibals. You go in there, they'll eat you and lick out your bones."

"Ain't no reason to go in," said the second one. "Not for canny folk."

They looked at her suspiciously. The first one spat again, near her feet.

Marra had found that the people inside were much more welcoming. They had shared their fire and given her the best directions they could offer.

I was worried about the wrong things.

As usual.

It had taken her a day and a half to get to the blistered land from the dust-wife's home. In the back of her head, Marra had a notion that it should have taken longer. She'd never heard of the blistered land before and it shouldn't have just been there, right there, practically on the doorstep.

Magic, maybe. Magic or worse. That a land like this existed at all. That the gods had destroyed it. That if you picked a direction and walked, holding the thought in your mind, you would come to it, no matter which way you went.

She did not like the thought. It meant that the blistered land might touch her own kingdom, that the gods that would punish starving people might someday reach out and touch her own. It was too close and too real and too hungry.

Marra pulled the owlcloth cloak around her shoulders and stepped out of the blistered land.

The curse tugged at her as she went, an itch like mosquito bites across her skin. She slapped at her arms instinctively, even knowing that there was nothing there.

The ground felt strangely hard underfoot, as if she had just stepped off carpets and onto stone. She looked around, blinking in the bright light.

She made ten steps, more or less, holding her hands against her chest, before someone shouted, "Stop!"

* * *

It was barely a season after Damia's funeral when word came down that the prince was willing to marry Kania.

"Not yet," said Marra's mother. "Not for a year or two. It wouldn't be seemly. But after that, to keep the alliance going."

Kania nodded. Her skin was darker than Damia's had been and she was at least six inches shorter, but at that moment, Marra thought they looked very much alike—resolute and strong and a little bit afraid.

"No . . ." said Marra, but she said it quietly, and no one heard.

It was absurd to think that Kania would die because Damia had. Damia's death had been an accident—that was all. It had been a tragedy. It was no one's fault.

Marra knew all these things. They did not shake the gnawing dread that had lodged itself under her breastbone. She felt as if the dread must be visible to other people, like a growth, and it seemed strange that no one ever commented on it.

"Be careful," she said to Kania one day. "Please. Don't . . ."

She stopped. She didn't know how to finish that. Don't get married? Don't walk down any stairs?

Kania gave her a sharp look. "Careful how?"

Marra shook her head miserably. "I don't know," she said. "I just feel like something's going to go wrong."

"Nothing will go wrong," said Kania. "What happened to Damia was an accident. It won't happen to *me*!"

Her voice rose sharply on the last word, and she turned and stalked away.

I've made a mess of it again. I can't say anything until I know more.

A year passed, and Kania went away to the north, with slightly less pomp than Damia had. Marra dug her nails into her palms and watched her go. Her sister was much too young, and no one was saying anything about it.

Before Damia died, Marra would have spoken up and demanded answers and explanations. Now she bowed her head and said nothing.

Everyone else knows. They must know. They are not talking about it for a reason. Why is no one talking about it?

"Don't cry," her nurse said, as she stood on the castle wall, watching the prince's horses take Kania away. "Try to be happy for her. You'll have a prince of your own someday."

Marra shook her head. "I don't think I want one," she said.

"Of course you do," said her nurse. She was hired to see that the princesses were dressed and fed and learned to walk and talk and smile politely, not to unravel the strands of their thoughts. Marra knew this and knew that she was asking for too much, so she said nothing more and simply watched the horses take her sister farther and farther away.

* * *

Marra went to the convent eight months later. She was fifteen. It made no sense that she would go to a convent, when she might conceivably marry a prince and bear sons, but Prince Vorling did not want that. Kania had not yet had a child. If Marra married and bore a son before Kania did, then that child might be a challenge to the throne of the little Harbor Kingdom.

Prince Vorling got what he wanted. The Northern Kingdom's knife was still at the little kingdom's throat, and now he had Kania as a hostage.

The queen explained this to her, although she did not use the word *hostage*. She used words like *expediency* and *diplomacy*, but Marra knew very well that *hostage* was lurking somewhere in the background. Kania was hostage to the prince. Marra's future children, if any, were hostage to Kania's fertility.

"You'll like the convent," said the queen. "More than you like it here, at any rate." She and Marra looked very much alike, round and broad-faced, indistinguishable from any number of peasants working the fields outside the castle. The queen's mind was as brittle-sharp as an iron dagger, and she spent her days delicately threading the web of alliances and trade agreements that allowed their kingdom to exist without being swallowed up. She had apparently decided that Marra could be withdrawn from the game of merchants and princes and safely set aside. Marra both resented her mother for being so clear-eyed and was grateful to be free of the game, and she added this to the store of complicated things piled up beneath her heart.

And she did like the convent. The house of Our Lady of Grackles was quiet and dull, and the things that people expected of her were clear-cut and not shrouded behind diplomatic words. She was not exactly a novice, but she worked in the garden with them and knit bandages and shrouds. She liked knitting and cloth and fibers. Her hands could work and she could think anything she wanted and no one asked to know what it was. If she said something foolish, it reflected only on her, and not on the entire royal family. When she shut the door to her room, it stayed shut. In the royal palace, the doors were always opening, servants coming and going, nurses coming and going, ladies-in-waiting coming and going. Princesses were public property.

She had not realized that a nun had more power than a princess, that she could close a door.

No one but the abbess knew that she was a princess, but everyone knew that she somehow was of noble rank, so they did not expect her to shovel the stable where the goats and the donkey lived. When Marra realized this, a few months after she had arrived, something like anger flared up inside her. She had been proud of the work she was doing. It was something that belonged to *her*, to Marra, not to the princess of the realm, and she did it well. Her stitches were small and fine and exact, her weaving uniform and careful. That she was still living under the shadow of the princess woke the stubbornness in her. She went to the stables and picked up a pitchfork and set, inexpertly, to work.

She was very bad at it, but she did not stop, and the next day she went back to it, even though her back ached and blisters formed on her palms. *It is no worse than when you first fell off a horse. Keep shoveling.*

The goats watched her suspiciously, but that did not mean anything, because goats watched everyone suspiciously. She suspected that they didn't think much of her shoveling technique.

"No one expects you to do this," said the mistress of novices, standing in the doorway of the stable. Her shadow fell down the central aisle of the stable, like a standing stone.

"They should," said Marra, gripping the pitchfork's handle while her blisters shrieked. She edged the tip of the tines under a clot of manure and lifted it cautiously.

The mistress sighed. "Sometimes we get novices who have never worked," she said, almost absently. "Some of them fear hard work. Then you get some who do not feel work should apply to them. And then again, some who wallow in it, who treat it like mortification of the flesh."

Marra flipped the manure into the waiting wheelbarrow and straightened up. Her back asked if she really, truly wanted to be doing this. "Which do you think I am?"

The mistress shrugged. "Eventually, everyone winds up in the same place. You do the work because it needs to be done, and it is satisfying to have it done for a little while." She took the pitchfork away and cleared a bit of stall with two or three expert strokes.

"Hold it like this. You are holding too close to the fork, you lose the leverage."

Marra took the pitchfork back and tried, cautiously. It was easier that way and seemed to weigh less. The goats, less amused now that she was doing it correctly, wandered off.

"I will add you to the rota," said the mistress of novices, flicking a bit of dirt from her robe. "When you have finished this stall, be done for the day. And speak to the Sister Apothecary about those blisters."

"Thank you," said Marra, almost inaudibly, and bowed her head. She felt as if she had passed some test, even if it was only in her mind, and she did not know what, if anything, she had learned.

Chapter 3

On the edge of the blistered land, Marra stood and looked around for the source of the voice. It was too bright here. She had gotten used to the dimness of the blistered land. Her eyes ached as if she were staring at a snowfield instead of a dusty road and a line of fences.

"I saw you," said the voice. She squinted against the light and saw the speaker. A man. Perfectly ordinary looking, in the gray-brown garb that everyone wore, here on the edge of the desert. There was nothing that stood out about him, except that he was shouting at her.

"Hello?" she croaked. Her voice sounded as harsh as the crows overhead.

"I saw you come out of there," growled the man. "You're one of them. One of the bad ones."

Marra shook her head. This was absurd. She'd broken bread with cursed souls, and of course it was a supposedly sane man who was going to try to stop her. It was ridiculous. It was . . .

Typical. The prince is sane, too, as men judge these things. I should probably have seen it coming.

"I'm not from there," she said, fighting the urge to defend the people inside. "I got lost. I'm from the Harbor Kingdom."

"The Harbor Kingdom is nowhere near here."

Despite herself, Marra felt a pang of relief. Good. The blistered land did not touch her own kingdom—not yet.

Her relief was short-lived. The man was carrying a shovel. Marra eyed it warily. Shovels were good for burying dead bodies, and also for making bodies dead in the first place.

"I traveled for a long time," said Marra. "To get here. Well, not here specifically. To the dust-wife." She wondered if the dust-wife's name would help. Surely everyone respected dust-wives?

The man spat on the ground. "Trying to raise the dead?" he asked. "The bad dead in there?" He took a step forward.

"No, I . . ." Marra retreated, darting a glance over her shoulder. Could she make it to the safety of the fog?

This is completely ridiculous. Did the hero Mordecai have to stop and explain about the poison worm to the locals? Did they try to chase him back into the swamps? Bad enough that Marra had failed in the task, but now this?

He took another step forward and lifted his shovel. "You go back in," he said. "You go back in or I'll kill you. You stay where you belong."

"But—"

She tried to explain. She really did. The words spilled out of her like blood from a wound, a jumble of explanations about the dust-wife and the bone dog and three impossible tasks and traveling on the coaches from the Harbor Kingdom, and after about thirty seconds, she realized that he wasn't listening to her at all. He was staring past her, into the fog.

Marra turned and saw shadows moving in the murky edge of the blistered land.

"Oh god," the man whispered, clutching his shovel. "Something's coming."

Marra froze, trapped between the shadow and the shovel, not daring to move. She could hear footsteps pounding on the earth, a rattling sound, and then . . .

It galloped out of the fog, an articulated ghost, bouncing on its forelegs. Briefly it rose up and swiped at her face with its nonexistent tongue, then dropped back down again.

"Dog," she said. Tears began to spill down her face. "Dog. You came back."

The bone dog gazed up at her from empty sockets, mouth open in a fleshless grin.

"M-monster!" shouted the farmer, scrambling backward. *"Monster!"*

Monster? Where?

Marra looked behind her, wondering if something terrible had come out of the blistered land. The skeleton dog barked soundlessly, bouncing on his paws, and Marra heard the rattle-bone click of vertebrae and wire.

She grabbed the dog by the backbone, trying to find a convenient way to hold him. You couldn't very well scruff an animal with no scruff. "Hush!" she begged him. "Settle down! Be quiet!"

The edge of the blistered land was calm. A crow cawed and it echoed in a space neither here nor there. The man was long gone and had left his shovel behind.

Monster?

And then she looked down and realized that her assailant had been talking about the skeleton of the dog.

Oh. Right. I suppose . . . yes.

She scowled. He was a *good* dog. He had excellent bones and even if she had used too much wire and gotten it a bit muddled around the toes and one of the bones of the tail, she'd think that a decent person would stop and admire the craftsmanship *before* they screamed and ran away.

"No accounting for taste," she muttered. She was still crying a little, but her tears felt as ghostly as the bone dog's tongue. "All right. Let's go back to the dust-wife and show her you exist."

* * *

Because she was a novice but would never take orders as a nun, Marra was not expected to attend services three times a day. Sometimes she did anyway. The services for Our Lady of Grackles were short. The goddess—or saint, no one was quite sure—did not care for complex theology. No one knew what she wanted, only that she was generally kindly disposed toward humans. "We're a mystery religion," said the abbess, when she'd had a bit more wine than usual, "for people who have too much work to do to bother with mysteries.

So we simply get along as best we can. Occasionally someone has a vision, but she doesn't seem to want anything much, and so we try to return the favor."

The statue of Our Lady of Grackles was a woman with a hood that fell in folds over her face to the lips. She had a small, wry smile, and four birds perched on her arms. Her altar cloths were embroidered with depictions of lesser saints. Since the goddess did not seem to want anything, the nuns offered prayers to saints that had no worshippers of their own. "Some of them probably aren't alive," said the abbess, lighting candles, "but a few prayers for the dead won't go amiss, either."

The convent shared a wall with a monastery, and if she had a chaperone, Marra could go to their library. She had never been terribly easy with reading, but there were books on everything, not merely religion, and she found books on weaving and knitting. It was worth puzzling out the longest words to learn new patterns. She pieced bits together on scraps and sometimes things worked and sometimes they didn't, but the burn of curiosity to see if the next thing would work, and the next thing, and the next, kept her forging ahead.

She could not remember ever feeling such a thing before. There was no call to nurture intellectual curiosity among princesses. She did not even quite know what to call it. It felt like a light shining in her chest and she could see just a little way ahead, and that was enough to keep her going forward. There was no one to tell her what she wanted to know or whether the information even existed. She had no one to share her excitement with, but she did not mind, because it did not occur to her that anyone else might care.

Because she was royal, and not quite a nun, Marra was allowed to keep going forward. When, once a season, the abbess wrote to the royal house and requested the payment to keep a princess, she mentioned that her charge was very fond of knitting and embroidery, and so fine wool and dyed thread found its way to the convent alongside the coin.

Her mother, the queen, sent careful, precise letters once a month.

There was nothing in them that a spy could have found interesting. The king had a cold. The apple trees in the courtyard were flowering. The queen missed her. (Marra did not know whether or not she believed this bit.) And one line, the same every month, "Your sister says that she is well."

When she was eighteen, Marra fell passionately in love with a young acolyte from the monastery who was apprenticed to the Brother Cellarer. He had beautiful eyes and skilled hands and she was utterly lost. They had four or five frantic, awkward couplings, and then Marra overheard him boasting to the other acolytes that he had bedded one of the king's by-blows. It did not matter that they jeered at him and didn't believe him. She went to her room and curled into a ball of misery and decided that she would die of a broken heart. Minstrels would write sad songs about how she had turned her face to the wall and died of the false-heartedness of men.

She could not quite make up her mind whether she wanted to be a ghost who would haunt the convent or not. It would be very satisfying to be a sad-eyed, beautiful ghost who drifted through the halls, gazing up at the moon and weeping silently, as a warning to other young women. On the other hand, she was still short and round-faced and sturdy, and there were very few ghost stories about short, sturdy women. Marra had not managed to be pale and willowy and consumptive at any point in eighteen years of life and did not think she could achieve it before she died. Possibly it would be better to just have songs made about her.

The Sister Apothecary came to her, the nun who doctored all the residents of the convent for various ailments, and who compounded medicines and salves and treatments for the farmer's wives who lived nearby. She studied Marra intensely for a few minutes. "It's a man, is it?" she said finally.

Marra grunted. It had occurred to her about an hour earlier that she did not know how the minstrels would find out that she existed in order to write the sad songs in the first place, and her mind was somewhat occupied with this problem. Did you write them letters?

The Sister Apothecary poured out two small measures of cordial and handed Marra one. "Drink with me," she said, "and I'll tell you about the first boy I ever loved."

It took three more measures of cordial and two more tales of woe, but Marra uncurled and told the Sister Apothecary everything. The Sister gave her a tea to bring her courses on, just in case, and went to the abbess, and the young man was reassigned to another monastery a week later. Marra was left feeling raw and hollow, and brooding over the fact that somehow "unknown noblewoman" had translated into "king's bastard daughter" in the minds of the monks.

Well. It was safer than being a princess. She was outside the hierarchy and so she had been assigned a story that made sense of her position. Marra felt embarrassed for her mother, because now everyone thought that the king had been unfaithful, and then suddenly it occurred to her that maybe he had been unfaithful and she did have half sisters out in the world and that was too large and staggering a thought, so she buried it immediately.

But her heart healed, as hearts almost always do. She brooded for a little time and then she stopped brooding. She had a powerful and thoroughly unrequited love for a visiting scholar with fiery red hair and soulful eyes, which left her in pleasant agonies. Rather than ghosts or minstrels, this time she fantasized about growing old in the convent and telling young novices about the great lost love of her life.

And time went on, and even that great passion became a fond memory, and the letters from the queen arrived, month after month, to tell her that her sister Kania was well.

* * *

When she was twenty and had spent five years in the little room with whitewashed walls and baskets of yarn and thread, she was summoned to the Northern Kingdom. Her sister Kania was about to bear a child at last.

It was strange to travel in the queen's carriage again. Marra was not confined to the convent and traveled often enough to the nearby village, but she walked or rode on the donkey cart with one of the sisters. To be in a well-sprung carriage with velvet seats, drawn by swift gray horses, was a forgotten luxury.

She stared out the window and thought how odd it all was, how very odd.

"You look very well," said the queen.

"Thank you," said Marra. She ran an appraising eye over her mother. It was like looking in a mirror, twenty-odd years into the future. The queen's hair was still black, though henna played a part, and her clothing was as carefully layered as armor, creating a shape with which enemy eyes could find no fault.

"Mostly corsets," said the queen, amused, watching Marra's gaze. "There's a trick to it, at my age. You must have a good figure for having born two children, but not so girlish that people suspect artifice and not so ripe that people think you are trying to be seductive."

"It matters that much?" asked Marra, looking down at her own plain robes. The material was very fine and there were grackles embroidered around the sleeves, but no one would mistake her as being from anywhere but a convent.

"For a queen? Yes."

Marra sighed. It seemed absurd. The abbess was stout as a barrel, and the Sister Apothecary had narrow shoulders and wide hips, like a pear, and both of them wore layered robes like Marra, except that the abbess also had vestments and the Sister Apothecary tied her sleeves back to keep from trailing them in the herbs.

"Clothing can be arranged for you," said the queen. "If you would like dresses instead of robes for the week." Her voice was carefully neutral, as if she did not wish to prejudice Marra's decision.

Marra looked at the queen's clothing and remembered how long it had taken her in the mornings to get ready, even at age fifteen. At the time it had seemed exciting. Now it seemed like so much work, and the eyes on her would be far less indulgent than the ones when she had been a teenage princess in her own family's castle.

I have forgotten whatever I knew. There would be maids and ladies-in-waiting to tend me and do my hair and powder my face, but I would have to sit for hours while they dressed me like a doll, and then for the rest of the day I would be afraid to eat or drink for fear of ruining all their handiwork.

"I would rather appear as a nun," she said.

Her mother nodded. "More robes, then," she said. "It is easily done. But you will be treated as a nun, not as a princess, you know."

"I think," said Marra, folding her hands to hide the calluses from shoveling manure, "that I would prefer it."

* * *

The Northern Kingdom's capitol was set on a hill above a cold, flat plain. There were few trees. The mountains in the background loomed like swords, but the city loomed higher, as if it had been made to stand against the mountains.

The first city had been walled, then had outgrown the walls, so a second set had been built, then a third, until there were five sets of high white walls and a main road spiraling up the hill between them to the palace.

The white stone glowed against the brown earth, but it was a chilly glow, like moonlight on snow. Marra felt very small compared to that immense white city, very small and insignificant, and yet she had the feeling that the effect was deliberate, as if the city was designed to make visitors feel insignificant in comparison.

Perhaps it makes it safer against invasion, she thought. *But it does not seem like a friendly place.*

The carriage passed through the gates, under portcullises edged like saws. Marra pulled the lap quilt more tightly around herself, as if the cold were seeping in. Then came the long, winding way up to the palace, through streets that wrapped in a circle, over and over, as if they were climbing the body of a coiled eel. There were eels in the river near the convent and sometimes people tithed them to the nuns. Marra had eaten a great many eels. She suspected that this one would stick in her throat if she tried.

At the palace, hardly anyone waited to meet them. Marra'd had a vague notion that there should have been a great show of pomp and royal favor and she had been braced to withstand it. When it failed to materialize, she felt off balance. "Not many people," she murmured.

"We are being put in our place," said the queen calmly. "We are here as Kania's family, not as royal envoys, and so we are being reminded that we are poor relations."

"What do we do?"

"We ignore it." And she proceeded to alight from the carriage as if she were the queen of this kingdom, not a poor relation at all.

Two footmen in livery flanked a woman who reminded Marra of the Sister Apothecary. "She's gone into labor," said the midwife bluntly. "Your majesty. It'll be hours yet, but it's been hours already, and the first time's always hard."

"Take me to her."

The palace was a blaze of color and hallways and tapestries. Marra was swept along in her mother's wake, following the midwife. She had also expected to go to a room and perhaps be able to rest or eat, but it seemed there was no time.

Am I going to be there? Am I actually going to see it?

Well, perhaps she was.

The midwife opened a door and there it was, a bedroom the size of a great hall, with a fireplace at one end. Whatever the failings of their reception, the Northern Kingdom did not stint the midwives for their princess. It looked like half an army had encamped in the room, and in the middle of it, in a bed like a battlefield, was the dim brown circle of Kania's face.

"You look radiant," said the queen, taking her daughter's hands. Marra lurked behind her shoulder, unsure what to say.

Kania did not look radiant. She looked exhausted and wan and her eyes were dark wells in her face. "Mother," she said, clutching the queen's hands. "Mother." She closed her eyes and swallowed. It sounded like a click in her throat.

"It will be over soon," promised the queen. "It hurts, but then it's over."

"I don't care how much it hurts," said Kania hoarsely. "I want this child out of me. *Now.*"

"That's every woman, when the time comes," said the queen. She stooped and kissed Kania's forehead. "Soon enough. I promise." She rose. "I'll get you something to drink," she said, and turned to demand tea of the ladies-in-waiting.

Marra looked after her mother nervously, then back to Kania. She had not seen any woman deliver before and she did not know what to expect, but the knowledge of Kania's hatred was tucked up under her heart. Would her sister even want to see her here?

"Marra?" whispered Kania.

"I'm here," she said, taking her sister's hand. "I'm here."

"You're here," Kania repeated. She looked past Marra's shoulder. "Where is Mother?"

"She went to get a drink for you," said Marra. "She'll be back soon."

"No time, then," said Kania softly. She beckoned Marra closer, until her lips were nearly beside Marra's ear.

"Kania . . . ?"

"Listen," hissed Kania. "Listen! If I die, don't let her marry you off to the prince. Run away. Ruin yourself. Whatever it takes. Don't let her drag you into this hell along with us."

Marra blinked. Kania clutched at her shoulder and might have said something more, but a contraction ripped through her and she shrieked, her swollen body bucking on the bed.

What is that? What was that? Marra looked around, panicking, because such a thing could not be normal, but the midwives were calm and acted as if it were every day that a woman's body writhed like a dying snake on the bed.

The queen returned. Kania gave Marra a last, searching look before dropping her hand. The queen tipped water into her daughter's mouth and made soothing noises, and the midwives circled like jackals, waiting for the babe to come.

Chapter 4

The babe, when it came, was a girl. Kania took this news with her lips white and set. She had screamed terribly through labor, but she was strong and healthy and the babe was strong and healthy and perhaps only Marra thought it strange that her sister took this news like a blow.

The queen lifted her granddaughter and smiled down at her, the broadest smile that Marra had ever seen. The prince did not come to visit. Marra had still never seen him. In her mind, he had become something other than human, a creature like a dragon, something large and powerful and uncertain.

The Northern Kingdom's palace certainly seemed as much like a dragon's domain as a human's. It was huge and rich and there were a hundred corridors and a hundred tapestries on every corridor and a hundred courtiers lurking, watching for signs of weakness. Even after Kania's babe was delivered, there was no privacy. She could not ask Kania what she had meant, or if she had meant anything at all.

Marra did not like the courtiers. She was, in truth, a little intimidated by them. The Northern palace was so much larger than the small, shabby one that she had grown up in, and that palace itself was so much larger than the convent. Had it truly only been five years since she had walked among them? It seemed like far longer, like an entire life had passed. She was glad that she had not chosen to wear the dresses that her mother had offered.

The courtiers bothered Marra, but for the most part, they did not bother *with* her. She was too minor a player to be worth cultivating. When they spoke to her, they were polite and careful, and after two days, she realized they thought she was simple.

Well, as far as they are concerned, I might as well be. These machinations are beyond me. I would rather look at tapestries and try to work out the stitches.

She met the king, who was very old. He had false teeth made of walrus ivory, and his mind wandered. Sometimes he was very sharp and sometimes very vague. When he had vague days, he wandered the halls of the palace and called Marra by her grandmother's name. The guards with him pretended that nothing strange was happening, and Marra pretended as well.

They stayed for a week, until the christening. The palace seemed very cold to Marra, even with all the tapestries on the walls. There were drafts in unexpected places, even in her room, and no matter how she tried, she could not seem to find out where they were coming from.

"That's the dead kings, I expect," said her maid matter-of-factly.

"Dead kings?" Marra sought her eyes in the mirror.

The maid nodded. She was younger than Marra, but she had lived in the Northern palace for most of her life and had taken pity on the princess's sister for her lack of worldliness. Marra rather liked her. She never stopped talking, but her chatter was a combination of harmless gossip and acute political commentary. When she told Marra, on the first day after the birth, that she must wear her hair in a particular arrangement, Marra bowed her head and allowed the maid to braid it as she saw fit. She was glad of it later, too, when she saw the way that the other women wore theirs. A simpler style would have called attention to itself by its very simplicity, and Marra preferred to simply fade from notice.

She had not, however, realized that the maid might be superstitious. "What dead kings?" she asked.

"Under the palace," said the maid. "That's where the crypts are. You have to keep them down there deep so that the frost doesn't heave them back up, but it means they're all cold and dry and they don't really go to bones as quick as they should. Tuck your chin, ma'am, so I can get this bit here . . ."

Marra tucked her chin obediently. In the mirror, her neck vanished into a plump roll. She wondered if the maid was going to continue on her own or if she needed to ask for more information. Fortunately, this was apparently a favored topic.

"All the dead kings are down there, and the dead princes, too. They say it's a whole palace of the dead down there. Each king got a room, you see, and the queen got her room next to his. If she had any babies who died, they put them in her room, and in his room . . ." She gave a small, pleased shudder. "In his room, they'd put the royal concubines, back in the days when they had them, yes? And if the concubines weren't dead when they buried him, why, they'd strangle them with a silken cord and put them down there beside him."

Marra watched her own eyes go wide in the mirror. "Goodness! What did the queens think of that?"

"I expect they were just glad to get their own room," said the maid practically. "But of course, some of the kings had more than one queen. If she died before she had any babies, they sent her back to her people, but otherwise, they buried her here, so sometimes the kings have three or four rooms branching off their room, and then the princes would also have rooms nested in there, so now it's like a maze down under the palace, and nobody knows how far back it goes. Sometimes people try to explore it, but they have to take a family tree in one hand and a map in the other, and they don't always come back." She wrinkled her nose. "The dead don't always lie easy, particularly kings, and they don't always approve of the way their descendants are running things, so they come up and walk around and disapprove. That's why there's so many drafts."

"Goodness," said Marra again. She would have liked to swear rather more strongly, but it did not seem appropriate for the princess's sister, who was also mostly a nun. "Are there so many kings as that?"

"They don't last that long," said the maid, matter-of-fact about the royal family's mortality. "It's hard to be a king, and the ones who don't die in battles waste away young. You've seen His Majesty, of course."

"He's very old," said Marra, thinking of the ivory teeth and the wandering mind.

"He's barely fifty."

"What?"

The maid laughed, but kindly. "Oh, aye, it's in the blood. My mother served his father *and* his grandfather, and she only retired last year. Some say there's a terrible magic over the kingdom and it's the godmother's blessing that keeps it all at bay, but the strain of it wears on them, poor souls. My mother, she said they burn themselves out keeping us all safe. Who knows, though? Anyway, that's why the palace under the palace is so large."

"Oh . . ." said Marra faintly, wondering what her sister had married into.

"There's some who say that it's not just the kings," added the maid. "You can't have a great big palace of the dead like that without grave robbers, can you? So it's all laid about with curses that rip the souls out of the robbers and wad them all up together, and they say that goes waddling and wiggling through the halls of the dead palace, looking for more souls to eat."

"Oh my."

"Makes you fair shiver, doesn't it?" said the maid cheerfully. She patted Marra's shoulder as if she were a horse. "You're all ready to go, ma'am. Best not be late for the christening."

* * *

It was at the christening, for the first time, that Marra saw Prince Vorling.

He was small. That surprised her the most. Her whole family had ordered their lives around his whims, and he had loomed very large in her mind. But he was barely taller than Kania, slim-hipped, with a narrow, angular face. He stood behind the golden cradle and smiled and smiled, his eyes as flat as river stones. He did not look as if he were aging out faster than a normal man, but perhaps it came on the kings all at once, or perhaps it was only a maid's gossip.

Still. She looked over at the king, his hair as soft and thin as that of the infant in the cradle. Could he really only be fifty?

The christening itself was dull. Courtiers stood around and pretended to be fascinated by the sight of a cradle that presumably held a child somewhere in the pile of lace and linen. As a family member, Marra was closer than she might have been, but as a very unimportant person in the family, her primary view was over her mother's left shoulder.

The cradle had golden ribbons on it. The king mumbled a name and then Vorling shouted his daughter's name in a carrying voice. Marra caught that the first name was Virian and then it dissolved into a welter of names that slipped out of her mind as soon as it went in. *Surely they cannot be saddling this child with all those names?* she thought. She wanted to give her sister a bemused look, but she could only see the side of Kania's face.

And now there will probably be speeches, she thought, and steeled herself to stand looking calm and composed and politely interested.

But there were not speeches. Instead, Vorling stepped back and said, "The godmother's blessing," and was silent. The courtiers, too, fell instantly quiet. The double door at the side of the great audience hall opened.

"The godmother of the royal house," said the herald in the doorway, and then he, too, stepped aside and a figure in gray came through the door.

The godmother was old, very old, older than Marra knew a person could be. She did not have wrinkles any longer. Her skin had drawn tight across her skull, almost translucent. Marra could see the shadow of bones in her face, as if there were light streaming through her like stained glass and the bones were the lead between panes of skin.

She moved very slowly. Her spine was curved, but in a way that gave the impression of a scimitar blade rather than old age. She leaned on a black cane and her progress toward the cradle took many minutes, but not one of the courtiers, nor even the prince, showed the slightest trace of impatience.

It occurred to Marra that the king was not treated with half as much deference as the godmother.

She wore dove gray, but her skin was so pale that it looked almost black by contrast. She made her slow way to the cradle, and it was not until she lifted her hand that Marra noticed the exquisite layers of lace that draped her sleeves.

Marra herself had tried making lace once and never again. It was ruinously expensive. Even the prince and the highest ranked lords only had it at their cuffs and hems, and here was the godmother wearing enough to buy a palace.

The lace swayed as she pushed the curtains of the cradle open, and one shadow-bone hand rested on the air over the child's head.

"This is my gift," said the godmother. Her voice was not loud, but it was so silent that it carried to the far corners of the room. "I shall serve her as I have served all her line, my life bound to theirs. No foreign magic shall harm them. No enemy shall topple their throne. As it has been for all the children of the royal house, so shall it be for her, as long as I draw breath."

The king bowed his head. The prince did as well. As the godmother turned and began to make her slow way to the door, the new princess of the Northern Kingdom began to cry.

Kania half turned as if to go to her, but the prince caught her arm and held it fast. A nursemaid hurried from the sidelines, her footsteps muffled on the carpet, and caught up the infant, hushing her with soft, frantic whispers.

Even at her own christening, she is not allowed to cry. Marra bowed her head so that no one would see her lips twitch. She, too, had been a princess once. *And I do not know that I would wish it on you, niece, but I am only a youngest daughter dressed up as a nun, and no one cares what I think either way.*

* * *

Returning to the convent was a relief. The white walls were restful and cool after the opulence of color. Marra had a head full of stitches and mangled a few bits of fabric trying to duplicate them all.

Several of the novices, still thinking her a bastard daughter, wanted to know all about the palace and the christening and the princess. Marra tried to answer but found herself with very little to say. Had the men all been very dashing? She didn't think so. Had the women all been very beautiful? She remembered the dark circles under Kania's eyes and the tightness of her lips. Had the prince been handsome? She truly had no idea. She tried to describe him and the only word she could come up with was *short*.

This was nothing the novices wanted to hear, and all the other things Marra could tell them were nothing she wanted to say aloud. Eventually they gave up asking, and both parties went away mutually disappointed.

The abbess had her own questions, which Marra was also mostly unable to answer. She was interested in Prince Vorling's fairy godmother, but much more so in the priests and clerics that had attended. "Did you see Archbishop Lydean?"

Marra spread her hands helplessly. "I don't know. Did I?"

"A young person," said the abbess. "The youngest ever named archbishop. They would have been with the Archimandrite, a very old man in blue robes."

Marra vaguely remembered the old man, who had been a blaze of cerulean in the crowd. Yes, she had seen him. He had coughed and coughed and looked like a shaking bit of sky.

"Ah!" said the abbess. "We have heard his health is not good. When he dies, Lydean will take the mitre and become Archimandrite, but there will be resistance because they are so young."

"All right," said Marra, conscious of politics swirling around her that had little to do with princesses.

The abbess patted her hand and went away again, and Marra tackled her new stitches and weeded the garden and let the convent's quiet settle over her like a blanket against the cold.

Six months later, a letter from the queen mentioned that Kania was pregnant again, which troubled Marra more than she would admit. It seemed very fast, and of course, the queen would not have mentioned it unless she was several months along. Marra had not really thought you could get pregnant so swiftly after giving birth, but the Sister Apothecary said that it was possible.

Months slid by, Marra expecting to be summoned at any moment for the birth and christening, until one day she counted on her fingers and realized that Kania would be eleven months pregnant at the very least. *She must have lost the child*, Marra thought, *or perhaps there never was one.*

She knew more about miscarriages now than a princess probably should. Her friendship with the Sister Apothecary had continued, and because she could read and research and wrote with a steady hand, she found herself doing small chores for the other woman. And then one day a farmhand was hauled in on a door, screaming from the pain of his broken leg, and Marra found herself holding the lamp and handing the Sister bandages, acting as a second set of hands.

Long after midnight, the Sister washed her hands in a bucket of bloody water and said, "You did well," to Marra.

The praise warmed her down to her bones because it was true and it was not for the princess.

It was a few days later when there was a knock on her door near midnight. Marra opened the door, puzzled—no one ever knocked so late, and Our Lady of Grackles only held midnight services on the solstices and equinoxes—and saw the Sister Apothecary there, holding a cracked leather satchel. "It's a birth," she said shortly. "You've seen one, haven't you?"

"One . . . ?" said Marra. "Only one."

"Then you're ahead of the Brother Infirmarian. He hasn't touched that end of a woman since he slid out of one. My assistant's down with the flux and I need someone to hold a lamp."

Marra gulped. She waited to see what she would do next, half-convinced that she would curl up in a ball and whimper, but instead she straightened up and said, "All right. Let me get on my shoes."

* * *

The labor went very much the same way that Kania's had, which seemed strange to Marra. *Then again, peasants and princesses all shit the same and have their courses the same, so I suppose it's no surprise that babies all come out the same way, too.* Having thus accidentally anticipated a few centuries' worth of revolutionary political thought, Marra got down to the business of boiling water and making tea.

It went more quickly than Kania's, at least, but it was still a long, tense, tedious stretch. Marra nodded off more than once and sometimes came to with the lamp in her hand and the Sister Apothecary crouching between the mother's legs, wondering if she was really awake or if she was having a strange sort of dream.

Dawn had passed and it was most of the way to morning when the baby emerged into the world, looked around, and burst into tears.

"You get used to it," the Sister told the infant, and handed the child to Marra, who stared at it with intense horror. It was bloody and wrinkly and reddish gray and looked like the sort of thing you would drive back to hell with holy water. "Um," said Marra.

"Is it . . . Is . . ." The mother was panting and could hardly breathe. "It cried. It's alive, right?"

"Oh yes," said Marra hurriedly. "Very alive." She stared at it, trying to find something else to say. "Has arms and legs. And, uh . . . a head . . ."

"That's good," said the mother, and began giggling with high, hysterical laughter. "Oh, that's good. You want them to have heads."

"Lady of Grackles have mercy," muttered the Sister Apothecary, but as she was saying this directly into the birth canal, no one but Marra heard.

Fortunately the afterbirth arrived immediately and the Sister swapped burdens with her. "Go and give that to her husband," she said. "He'll know what to do."

Marra bowed her head and fled.

The husband was a farmer with a young face and gnarled, ancient hands. He took the afterbirth as reverently as if it had been a child itself. "Will you help me then, sister?"

Marra swallowed. "I'm . . . I'm not a sister. Not all the way."

He smiled a little. "Don't have to be. Not for this."

She walked with him and picked up the spade he pointed to. They buried the strange, muscleless piece of birth meat under a hickory tree, down among the roots. "Oak's usual," said the farmer, sitting back, as Marra patted the earth into place. "Oak's strong. But hickory's lucky. We've got two strong children already, and the third could use a little luck to make their way."

Marra stifled a sigh, thinking of her own godmother, who had given them gifts of health and princes. A little luck might have smoothed the way for all of them.

She went with the Sister the next time she was called out as midwife, and she was called out often at night because the town midwife was old and slept soundly. Once or twice a month, there would come a tap on Marra's door and it would be the Sister going out to tend to a woman laboring.

She was never asked to do more than hold hands and bring water, but she learned nevertheless. Among other lessons, she learned to pretend not to hear the terrible threats uttered by women in labor. Strange as it was, this set her mind at ease. Kania could not have meant what she had whispered in Marra's ear.

It was the labor—that was all it was. When the miller was brought to her bed, she threatened to put her husband's balls on the millstone and grind them fine if he ever so much as looked at her again.

She saw babies born and mothers die. She saw mothers have an easy birth and then the bleeding simply never stopped, until they died white and bloodless against the pillow. She saw a birthing hook and how it was used to extract babies who had not survived long enough to emerge.

It was the fifth or sixth or tenth labor, as they walked back to the convent, that Marra could no longer keep silent. "It's so *stupid*!" she said.

The Sister glanced at her mildly. "They both lived," she said. "That's a good outcome, in my book."

"Not that," said Marra. Both mother and child had lived, although it had been a harder labor than anyone was happy with. "Just . . . Lady of Grackles! We lie on our backs or sit in a chair and push out a thing that's too big to fit so that everything's torn bloody! What a stupid, *stupid* way to bear!"

"Oh, that," said the Sister. "Yes. I've often thought so. Cows have a much better time of it. Goats and sheep, too. Granted the legs are a bit harder to untangle, but it's not half the mess of humans."

"I won't do it," said Marra.

"Nobody's asking you to," said the Sister. She paused. Marra was fairly certain that the Sister knew exactly who and what she was, and who her parents were, and was trying to find a way to phrase her next sentence. "Well, not at the moment, anyway. And if someone should . . . ah . . . well. There are ways."

Run away. Ruin yourself. Whatever it takes. Don't let her drag you into this hell along with us.

Marra licked her lips. Had they used a birthing hook on Kania, for the child who had gone much too long without being born?

"Ways?"

The Sister glanced around, as if someone might really be eavesdropping in a remote hedgerow in the hour before dawn. "Ways," she said. "Herbs, mostly. Sponges soaked in lemon juice. None of them work perfectly, and anyone who says they do is lying to you. Most of them are dangerous. Sometimes everyone dies anyway, and there's nothing to be done. But there are things that can make pregnancy less likely."

Marra's heart leapt. Could she find out? Could she tell Kania? The entire point of queens and princesses was to act as broodmares for royalty, but if there were ways to prevent it . . .

"I want to know," she said. "All of them."

The Sister Apothecary sighed. "It can be done," she said. "But not tonight."

* * *

The Sister was as good as her word. It was all rather abstract at the moment for Marra, but she memorized the methods and even brewed an entire vial of extract, with the Sister standing over her to make certain she did it correctly.

"You care very much about this," said the Sister.

Marra shrugged. She did not want to care. She did not want to think that her time in the convent might come to an end, that she would be dragged back out onto the game board with all the other pawns and princes.

But if I am, I will not go unarmed. I won't. I have to learn. And maybe I can tell Kania. She had already seen women wearing themselves out from too much bearing.

There was a letter in her room now, another polite, correct letter from her mother, and at the end, her mother had written that Kania was pregnant again.

This is too much. Surely it is too much. She is wearing herself out to bear an heir, and if she dies . . .

Marra told herself that it was fear for her sister that drove her on, not fear for herself. She clamped down on the traitorous little whisper that said that she would have to take her sister's place as broodmare to the prince.

I will not. I will not. *But it will not come to that. I will learn . . .*

Chapter 5

In the spring of Marra's fifteenth year at the convent, a fever went through the kingdom. It laid Marra low for many days, and when she struggled to her feet at last, it was to discover that the abbess was near death. For nearly a week, it was touch and go. Because she had recovered, Marra was allowed to tend to the older woman. In truth, there was not much to be done except to sit in the room and practice her needlework and listen to the rattle of breathing that would not quite be still.

The abbess recovered, but there was white in her iron-gray hair, and she moved more cautiously than she had done. She needed a cane to go up stairs and it clearly infuriated her. The abbess had never been patient with her own weakness.

Marra herself recovered well, though there were days when she only dozed at the window and could not will herself to move. Even the view from the window reminded her of plague. They lost two novices, and the old man who sold goat milk was replaced by his son, who told them quietly that his father would not be coming back.

She was gazing out the window, not quite awake, thinking long unraveling thoughts, when there was a tap on the door and the Sister Apothecary was waiting.

"It's bad news," she said, holding out a letter. "The abbess asked me to bring it to you. She would have done it but she can't handle the stairs. I don't know what it is, but it's not good."

Marra broke the seal. If the Sister said something else, she didn't hear. Her heart was pounding too hard in her ears. If the abbess had been informed of the contents, then it must be bad; it must be . . .

I regret to inform you that the fever took your niece, Virian. The funeral will be held as soon as the family can travel to the Northern Kingdom. If you are well enough to travel, a carriage will be sent to fetch you.

"Oh," said Marra. She was horrified to find that the sensation she felt was relief. It was not her mother, not her sister, not her father. Her heart ached for Kania's grief, but part of her said, *It is only a child you saw for a few minutes at her christening and never again,* and she hated herself for feeling that way, but the loss was at a remove and her love was an abstract love, not one born of close familiarity.

"My niece," she said, realizing that the Sister was waiting for an answer. "My niece has died of the fever. There's a funeral. I have to go. I . . . someone should be told . . . I don't know what I do next, but they're supposed to come and fetch me . . ."

Someone did. Two days later, she was in a carriage traveling north. The horses were black, the bridles were black, the coachman clad in charcoal gray. The Northern Kingdom was showing off its wealth again, and Marra found herself crying, not for her niece but for Damia. *Late again,* she thought. *That was so many years ago. You're being slow again, only mourning now. Probably you'll actually get around to crying for your niece in a decade or so.* Which was comforting, in a foolish way, because maybe that meant that she was not a complete monster. She had been wondering since her first instinctive relief.

She was met by a footman who led her to Kania's chambers. It was all so much like the first time that she half expected Kania to be in labor again. But her sister was not. She was standing at a window, with her mother's arm around her, and the first thing that Marra saw was the roundness of her sister's belly.

"You're pregnant again," she blurted. There had been other letters over the years, announcing pregnancies, but never births. Eventually they had stopped coming, and Marra had thought that perhaps Kania had stopped trying. *Perhaps she has only stopped telling people.*

Kania and the queen both looked at her. Kania had blue circles under her eyes and her face was swollen, but she was still so clearly her mother's daughter that it was like being studied by the queen and her reflection. Marra managed a stammering apology, or perhaps it was only a stammer and Kania took pity on her instead. "I am," she said.

"You . . . um. Felicitations. I'm sure you must be very . . ." *Oh hell. How can she be happy? She just lost her daughter, the one that was already born.* Marra looked around the room wildly, hoping that the right words would come but they didn't, and eventually the silence stretched out so long that no words could have fixed it.

The queen sighed, but Kania gave a strangled laugh and came across the room to embrace Marra. "I'm glad you're here, Sister," she said.

"I'm sorry," said Marra miserably. "I'm sorry for Virian, for you, or— I'm so sorry. I'm not good at this."

"It's all right," said Kania. "I'm not, either." She wiped her eyes and stepped back. Marra thought perhaps she wasn't very far along, but her clothes were cut to show her belly, or perhaps she was one of those women who began to show almost immediately.

"Can I do anything?" asked Marra. "Anything at all?"

"There is nothing to be done," said Kania. "Sit with me. The funeral's tomorrow." Marra nodded and they sat at the window and she tried not to say anything too horribly foolish, with the result that they mostly sat in silence.

There was a family dinner that night. It was strained and everyone picked at their food. There were too many courses, all of them far too rich, and the servants took them away again, barely tasted. Marra watched turtles go by, cooked in their shells, and quail stewed with apricots, and venison in lingonberry and truffles and trifles and wondered who in their right mind served such a thing to mourners.

The old king was having a vague sort of day, intercut with moments of lucidity. Vorling's smooth, handsome face was smoother and colder than Marra remembered. She wondered if he was beginning to age like the old king had. She had no idea how old he was. Forty? Forty-five? He did not look old. He did not look young. He looked like carved marble. Kania, beside him, was all too clearly flesh. Her wrists and ankles were swollen and her skin was puffy.

Marra wanted to grab her hands and beg her not to get pregnant again, to dump everything she'd learned about preventing conception into her sister's lap.

She did not, because even she was not so far gone as to do that at dinner, particularly not with the husband who had bought her sister to give him sons. She fiddled with the stem of her wineglass and waited for the endless courses of food to just go away. Finally they did. The last plate was removed and the king stood and everyone else got to their feet as well.

"Tomorrow," said Vorling. His eyes flicked over Kania. "Clean yourself up for it. You look a fright."

Marra inhaled sharply. Had he really said that? Had she misheard? Why was no one else reacting? That was shockingly cruel. She couldn't really have heard it.

She glanced at her mother's face, seeking confirmation, but the queen's face was utterly calm, the same calm that she wore when speaking to enemies and diplomats. The two attendants who helped the king began to lead the monarch gently toward the door, and Vorling followed.

"I would like to stand vigil for my daughter tonight," said Kania to Vorling's back. "In the chapel."

Vorling turned. Marra saw his lips thin, saw them start to form a denial, but the old king looked at her and smiled blearily and said, "Yes, yes, right and proper . . ."

Rage flashed across Vorling's face. It was so strange and unexpected that Marra almost didn't recognize it. For a moment she thought that the prince was in pain or about to have some kind of fit. Then it passed and his face resumed that flat, smooth tranquility.

"I will send guards," he said.

"I would prefer to keep vigil alone," said Kania. Her voice shook a little, as if she were asking for some enormous favor. "But I will take my sister with me for comfort."

Vorling's face turned toward Marra. There was something masklike about his expression, and Marra wanted to take a step back, but Kania was also looking at her, and so was the old king.

"Yes, of course," she murmured, folding her hands inside her sleeves. "I would be honored."

"You must keep a guard," said Vorling.

"I must mourn," she said. "A nun is chaperone enough, I think."

Marra wanted to say that she was not really a nun, but she knew that her sister knew that, and if her sister thought it was important enough to lie, she would not be the one to expose her.

A tear slid down the old king's face, and he wiped it away. His wispy hair seemed to float as he nodded. "It's proper," he said. He nudged his son's shoulder. "You have to let the ladies weep in their own way."

Vorling's lips tightened over his teeth. "My guards will escort you," he said in a clipped voice, and he turned on his heel and walked away.

* * *

The guards came for Marra that night after dinner. She had sent the maid away and was staring at the tapestries in her room, pacing from one to another. They mostly showed treaties being signed and were remarkably tedious, but she had to admire the craftsmanship that suggested writing on pages without actually spelling out the letters. *That is a fair bit of design. I wonder if I could do that . . .*

One of the tapestries billowed in a draft, perhaps from the palace of dust underfoot. Tomorrow her niece would go to join the ancient kings. It seemed like a cold and lonely place to send a child.

Someone knocked on the door, then opened it immediately. Two guards came in, wearing the white cloaks of the prince's personal guard. "You are sent for," said the taller of the two.

Marra nodded. It occurred to her, somewhat belatedly, that guards might address a princess with a little more respect, but here in this place built on dead kings, perhaps there was no great worth to a princess. She walked behind them, her head bowed, and concentrated on looking as much like a nun as she could.

Lady of Grackles, forgive me for this deception. It seems like it must be important.

The chapel where her niece's body lay in state seemed larger at night, with candles flickering and the shadows looming in the corners. Kania stood just inside the door, her face blank, as if she had stepped away from her own face for a little while and retreated somewhere deep inside.

There were two more guards with her, also clad in white. The four of them went through the chapel, looking in each pew and each shadow. It struck Marra as almost a parody of watchfulness. There were no places to hide in the chapel. Were they trying to impress her with their care? Seeking assassins under the pews?

She was half-surprised that they did not look inside the closed sarcophagus, but they left it alone. When they had scoured the room, the leader of the four nodded curtly to Kania and they left the chapel. Marra heard a bar grinding into a socket as they were locked inside.

"That was . . . thorough . . ." she murmured.

Kania snorted. "The prince fears that I keep lovers under every bush," she said. "If the king had not thought that it was *sweet*"—she rolled the word on her tongue and spat it out with scorn—"I would not have been allowed even this much solitude."

"Oh," said Marra faintly. She swallowed. Kania? Keeping lovers? She understood all the words, but they did not seem to line up in her head. "Oh."

They knelt together at the rail before the coffin. Kania settled heavily, her belly swollen against her legs. Marra wanted to tell her that it was too many pregnancies, ask her if she knew about the ways to stop from conceiving, but how could you do that in a room with a dead child? Instead she bowed her head and tried to pray. *Our Lady of Grackles, please . . . please . . .* She could not think of anything to pray for. What did you ask for when a child was dead? *Please make this as easy on my sister as you can,* she thought finally. That seemed like the only thing worth asking for.

She stared at the stone coffin and thought again of how she had felt relief that it was only her niece who had died. Shame washed through her. She dropped her eyes to her hands.

"You learned to pray in the convent," said Kania quietly.

"I suppose," Marra said. "Mostly I learned about ways to weave and embroider. And how to shovel a stable. And lately, how to deliver a baby." She glanced over at Kania, wondering if this was an opening, but her sister said nothing.

They continued to kneel. The candles burned down slowly, a drop of wax sliding down the pale pillars.

After what seemed like an hour, Kania said, "My daughter is in this coffin, and I do not feel anything." She gazed at the small sarcophagus, dry-eyed. "Did your convent teach you what to do about that?"

Marra swallowed hard and shook her head.

"They took her from me as soon as she was born," Kania said. "You remember? I did not hold her, not even for a moment. They took her to her father, and then to the wet nurse. She had an army of nursemaids and tutors. I saw her for a few minutes a day at most." She shook her head slowly. "There were so many things I missed, and I did not even know that I was missing them. She took her first step and spoke her first words, and I heard from the nursemaids."

"Perhaps you mourned then," said Marra, hoping desperately that it was true. *I didn't mourn her, either, and now it seems like no one is, not really, and that's not right.*

"Perhaps. But I should be mourning now," Kania said, sounding thoughtful. "I should be destroyed. This should be the greatest pain that a mother could know. And yet it is as if a stranger's child had died. I feel badly for that stranger, but it does not seem as if it has anything to do with me."

"I'm sorry," croaked Marra. *Our Lady of Grackles, please tell me what to say. Our Lady of Grackles, please fix this because I can't.*

"I am, too." Kania shifted her pregnant bulk, grimacing. She put a hand to the small of her back and winced, then stretched her arms out along the prayer rail. "They took my daughter and now they have taken even my ability to mourn her. The children I lost before they were born—they felt more real than this."

It would have been an opening to talk to her about the lost pregnancies. It would have been the time. But Marra's gaze was transfixed on her sister's wrist, on a line of livid purple marks there.

She held out her hand, trembling a little, and the marks matched. Fingerprints. A man's hand, larger than hers, but fingerprints nonetheless.

"Kania," she said hoarsely.

Kania looked down at her arm and pulled the sleeve to hide the marks. "Ah," she said.

"Were those . . . how did you . . . ?" Her throat closed up. They could not be what it looked like. *It was an accident—surely it was an accident. She fell and he caught her . . .*

"Normally he's careful not to leave them where they show," said Kania in a voice so weary that the carvings on the walls should have come to life and wept. "But since I'm pregnant, his ability is limited. And he was very angry that I would keep a vigil alone."

Marra stared at her. The words fell into her like stones into a well, and she could hear them rattling down into her mind, but they did not seem to make any sense. They could not *possibly* make sense.

"He . . ." She had to stop and swallow. Her throat was suddenly dry. "He . . . he hurts you?"

Kania gave her one of those quick, sharp looks she remembered from childhood, when she had been too slow to realize something. It was the same look that she had worn when Marra had refused to believe Damia was dead. Marra flinched back as if it were a blow.

"Of course he does," said Kania. "Though he mostly stops when I'm pregnant. He doesn't want any more miscarriages. He gets them anyway." She smiled sourly. "Although it's not much of a respite, because he saves up a great deal of anger in those months. You'd think he'd have whores to take it out on, but the man's got a horror of bastards and bastardy, so it's me or nothing."

"The prince," said Marra, feeling as if she were still half a step behind the conversation. "The *prince* is doing this?"

Kania gave her another sharp look. "Of course. Who else?"

"But someone has to stop him," said Marra. "The king . . . or . . ."

She trailed off, because who could stop a prince? Did you call the guard on them? You couldn't do that, could you?

"The king is in his dotage," said Kania. "You saw. He shows up at ceremonies and mumbles and waves, then goes back to bed. Vorling is the true ruler here. Has been for years."

"How long has this been going on?" whispered Marra.

"Since the beginning."

"Oh." Marra swallowed. No king. No guards. No help. "Come home, then. Leave him and come home where he can't get to you."

Kania's look was almost pitying. "And he will declare war on our country for breach of contract. Do you think I haven't asked? I haven't even been allowed home for a visit. I told you he's terrified of bastards. It goes both ways. If I'm allowed out of his sight for a day, he's sure that I'll be pregnant by some other man. He tells me he'll have no bastards on the throne. It's the spell, you know. The godmother's blessing. No enemy shall take the throne—but only as long as the bloodline continues. A bastard on the throne means the Northern Kingdom falls. Or so he believes."

Each word rang out ugly, like the chop of an axe into heartwood. Marra shook her head slowly. It was baffling. Appalling. It made no sense. "But you wouldn't do that!"

Kania gave a short, hoarse laugh. "In a heartbeat," she whispered, dropping her voice. "In an instant. If I thought I could have a child that did not carry that monster's blood . . ."

Marra stared at the coffin, because she could not look at her sister's eyes any longer.

"He was away on a military campaign early on," said Kania. "It lasted for years. When he came back, he would not touch me for nine months. To be sure, he said. To be absolutely sure." She gave another hoarse laugh. "Those were the best years of my marriage. Except that I was still young and fool enough to think that he might change."

Marra took a deep breath. "Then you must kill him," she said, her own voice barely above a whisper. Could the guards on the door hear her? She dropped it even lower. "Stab him when he's asleep."

Kania looked at her with pity and despair. "He does not sleep with me."

"Then . . . when he . . . you know . . ." Marra felt herself turning bright scarlet.

Kania's face softened as she looked at her sister. "His guards are with him, even then," she said very gently. "I think it excites him to know they watch."

The whole world seemed to slew sideways. Marra had never thought . . . never even dreamed . . . "Oh," she said.

She couldn't deal with that. There was no place in her head to put that piece of information. She tried to think of something else, something that would fix things. Kania sat in silence, her hands folded, looking at the coffin of the daughter she had not been allowed to love.

"If . . . if you had an heir," said Marra, "if you bore him an heir, would he let go? You could go away. Somewhere else. A separate estate, or back home? Something. He wouldn't need you anymore."

"He would not need me anymore," agreed her sister. "And the moment he does not need me, the moment that he has a son that will rule both our kingdom and his, then my life will be worth less than the lowest peasant. I will not die quickly, but I will die."

"Then you can't have any more children!" said Marra hopelessly. Her mind was full of horses with black bridles, a funeral procession of mourners, the wrapped body that must be Damia's. "You can't! One could be a boy!"

And if she does not bear children, she will no longer be useful to him. He will kill her and marry the next sister in line, to get that son.

The next sister.

Kania gazed at her steadily and Marra realized that her knowledge must be written across her face.

"You see how it must be," said Kania softly. "If there is a way out, I cannot find it." She drew herself up, every inch a queen. "But I endure. For the sake of our people, I will endure."

* * *

The next three days were nauseating in the dullness of their horror. Marra did not dare speak to anyone about what she had learned. The prince would hear. He must. Kania had not dared to speak of it except in the chapel, to her sister and the body of her daughter. *I do not dare speak of it to anyone. He will know. He will know.*

But just as there was no speaking, there was no way to stop thinking about it. There was no moment, waking or sleeping, when it was not burning in Marra's brain. She choked down dry toast and dreamed about the marks on Kania's arms, and the only mercy was that everyone took her horror for grief.

Her niece's coffin was interred in the crypts below the palace. All Marra could remember was great iron doors opening, then a procession through a maze of cold stone corridors. She walked behind Kania with her hands tucked into her sleeves and watched Vorling's face and realized that she had never hated before now. This must be what this new feeling was. It took up so much space in her chest that she did not know if she could breathe around it.

When she and her mother left the Northern Kingdom, relief took her so strongly that it felt like joy, as if she might fling herself out of the carriage and dance in the road. *I cannot be relieved. Kania is still trapped. I was never the one in danger. I do not deserve to feel this way.* But she felt it anyway and the shame of it struck her in waves, but when they ebbed, the wild joy of being away from Vorling's palace was still there.

She stayed only one night in her father's palace. Her old room was still kept for her. Even a small, poor kingdom can usually afford to keep a princess's room for her. It was much too young, filled with stuffed toys, and Marra was thirty years old now. *But I can hardly ask them to change it, for a room I use one night in a decade. That would be wasteful.* The abbess would have looked down her nose at the extravagance, which might have gone to feed the poor, and the Sister Apothecary would have shaken her head and laughed.

There was one thing that she could do, though, in her father's house, and one thing only. Marra took her courage in both hands. It had not occurred to her that living as a nun might have robbed her of bravery, and yet facing her mother seemed far more alarming than it ever had when she was a child. She was too aware that the other woman was the queen first and her mother second, and that Marra herself was a small, insignificant piece in the game.

"I need to talk to you," she said, when her mother looked up at her. "Uh, Your Majesty. Mother. Please."

Well, that was even worse than I expected, she thought. She had never been terribly clever with words, but apparently she had lost what little skill she'd ever possessed.

A line formed between the queen's eyebrows. "Leave us," she commanded the waiting women, and they filed out, glancing curiously back over their shoulders.

"Kania's in trouble," said Marra, as soon as the door closed behind them.

The queen cocked her head to one side. "How so?"

"It's the prince." Marra swallowed. Her throat felt very dry. *She's listening—that's something.* "Prince Vorling. She's scared. She's very scared. I think . . . I'm pretty sure . . ."

She could not say the words. They were right there in her head. *He's hurting her.* And yet she couldn't seem to get them out. *I can't say it. Why can't I say it?*

It felt as if she were about to say something horrible and shameful. Her throat wanted to close up, to prevent her from saying such awful things, even if they were true, even if it wasn't Kania's fault, it was Vorling, but for some reason even just saying the words seemed impossible. She swallowed. Her face felt hot.

Say it. Say it. She thought of the line of violet fingerprints again and tried to focus. Why was this so hard? Kania hadn't asked for her help, but she had to get the words out. Their mother would fix it. The queen fixed things—it was why their father had married her. She understood politics and expediency and she would fix it somehow.

"He's . . . he's doing . . ." Marra took a deep breath. *Say it. You have to say it.* "He's hurting her. There were marks. We have to get her away."

"Ah," said the queen.

Does she believe me? What if she doesn't believe me? All the memories of childhood reared up in her head, all the childish lies, Kania saying that she was just jealous because she didn't have a prince . . . *Oh, Lady of Grackles! What do I do? Do I drag her back to the Northern Kingdom and show her Kania's arm with the marks?*

The thought was absolutely shattering. She watched as the queen bent her head over the bit of embroidery in her hands. Marra could identify the stitch from where she stood, a cranefly knot, and thought that she would have done it better and more neatly. That gave her a tiny shred of courage, that she was more skilled at something than the queen, and she had so little courage left.

"Prince Vorling is a monster," said the queen crisply. "He is undoubtedly hurting her in all manner of ways, although he has learned not to do anything that might cause a miscarriage. We shall hope the next child is a son, so that your sister has some chance of retiring from his immediate attention."

Marra's mouth hung open, but there were no words in her throat. *But he won't let her go. He'll kill her, then.*

"Until she has a son, however, she is at his mercy. And so are we."

"But . . ." croaked Marra.

The queen yanked the needle through the fabric with an impatient flick. "Think, Marra! We are a very small kingdom and his knife is at our throat. If the protection of the Northern Kingdom is withdrawn, then the Southern Kingdom marches on us to seize our harbor."

"But . . . but they didn't before . . ." Marra felt as if she were stumbling through the steps of a dance that was far more intricate than she had believed.

"They did not, because the Northern Kingdom would have stopped them. If not for our sakes, so that the South did not control the harbor. But if the Northern Kingdom let it be publically known that we had fallen out of favor and they were no longer interested in defending us, then we will have Southern troops surrounding the castle in a fortnight."

Marra tried to imagine the fields around the castle sprouting with tents and swords and pikes and could not.

Another stab of the needle into the cloth. The stitch would be too tight and would pucker the fabric. "Or," said her mother, "if we defy Vorling before he has an heir that might conceivably inherit our throne, he well might decide to march on us himself and raze this entire city to the ground in a single bloody day."

Marra swallowed. "But Kania . . ."

"Is threading a very dangerous needle right now. Did she ask you to get her out?"

"No . . ." Marra felt as if she were standing a few paces behind herself, completely outside the world that could be so strange and cruel and complicated. "No, I . . . no."

The queen nodded.

She wanted to say so much more. She wanted to say that Kania thought that a son would be the death of her, but maybe Kania was wrong or perhaps the queen was wrong or perhaps everyone was wrong and nothing could be made right. But another thought was beating at her skull like a moth against a windowpane.

"Did you know?" asked Marra. "Before?"

"I knew that he had questionable appetites," said the queen. There was nothing in her face or her tone that asked forgiveness. "I had hoped he was wise enough to keep them quiet. I did not think he would be fool enough to torment his wife to miscarriage and death." She shook her head, her lips a grim line.

Death? But . . . It took far too long before it finally occurred to Marra that her mother was talking about Damia, not Kania.

Oh.

Oh.

So he did kill her.

And Mother knew.

She did not know how to feel. It was too huge, too strange. She did not know if she wanted to weep or rage or throw herself from the castle wall. There was nothing in her heart or her history that told her what to do with this new knowledge. It was too big. She had to shove it aside and focus on Kania or else she would be lost completely.

"We could get her away," said Marra hopelessly. "She could come and stay with me. Take orders with the sisters. He couldn't get her, then."

"Marra," said the queen, her voice softening. "Marra, love, do you think a man who tortures his wife and would wipe out a kingdom on a whim would be stopped by an abbey's walls?"

She was still standing too far back from herself, trapped in amber. She watched herself bow her head and say, "No. Of course not."

The fury rising inside her was doused at once. Her mother had known, and she had also known that there was nothing she could do. It was too late. Perhaps it had been too late since Vorling came courting Damia, many years before.

Don't let her drag you into this hell along with us, Kania had said, her eyes dull with agony, clutching at her sister's robes. *Run away.*

The knowledge bloomed inside her like blood soaking through a bandage. Prince Vorling had picked a tiny, vulnerable kingdom who could not fight back. He had done it deliberately. He had married their daughters, knowing that he could torment them at a whim, and they would have to take whatever he gave, to keep their people safe.

. . . Oh.

"Don't do anything foolish," said the queen. "Don't talk to anyone about this. If word gets back to the prince, it will go badly for your sister." She set her embroidery aside. "I don't talk about it, either, for the same reason."

"Will she be all right?" asked Marra. She knew that the answer was no, but she wanted the queen to comfort her, to tell her that everything would come out for the best, the way that she had when Marra was very young.

"She's managed this long," said the queen. "She is riding a dragon, and all of us in the kingdom are riding along with her."

Chapter 6

Marra had spent fifteen years in the convent all told. Half her life, barring a few months. She could embroider and sew and knit, and she knew, perhaps, a little more of politics than an ordinary nun might. But she could do nothing to save her sister.

She had thought that returning to the familiar routine of the convent would soothe her, but it did not. Days after her return from the Northern Kingdom, Marra still could not settle. She went back and forth, her fingers itching with inactivity, unable to bear the stillness of the convent. What could she do? She had to help Kania, but she could not, but she had to but she could not but . . .

"Are you in love or pregnant?" asked the Sister Apothecary.

"Neither," said Marra, somewhat horrified.

"Don't look so appalled. You're as jittery as a grasshopper, and those are the two ailments I know of that start that way."

"No," said Marra. She trusted the Sister Apothecary a great deal, but she remembered what the queen had said about word getting back to the prince . . . "No. I'm worried about my sister. She's . . . she's had a lot of pregnancies. Very quickly. And she lost a few and . . . you know."

"I know," said the Sister Apothecary heavily. "I see it all the time. 'One child, one tooth,' as the peasant women say, and half these poor women have no teeth left to spare. They wear themselves out bearing. But your sister is a princess, and princesses get better care than the rest of us. She is in good hands."

It's the prince's hands I worry about. Pinching and grabbing and bruising . . . She remembered the line of violet fingerprints on Kania's wrist.

"I have to do something," she muttered, pacing back and forth, worrying at her own wrists with her fingers.

"It's not yours to fix," said the Sister Apothecary. "You think I wouldn't stop women from catching pregnant until they die? But you don't get that choice. You can't go around kicking their husbands out of bed. I can mix up bushels of special tea, but I can't force them to drink it."

Marra stared down at her hands. "I have to do something," she said.

"Good luck," said the Sister Apothecary, saluting her with a glass of cordial. "If you find a way, let me know."

* * *

Days stretched into weeks, while Marra fretted and dug her nails into her skin. The abbess was worried, but the Sister Apothecary mixed up a salve for her scratches and simply said, "You're kicking against the world, that's all."

This was true, so far as it went, but Marra resented it. It was the sort of thing you were supposed to get out of the way when you were sixteen, not thirty. *I have always been slow for my age, but this is too much.*

Weeks became a month, then another month, then another, while Marra did nothing but pace and worry and feel increasingly useless. *I should do something. I should be able to do something. I should be able to fix this somehow.*

She could not think of a way. It was a job for heroes, perhaps, and Marra did not know how to be a hero. She lay awake at night, chasing phantoms behind her eyes, reliving the moments in the chapel over and over, the moments with her mother over and over. She made dramatic plans in the darkness and discarded them in daylight. She would go and ask for an audience with Vorling and stab him. (No, the guards would stop her.) She would attempt to seduce Vorling on condition of the guards being sent away and *then* stab him. (She was nearly a nun—what did she know of seduction?) She would take plants from the Sister Apothecary's store and poison

him. (How would she even get close to his food?) She would . . . she
would . . .

Apparently she would do nothing. Every course of action ended
with Marra dead and her sister or her kingdom destroyed. The plans
played out in her head night after night, all of them useless.

Worthless plans. Worthless Marra. What good am I to anyone?

It occurred to her that Kania's pregnancy was well advanced by
now. *If she's showing, maybe she's safe. She said he leaves her alone when
she's pregnant. Mostly.* She thought of her sister's clothes, the way
that she had seemed to be showing so very early. It did happen that
way, sometimes, but Kania was no fool, and perhaps her dressmak-
ers had cut her clothing so that her pregnancy was obvious.

Assuming she hasn't lost this one, too.

But it was not the baby that she lost next. Instead the word came
down, not from letters but from gossip, that the king had died and
Prince Vorling was now King Vorling of the North.

Is this better?

Is this worse?

Are more people watching him?

But he is the king and no one can stop him now.

She had no answers. She did not know whether this was good or
bad or terrible, whether Kania had been thrown a lifeline or given
a death sentence. She could not even get her mind around it. *King
Vorling* made no sense. He was still *Prince Vorling* in her head. She
remembered that flash of rage when Kania had asked to hold a vigil
for her daughter. How could a man like that be a king and hold a
whole kingdom at his fingertips?

She took to weeding the garden with savage intensity, ripping out
dock and plantain and rabbit tobacco, her teeth grinding in her jaw.

If I were a man, I would fight him.

*If she were a man, no one would force Kania to try to bear child after
child. If I were a man, I would not be the next in line to be married if
he kills her. If we were men . . .* She stared at her fingers curled in the
dirt. It did not matter. They were not and the history of the world

was written in women's wombs and women's blood and she would never be allowed to change it.

Rage shivered through her, a rage that seemed like it could topple the halls of heaven, then vanished under the knowledge of her own helplessness. Rage was only useful if you were allowed to do anything with it.

She was still staring at her hands when she heard two of the lay sisters talking. "I don't know what to do," said one. "I'm out of ideas."

"Go to the dust-wife," advised the other. "She knows things."

"What sort of things?"

"You know. Magic."

Marra looked up sharply. Too sharply as it turned out. They saw her and moved away hurriedly, lowering their voices, but the seed was planted.

The dust-wife.

In this part of the kingdom, every graveyard of any size had its dust-wife. Marra was vaguely aware of their existence, but she came from the western side of the kingdom, and there was a definite difference. On the seacoast side, churchyards buried a dog to guide and guard the dead—church grims they were called. On the eastern mountain side, there were dust-wives. (In one or two places in the middle, there was both a dust-wife and a church grim. "They're no trouble," said one dust-wife of the grim, "and it's good to have a dog about the place.")

Dust-wives lived in little houses by the cemeteries. They operated as combination witches and gravediggers, digging the holes and laying out the dead. Even when a dust-wife got too old and frail to dig the graves herself, she would totter out with a spade and move the first spadeful of earth before hired hands did the rest. Otherwise, there was a chance that the dead might think the diggers were graverobbers, and their curses would be upon them, if not for the dust-wife's blessing.

It was said that the dust-wives could speak the language of the dead and that they knew all the secrets that lay beneath the earth. When a dust-wife died, she was cremated and her ashes were spread across her graveyard, so that each dust-wife who came after might keep the wisdom of her predecessors near at hand.

Marra pulled her cloak's hood up over her hair and went out to find the dust-wife. The convent had its own tiny cemetery, but those souls belonged to Our Lady of Grackles. She had to go into the town to the big church, consecrated to Our Lady of the Harvest, to the graveyard there.

The dust-wife was working outside, tending the graves. She was a fat, sturdy woman with a pink face. "Good afternoon," she said, smiling. "Can I help you, lass?"

"I need a spell," blurted Marra, then stood there, unsure if she had committed some dreadful social error. Were you supposed to make small talk with a dust-wife? Beg? Offer money? "I'm sorry. I don't . . ." She put her hands to her cheeks. They felt hot.

The dust-wife pushed herself to her feet and patted her hand gently. "Let's start at the beginning. My name's Elspeth. What's yours?"

"Marra," said Marra, before it occurred to her to lie.

"Good, solid name. Like our princess. Come sit down and tell me what's wrong."

Marra took a deep breath. Her mother's warning hung heavy in her mind. How much could she say? "My sister is married," she said, sitting down on the wall beside the dust-wife. "He's . . . he's not good. She stays pregnant so he won't beat her. But it's hard on her. She loses them sometimes, and then it's worse. I can't . . . I have to help her. But he's . . . um. Not going to let her go." She stared at her hands.

"Poor girl. That's hard. Does he have the rank to get away with it?"

Bursting into hysterical laughter would not help anyone, so Marra simply said, "Yes."

Elspeth leaned back, face grave. "What would you have me do, child? It does not sound like barrenness will help her. I could give you a charm to make childbearing easier, but I tell you true, it's little enough and it cannot save a babe that does not wish to come into the world."

Marra closed her eyes and thought about treason and regicide and whispered, "Can you give me a spell that kills him?"

The dust-wife was silent for a long time. Marra opened her eyes, expecting to see horror, but Elspeth's eyes were full of sorrow and understanding. "No," she said. "If I could, I might, though I'm not an executioner and I'd need to know more before I bloody my hands. But the sort of magic you're asking for is far beyond me. That's real power, not charms and knowing and listening to the dead." She looked away, apparently measuring her words carefully, then said, "If you go to the capital, there is a woman, I am told, who knows much of poison."

Marra shook her head. The prince employed a food taster, of course, but she could not very well explain that. "If he was poisoned, they would think of her immediately," she said instead.

Elspeth reached out and took her hand. Marra thought for a moment that the woman was offering her comfort, but the grip was too tight. She looked up, startled, and the dust-wife's eyes had gone strange and slack, the pupils huge, the irises nearly gone.

The eyes of the dead, Marra thought, and then, *Damia's eyes must have looked like this.*

Then Elspeth blinked and her eyes were normal again. She dropped Marra's hand and rubbed at her face. "Well," she said, almost to herself. "*Well* then. So that's how it is."

"I'm sorry?" said Marra.

"The dead could help you," said Elspeth. "But you need a real dust-wife, one married to clay and bone and grave dirt, not an old herb witch good at digging holes." She squinted and winced, as if the brightness of the day pained her. Marra watched a tear leak from the corner of her eye and run down her cheek.

"Where do I find someone like that?" asked Marra.

"South," said Elspeth. "South and east. Not here. Go around the south side of the mountains. The dry plains, you know?"

Marra nodded. Her father had taken the princesses there once, part of a royal procession, the whole land bone-dry, stone-dry, kicking up vast clouds of white dust as they traveled. "I know it."

"There's a great necropolis there, but you don't want that. Stop before you get there. The mountainside and the carved caves, the abandoned dwelling and the skulls of bulls. There. There's a dust-wife who's worth the name. The dead would crawl on their knees to give her their secrets."

Marra nodded again. "Thank you," she said, sliding off the wall.

"Don't thank me," said Elspeth. "Come back to tell me, after it's over."

Thinking of the long journey southeast, Marra shook her head. "I may not live to do it," she admitted.

"I know," said the dust-wife gently. "But I'll still be able to hear you."

* * *

It was a long road. The only person she told was the Sister Apothecary, who looked at her with steady eyes and then handed her a purse full of coins and a bag full of tea leaves. "Magic," she said. "Magic is beyond my skills. Come back as you can, and if you can't, I hope fate is kind to you."

Marra no longer had much faith in fate. She had been born a princess, which should have been lucky, but the price for never going hungry was to be caught in a struggle between people too powerful to call to justice.

She also rather wished that the Sister Apothecary would tell her not to go, because then she would have something to push back against. She was used to being stubborn, but having people agree with her was off-putting and didn't give her much to work with.

With the Sister Apothecary covering her absence, she pulled up her cloak and went into town again. The dust-wife directed her to a shepherd taking fleeces to market in Low Bandai to the south, and Marra rode with him clear to the city. The shepherd seemed to like company but did not talk a great deal, and that suited Marra, who had little to say that wasn't *Oh god oh god what am I doing oh god . . .*

From Low Bandai, there were coaches that traveled in all directions. She parted ways with the shepherd and took one southeast as far as it went, then another. She hoarded her coins for food and slept either in the coach or on benches while waiting for coaches. She was tired and snarly and often the hood of her cloak was to cover the wreckage of her hair, but her stock of coins did not go down as quickly as they would have if she demanded rooms at an inn.

No one would have mistaken her for a princess.

It was frightening the first time she had to go and request a seat on a coach. She had never done it, and she was afraid that she would say something so foolish that the driver would laugh at her and refuse her a seat. But she screwed up her courage and said, "I need to go to Essemque," and the driver named a price. She handed up a coin and he nodded and told her that the coach left in twenty minutes and to be on board.

The next time was easier, and the next after that. She got used to the coaches and she learned that being crammed inside was a recipe for rattle-bone nausea, but it was the cheapest way. She was not certain where this sudden frugality had come from, but something in the back of her mind whispered that there was no help coming and if she ran out of money, she had no real way to earn more. Her only skills were embroidery and weeding gardens. *I suppose I could sell my body, but I'm not sure how one does that, either.* It seemed like it would be a lot more complicated than getting a seat on a coach. Did you approach people, or did they approach you, and how did you start a conversation that ended in money for sex? Was there an etiquette?

This was not the sort of thing one was taught at convents. It was easier just to sleep in the coaches.

Sleep by bone-jarring sleep, she made her way south and east around the tail of the mountains. It occurred to her that the abbess had probably had to tell the queen that she was missing. Had she run away? Could you really run away when you were thirty years old?

She was lucky, as such things went. No one bothered her—much. Only once did a man try to engage her in conversation that proved dangerous.

"Where are you going?" he asked her, sitting opposite inside the coach. He had all his teeth and she could see each one in his smile.

"South," she said.

"Which city?"

Marra shrugged. "South," she said again, trying to hide the way her pulse jumped. Had he recognized her? Why was he asking?

He asked her name and she looked at him in silence. He asked more questions—where she was going and did she have family there—and when she did not answer him, his tone turned ugly. He spit an insult at her, heedless of the other passengers listening.

It was a middle-aged woman who saved her, leaning over and snapping her fingers in front of the man's face. "You rude young fool," she growled. "Can't you see she's a nun? Why are you taking your temper out on a nun on pilgrimage?"

The man was in the middle of cursing the woman when her words sank in. He stopped in midobscenity, the consonants getting lost on his tongue, and stared at Marra in her travel-stained robes as if seeing her for the first time. "A nun?" he said.

Marra seized the opening. "I serve Our Lady of Grackles," she said to the woman. It was not as much of a lie as it might have been. "Thank you." *Lady, forgive me.*

The man mumbled something, flushing, and did not bother her any longer. He left at the next stop. The middle-aged woman sat with Marra until the next coach came, though, her eyes weak and watery and sharp as flint behind the weakness. "Tell them you're a nun right away," she advised. "There's many a man who'll not think twice to mistreat a woman but who lives in fear of a habit and a holy symbol. Might save you some trouble along the way."

Marra nodded. After that she tried to walk like the abbess, to fold her hands into her sleeves as the sisters did. She had a carved grackle-feather necklace that her mother had sent her, which she had thought to sell, but she wore it on the outside of her clothing instead. It looked enough like a clerical medal to buy her a little more space on the coaches, a little more distance around her. People who would jostle Marra the woman would step aside for Marra the nun.

And Marra the princess? she thought, bemused. *Would they stand aside for her?*

The issue would never arise, of course. A princess did not ride on common coaches. She did not sit on the benches of common coach yards, or fall asleep with her head against the wall. The princess she had been was dead now, as dead as Damia in her grave, as dead as the children that Kania tried and failed to bear.

* * *

At the last town before the great necropolis, she made her way to the churchyard, where she found the local dust-wife, a woman so old that she could barely hold the spade to turn the earth.

"I am looking for the dust-wife," Marra said. "The . . . the powerful one."

"Ah," said the old woman. "I know who you mean. Walk out of town toward the rising sun until you see two walls, a little higher than a man's head. There's a gap between them, and lots of loose stones. Walk across them, and you'll see a flat place full of graves, and a little stone ridge. Her house is built into the ridge."

"Thank you," said Marra.

"Be careful," said the old woman. The dead looked out through her eyes, and Marra wondered who exactly was issuing the warning. "Be polite. She's not like a devil—she won't try to trap you in words—but she knows too many things."

It was on Marra's tongue to ask how you could ever know too many things, but then she thought of all the things she had learned about Prince Vorling and Damia's death. She bowed to the dust-wife, as a princess never bowed to anyone, and the dust-wife sighed and watched her trudge away to the east.

* * *

The walls were not so high as a man any longer. Perhaps they had been taller in the old woman's youth, or perhaps memory had increased them. Marra walked between two shoulder-high walls and looked across hundreds of loose, flat stones, each the size of her hand, with writing in some language she did not know.

Set within the sea of stones were little oval buildings, like bee-hives without openings. Marra knew at once that they were graves. You saw such markers sometimes, even in the north, usually where a family had their own plot.

The flat stones made for uneven footing. She set her feet carefully. If she had to run, she would risk breaking an ankle or worse. They rattled and slid underfoot, talking to each other in stone language, saying all the words they had been saving up until the next time a human walked across them.

Marra was watching her feet and so not looking up much, when she heard a sound that surprised her, not for its strangeness but for its familiarity. It was not a sound she expected, here in a strange, stony plain on the edge of ancient graves. She looked up.

Bok, said the chicken again, turning its head to look at her more closely.

Marra let out a gasp of laughter. There was a stony rise and a round house built into the side of it. In the yard in front of the house, a small flock of chickens scratched and wallowed in the dust. As she watched, one hen leaned over and pecked one of her fellows, who squawked and ran off into the stones.

The house was very like the beehive graves in construction, layers of stacked flat stones but with a dark, yawning mouth. It would have been alarming if the chickens weren't out in front of it, being so relentlessly chicken-like. It was hard to be frightened of the un-known when the unknown kept chickens.

"Yes, yes," she heard someone say inside. The voice was not thin or querulous, and yet something about it suggested great age. "Yes, I hear you. We've a visitor, I suppose."

Marra froze, unsure whether she should approach the house or knock or call out. One of the hens decided that a human standing still was an extreme threat to chickens everywhere and ran away, cackling in alarm.

"Well, come on," said the voice. "I'm not getting any younger." And then, almost as an afterthought, "Mind the brown hen. There's a demon in her."

Marra looked around but saw no brown hens in the immediate vicinity. She took a deep breath, squared her shoulders, and stepped forward to meet her destiny and win the tools to kill a prince.

Chapter 7

The first task was the easiest one, in a way. "It's straightforward, anyway," said the dust-wife. "This is owlcloth." She ran her hand down the fabric. It did not shimmer or shine in the light, but there was something about it that confused the eye. There were a half dozen ragged pieces laid out across the flat roof of the dust-wife's home. "Make a cloak of it. You must spin the thread yourself." She gestured to a wooden drop spindle and a distaff and a coarse mass of something only slightly more substantial than smoke. "With that."

Marra frowned. It seemed too easy and she was suspicious of things that seemed easy. She had spun thread before—everyone in the convent spun on drop spindles all the time while talking or sitting or even praying. It was the only way to keep the weavers supplied with thread. You needed six sisters with spindles for even one sister weaving.

She reached out and touched the smoky mass and snatched her finger back at once. It smarted as if she'd been stung. She stuck it in her mouth to cool it.

"Nettle wool." The dust-wife did not look smug, which was the only thing that made it bearable. "You must spin it into thread to sew the owlcloth together. It will hurt you if it can."

"They used to make cloth of nettle thread," said Marra. "It can't have been like this."

"Oh, no. You let the stems stand in the field for a few months and it acts like anything else. This is the wool of a ram who was trapped in brambles for a hundred years, while the thorns grew into his blood and his eyes." The dust-wife nudged the wool with her boot.

"Is that true?" asked Marra skeptically.

"Probably not. But it's evil, enchanted stuff, nonetheless." She straightened. "You have from dawn to dusk and back again. There's water in the jug." She swung herself down on the ladder and left Marra alone on the roof with the wool that could not be spun.

* * *

She did it in the end, of course. She had the same bitter feeling as when she had shoveled the stable—*I will do this. You will not stop me.* She tried a half-dozen different ways to cover her hands, only to find the fabric too clumsy to work with or too thin to offer any protection. Finally she stared at the mass of smoke and thought, *I am doing a heroic task and heroic tasks are not done by half measures. It's only pain. Kania's pain is so much worse than mine.* And she plunged her left hand into the mass of smoke and nettles and began to spin.

It burned and stung and blazed against her flesh. She hissed and cursed and bent over her hand. *No. Keep going. You can't stop once you've started.* She thought of every birth she had ever seen. Those women had been in far worse pain and they had done it, because once you started, you couldn't stop. She would do this. *Left hand only. I will need the right to thread the cord.* She could protect her right hand with fabric for this bit but she needed her left to pull the wool onto the distaff and there was no protecting it.

She was clumsy with her left hand, but it did not have to be done well, only done. Her fingertips turned angry red and her knuckles began to swell, but that did not matter. She only had to keep her fingers in position and let the angry smoke flow through them. The sun crawled overhead. The web of skin between thumb and forefinger hurt and hurt until it stopped being pain and became something else entirely.

It was hard to keep the drop spindle going slowly enough. She wanted to rush through it. But a faster spin meant finer thread and she wanted coarse, heavy stuff to hold her cloak, so that she need not use so much of it. She bit the inside of her cheek bloody and stared at her clawlike left hand and wondered if she'd ever do anything much with it again.

At last she had enough. Probably. The nettle wool was nearly gone, leaving only a great sharp thorn as long as a sheep's foreleg, with a point that could have pierced a man's heart. She dropped the spindle and clutched her ruined hand to her chest. It was red and violet and the joints were swollen thick. When Marra tried to open her fingers, she could feel the tendons grating against bones and could not contain her scream.

She looked up. The sun was on the far horizon and the shadows were turning blue. She drank water, holding the jug with her right hand. She tried to pour a little over her left. It didn't do anything. She cried a little, and that didn't do anything, either.

Marra had saved her right hand for the delicate work. She took a deep breath and then worked the thread loose from the spindle while her flesh blazed as if it had caught fire. The thread came off lumpy and ugly and uneven, but there was nothing to be done. She had no more nettle wool to spin anyway. She wished that she could ply it, but she did not have enough time and she did not know how much more pain she could endure.

There was no needle. She stared at the owlcloth scraps and the thread in her hand and could not believe that she had missed that. *There's always a needle,* she thought wearily. *I am an embroiderer; I always have a needle.* She started laughing softly to herself, the broken laughter of a mortal wound. All her needles were in her room at the convent, carefully jabbed into a pincushion shaped like a little white rat. It had been a gift from the Sister Apothecary.

She looked over the rooftop, looking for a shape she had missed, the wink of bone or metal in the moonlight. When had the moon come up? Had it been that long already?

Marra did not find a needle. Instead she saw the dull gleam of light on the bitter thorn at the heart of the nettle wool.

She picked it up in her swollen fingers and looked at the point. It was sharp enough to serve as an awl. She would have to push the thread through with her fingers and then grab it on the other side and pull it through and it would burn and burn and her fingers would stop working and then, Lady of Grackles help her, perhaps she would have to use her teeth.

Did you think impossible tasks were so easily done?

She looked at her sad, misshapen pile of thread and the soft, shifting owlcloth, and she cried a little more, and then she bent her head over the fabric and set to work.

* * *

"God's balls," said the dust-wife a week later, looking at the bone dog. "You did it." She did not sound happy about it. She hadn't sounded happy about the cloak of nettles, either, when Marra had come down with her ruined hands and her swollen lips and dropped the owlcloth garment at her feet.

"I did," said Marra. "Where do I begin the next task? Moonlight in a jar of clay?"

The dust-wife groaned. She got up without answering and went to rummage in her pantry. Eventually she found a pile of chicken bones and tossed them to the bone dog.

Marra had a vague notion that chicken bones were bad for dogs, but she also wasn't sure that there was anything in the bone dog to be injured. He lay down happily and began to gnaw. Bits of splintered bone rained out of his neck as he swallowed.

The dust-wife pulled out a chair at the table and slumped into it. She was tall and bony and stoop shouldered where Marra was short and round. "Do you know why you set someone an impossible task?" she asked.

Marra scowled. This was the sort of question that she hated, the kind that made her think that the other person was trying to be clever at her expense. But the dust-wife had dealt fairly with her, so she tried to think of an answer. "To see if they can do it?" She racked her brain, thinking of all the old legends: Mordecai and the worm; the white deer who loved a human and her terrible quest to save her lover; Little Mouse who killed the dragon on her wedding day. "To see if they are heroes?"

"Heroes," said the dust-wife with an explosive snort. "The gods save us all from heroes." She gazed at Marra, her normally expressionless face lined with sorrow. "But perhaps that's the fate in store for you after all. No, child, you give someone an impossible task *so that they won't be able to do it.*"

Marra examined this statement carefully from all directions. "But I did it," she said. "Twice."

"I had noticed," said the dust-wife grimly. "And quite likely you will do the third task and then I will be obligated to help you kill your prince."

"He isn't *my* prince," said Marra acidly.

"If you plan to kill him, he is. Your victim. Your prince. All the same. You sink a knife in someone's guts, you're bound to them in that moment. Watch a murderer go through the world and you'll see all his victims trailing behind him on black cords, shades of ghosts waiting for their chance." She drummed her nails on the table. "You sure you want that?"

"He killed Damia," said Marra. "He's torturing Kania. He deserves to die."

The dust-wife said nothing. For a little time, the only sound was the crunch of bones and the patter of splinters on the floor.

"Lots of people deserve to die," said the dust-wife finally. "Not everybody deserves to be a killer." She sighed heavily. "I can't change your mind, can I?"

"No."

"Right." The dust-wife scooted her chair back, reached up one long arm, and hooked a jar from the shelf. "Here," she said, passing it to Marra. "Open it."

The jar was heavy earthenware, squat, completely unremarkable. Marra opened the lid cautiously. Moonlight bathed her face, a streaming blue-white radiance.

"Close it again," ordered the dust-wife. "There. The moon in a jar of clay. Give it back to me, please."

Marra, by now thoroughly bewildered, closed it and passed it back to the dust-wife. Her eyes felt dazzled by the moon that had shown at midday inside the house.

"There," said the dust-wife. "You have given me moonlight in a jar of clay. Well done. That's the third task."

"But . . ." Marra stared at her and the little clay jar with the moonlight inside. "But I didn't earn it. I didn't do anything."

"It was an impossible task," said the dust-wife. "The other two should have been impossible, but here you are with a bone dog and a cloak made of owlcloth and nettles. Catching the moon would have broken you, though. That's not a task for mortals who want to keep their hearts."

"But . . ."

"I didn't want to do this," said the dust-wife. "That's why I gave you the impossible tasks, so you'd fail and go away and not ask any more. I don't like travel and I don't like going places and I'm going to have to find someone to watch the chickens. And also this is a fool's errand and we'll probably all die."

"But . . . ?" A hope began to bloom in Marra's heart. She fought it down, telling herself that she must be mistaken.

The dust-wife shook her head. "You want a weapon against a prince. Well, I haven't got a magic sword or an enchanted arrow or anything nicely portable." She leaned back in her chair. "So. Your weapon against the prince. That's me."

* * *

Setting out from the dust-wife's home took longer than Marra liked. "Three days," said the dust-wife. "I've got things to pack and things to settle." In the yard, the brown hen stared down the bone dog, apparently unfazed by his lack of eyes.

"Kania could be dead in three days," said Marra.

"Then she will die," said the dust-wife implacably. "Because it will take us weeks to walk to the capital of the Northern Kingdom, particularly given the stops we must make along the way."

Marra took a deep breath and schooled herself to patience. Even a princess learned patience in a convent, and what the nuns had not taught her, she had learned from knitting and weaving. Haste led to dropped threads and mangled socks. They could not afford haste with Kania's life.

Besides, she thought bleakly, *you have waited many years already. If you had noticed her bruises five years earlier, or ten, it would all be done already.* The bone dog, tired of being stalked by a chicken, flopped down on his side in the yard. It was impossible to tell when he was sleeping, but there was a sense of relaxation in the slow up-and-down movement of his rib cage.

"What's his name?" asked the dust-wife.

Marra blinked at her. "Who?"

"The dog, child! Dogs have human names. It's what keeps them from being wolves."

"Uh . . . uh . . . Bonedog?"

"Are you asking me or telling me?"

"His name is Bonedog," said Marra more firmly. In the yard, Bonedog rolled over and wiggled his backbone in the dust.

"Imagination is not your strong suit, is it?" asked the dust-wife. A smile cracked the planes of her face. "That's not an insult, child— don't look so surly. For this sort of work, you want feet on the ground, not castles in the air."

The brown hen came around the side of the house, saw Bonedog, and advanced like a general leading a host. She pecked Bonedog's tail and was rewarded with a ghostly yelp. Bonedog rolled to his feet, puzzled, and the hen ran off cackling in triumph.

The dust-wife took out a cloak made of bottles and pockets and tabs, like a walking cupboard, and spun it around her shoulders. Marra was surprised that she didn't rattle when she walked. Then she took it off again and began filling the pockets and bottles from the jars on the wall, decanting drops of liquid and placing odd packets. Marra watched her pack up feathers and mouse skulls and bits of lint and finally said, "What is the good of all that?"

Hummingbird feathers gleamed as the dust wife slipped a tiny bird skin into her pocket. "No idea," she said. "Most of it probably won't do us any good at all. But I agreed to help and that means you get the best I can do." She licked her fingers and placed three small black beads into a wax paper envelope, then paused. "Show me your hands."

"Eh?"

"Your hands. You're favoring them."

Marra held out her hands. The joints were stiff and the red puffiness where she had gouged herself with wires had gotten worse.

"Saints and devils," said the dust-wife. "Open wounds in the blistered land. Hold still." She got down a jar from the shelf.

"Is it bad?" asked Marra.

"It would probably kill you in a week or so," said the dust-wife, bending over her hands. "You'd get a taste for human flesh first, though, which would be exciting for everyone . . . Oh, don't look so stricken." She unstoppered the jar. Marra smelled honey, but the liquid that the dust-wife dabbed onto her wounds was red as fire.

"What is it?"

"Rust honey. Made by clockwork bees." The dust-wife rubbed it into the joints of Marra's fingers, muttering words that Marra couldn't quite make out. Eventually she sat back. "That should do it. Tell me if you get the urge to take a bite out of someone, though."

"There's a long list of people I'd like to bite," said Marra, a bit dryly.

The dust-wife snorted. "Fair enough. Just tell me if you get the urge to chew afterward, then."

Marra cradled her hands together, flexing her fingers. Already her knuckles seemed less stiff. She wondered if the words that the dust-wife had said had been magic, or if it was all the work of the honey.

She drifted to sleep in the corner, still wondering, soothed by the sound of the dust-wife moving around the room, the jars rattling, as the old woman packed away bits of magic inside the folds of her coat.

* * *

The brown hen rode on top of the dust-wife's staff, on the bone crosspiece. Her body moved as the staff moved, but her head stayed level in that peculiar way of chickens. Marra was first incredulous, then amused.

"You're bringing the hen?"

"She's got a demon in her," said the dust-wife. "It'd be rude to leave her for the neighbors to deal with."

The hen rode until midmorning, whereupon she would stretch, walk down the dust-wife's outstretched arm, and climb into her pack. The top flap was left open for just this reason. The hen would sit there for about a quarter of an hour, give a single pleased cluck, and then saunter back down the arm and onto the staff again. The dust-wife would pause, retrieve a single large brown egg from her pack, and tuck it into a safe pocket. In the morning, she would cook the egg, divide it in exact halves, and share it with Marra.

Half an egg did not make a terribly satisfying breakfast, but it was a great deal better than nothing. Sometimes Bonedog would flush a rabbit and kill it and they would stop and roast the rabbit. Sometimes a farmer would sell them eggs or a loaf of bread, although the dust-wife had to go alone to ask, because if the farmer saw Bonedog, there would be questions.

For the same reason, they could not take coaches, or even beg rides on farm wagons. They could not ask to sleep in barns where it might be warmer. There was no way to disguise Bonedog. Their progress back to the northwest slowed to a crawl.

"This won't do," said the dust-wife, the third or fourth day. "Your sister will have died of old age before we reach her, and I'll be so bent over from sleeping on the ground that I'll be cursing your prince's kneecaps."

"What do we do?" asked Marra. They had put a collar on Bonedog, although it was more like a knot with a loop tied around his neck bones. She slid a hand through the loop protectively. She could not leave him. She'd brought him back to life and that felt like a bargain to her, even stronger than the bargain that humans made with living dogs who loved them.

But I cannot let Kania down, either.

"No need to look so downcast," said the dust-wife. "The moon is full and the goblin market's still in season."

"Eh?"

"The goblin market," repeated the dust-wife. "Lords of Earth! What do they teach you in a convent, anyway?"

"Not much about goblins," said Marra. "I could tell you a great deal about knitting bandages and drying herbs and the feast days of lesser saints."

"Well," muttered the dust-wife, in the tone of one determined to be fair. "That's not completely useless, anyway. Whose feast is it to-day, then?"

Marra had to stop and work out the date. "Saint Ebbe," she said finally. "Patron of boar hunters."

"Hmm. Well, boar are cunning and fierce and hard to kill, much like your prince, though I respect the boars rather more. We could do worse than to offer prayers to such."

Marra bowed her head dutifully and offered a prayer. So little was known of Saint Ebbe that there was no specific form, so she used the standard invocation that could be applied to any saint—"Saint Ebbe, watch over us. Saint Ebbe, protect us and keep us from harm. Saint Ebbe, intercede for us . . ."

She was surprised when the dust-wife joined in on the final "May it be so." The old woman had not struck her as religious.

But I could easily imagine someone making a saint out of her, a hundred years hence. Maybe some of the saints were like that, too—cranky, old women with strange gifts. She remembered the one icon she had seen of Saint Ebbe, a gray-haired woman with her foot on a boar's snout, holding it pinned. Both she and the boar had been grinning. She'd thought at the time that perhaps the icon painter hadn't been very good. *But if I were going to paint the dust-wife as a saint, she'd have a brown hen with her, and that hen grins—I am nearly certain of it.*

She realized that she had gotten distracted. "The goblin market?"

"What it sounds like," said the dust-wife. "The marketplace of the goblins and the fair folk, and whatever humans go wiggling and wandering in. Curses and treasures in equal measure. And ordinary things as well, of course."

"The fair folk?" Marra licked her lips. "Is it dangerous?"

"Deeply," said the dust-wife. "But everywhere's dangerous if you're foolish about it. The goblin market has rules, and if you obey the rules, it's no worse than anywhere else." She considered for a moment. "At least if you're there outside the dark of the moon. The rules change in the dark, and sometimes they change minute to minute. Full and waxing are more forgiving. We'll go tonight."

"Where is it?"

"Doesn't matter." The dust-wife's mouth crooked up at the corner. "If we can find a stream, it's easier to get there. If not, we'll go by fire."

Marra had to be content with that, because no further information was forthcoming. She added the goblin market to things that she had to worry about, and felt anxiety gnawing inside her rib cage.

In the end, it was frightening but not difficult. There was a broad, shallow stream washing across the stones a few miles away. They walked along it in the growing dusk and eventually came to a shallow ford, full of round gray pebbles that glinted black where the water rushed over them.

"Hmm," said the dust-wife, sounding distracted. "Hmm . . ." She held out a hand to stop Marra moving. "Yes. There's one here. There usually is at a ford."

Bonedog, bored, sat down and began trying to lick his nether regions. Since he had neither tongue nor anything to lick, this accomplished nothing but seemed to please him.

The dust-wife drew a line in the pebbles with the tip of her staff, while her hen, half-asleep, muttered in annoyance. "Don't talk to it," she said.

"Talk to what?" said Marra, and then the dust-wife called up the dead.

Chapter 8

Marra's first indication was that the crickets fell silent. In the distance, a bird sang *oh-die-will, oh-die-will,* and as the crickets stopped, it sang more loudly. The river's hiss and roil seemed to slow, and then, very distantly, Marra heard splashing as something approached.

"There's something coming," she said. Bonedog quivered with alertness.

"Hush," said the dust-wife. "The drowned ones are tricky."

Marra closed her mouth on whatever she was about to say, but something else answered the dust-wife, a burbling liquid sound that might have been a laugh or a sob.

A shape was coming upstream. The moon was just high enough to throw cold, glittery light over it. At first Marra thought of beavers, otters, swimming creatures, but no otter had ever been so large, nor had a face like that.

The dead boy swam upstream, quick as a fish, and rose to his feet. Water streamed from his mouth and his empty eye sockets. His skin had swollen and split his clothes, a pale, bloated thing with flesh puffing out between strands of waterweed.

I will not be sick, thought Marra. *I will not. There is no blood. It is not as bad as that time the farmhand broke his leg and the bones stuck out. It isn't.*

Whatever the dust-wife said, Marra missed it. She was only vaguely aware of the other woman speaking at all. Then the dead boy replied, a hard gurgling as if wires were piercing his drowned throat, and Marra stopped hoping not to be sick and began hoping that she wouldn't faint instead.

"Good," said the dust-wife. "Which way?"

The drowned boy lifted his arm. His fingers had swollen together into a white mitten. He pointed upstream and gargled an answer.

The dust-wife nodded. "Do you wish ending?" she asked as brusquely as if she were negotiating with a farmer for a loaf of bread.

Another gargle. His face turned toward Marra and she knew that she should feel pity, not horror, but there was something strange and leering about the way he moved, as if he knew that she was frightened and delighted in it. He made a beckoning gesture with his swollen hand and then gulped with laughter when she shrank back.

"Enough of that," said the dust-wife. "She's not for drowning."

More laughter. He took a step forward, the water hilling up around his legs as if it were sand, then another.

The brown hen made a low, hostile noise. The boy froze, looking up. For a long moment he stared eyelessly at the bird; then he lowered his head.

"Cock's crow and demon's heart," said the dust-wife. "Don't test me, boy."

He gurgled sullenly but retreated.

She reached into a pocket and pulled something out. Marra couldn't make out the shape in the dimness. She tossed it over the stream and the drowned boy caught it with his bloated white hands.

"Go on, then," said the dust-wife, flicking her fingers dismissively. "Back to the water, and mind you don't pull down a traveler unless they break the covenants."

The drowned boy hunched his shoulders and turned away. The moon dripped light over him as he walked down the riverbed, sinking deeper with each step, until he dove like an otter and was gone.

"Bleah," said the dust-wife. "The ones who die by water go bad as often as not. Something about the water turns them dark. Give me bones in the ground any day."

Marra held her hand over her mouth and concentrated on breathing until her stomach stopped lurching. "Why did you summon that?" she asked finally. *What kind of monster is walking with me? What am I about to unleash? She's not just an old woman with a chicken . . .*

You knew that already, she answered herself. *You knew that, which is why you came to her. You want to kill a prince. Don't get squeamish now.*

"Directions," said the dust-wife. "Which he gave, although he would have liked to pull a much higher price than I was willing to pay."

"Directions?"

"Indeed. Now, follow me, and let's see what they were worth."

Apparently, they were worth a great deal, because within twenty minutes they reached a gnarled tree that overhung the bank.

"There," said the dust-wife. One of the tree roots stuck out over the water. "Earth and wood and water." She reached into a pocket and pulled out a cord with a stone tied to the bottom, then tied it to the root so that the cord fell down into the water. "Hold your breath," she said, almost as an afterthought, then ducked into the arch formed by the cord and the root and the overhung bank.

She took two steps, splashing, and passed through the arch. She came out the other side, looking just the same to Marra, and yet the sound of her footsteps in the water seemed to come from much farther away.

Bonedog cocked his leg meditatively on the tree root. Nothing happened, but it seemed to satisfy him. Marra supposed that he was already holding his breath, insomuch as he didn't breathe at all. She took a deep gulp of air and walked through the root archway.

Nothing obvious happened. It wasn't like the gluey sensation when she walked out of the blistered land. But a few steps later, her ears popped, and when she turned her head, everything seemed to move a fraction of a second slower than it should have, as if her eyes were struggling to catch up.

She scrambled up the riverbank. The dust-wife stood impatiently, tapping her staff. The brown hen grumbled.

"Does the chicken hold her breath?" asked Marra.

"She's got a demon; she doesn't have to." The dust-wife turned and began to walk back the way they had come.

Wait—that wasn't just a figure of speech?

"Do you mean that your chicken has a *literal* demon in her? Not that she's just a . . . a bad chicken?"

The words sounded incredibly foolish as she said them, and the dust-wife's look indicated that they did not improve upon hearing.

"Girl, have I given you any indication in the last week that I joke about *anything*?"

"How did you get a *demon* in your chicken?"

"The usual way. Couldn't put it in the rooster. That's how you get basilisks."

Marra opened her mouth to ask what the usual way was, then stopped because there was an enormous staircase in the ground that had most definitely not been there when they had walked by earlier.

It had broad stone steps, easily wide enough for two horses to pass abreast. Marra could not possibly have missed it. The steps ran straight down into the ground, ignoring the existence of the nearby river that should have turned them into a waterfall. The dust-wife walked down them without pausing, not even ducking her head.

It was dim for the first few steps but green light illuminated the lower stairs. Marra looked around for the source, then wished she hadn't. In alcoves on each side of the stairs, a firefly the size of a house cat blazed with light.

"Where does this go?" she whispered, hurrying to catch up with the dust-wife. The fireflies ignored her, but their antennae moved slowly in the air. "Who made this?"

"To the goblin market," said the dust-wife. "But in answer to your second question, I don't know. I'm not entirely sure it was made, in truth. Some things come into being once it's inevitable that they will exist."

Marra was still trying to parse that one when the stairs ended at a landing above a sunken room, and Marra gazed down into the goblin market.

* * *

It looked like a market, but such a market as Marra had never seen. There were jeweled pavilions crowded next to mud huts and hide tents and things that looked like upside-down bird nests. The aisles between were crowded, but the people within them did not move like a crowd. They moved like dancers, some light, some heavy, some in circling, solitary waltzes. They reminded Marra far more of the courtiers in the prince's palace than of the town on market day.

She had been a little afraid of the courtiers, and now she was more than a little afraid of the people here. The courtiers, for all their cloth and starch and politics, had been human, and some of the crowd here were obviously . . . not.

And I am here with a dog skeleton at my heels and a woman with a chicken on her staff, so what must they think of me?

"Don't stare," murmured the dust-wife, "but don't look away if someone looks at you. Show as little weakness as you can. Agree to nothing and accept nothing until you know the price."

With that, she stepped forward into the crowd, and Marra hurried after her.

The majority of the crowd had looked human from a distance, but once she was among them, she had her doubts. Some were human shaped but had green or blue skin. A number had horns rising from their foreheads, short and pointed as antelopes'. One woman walked by with a rack of antlers that would do any stag proud, and small black birds seated on each tine, wearing silver collars around their necks.

Others were not even human shaped. A trio of boars in starched collars, walking on their hind legs, went grunting past. Six white rats, each nearly three feet tall, carried a palanquin on their shoulders. And who could guess what lay beneath the pale braids that covered that figure from head to toe?

Where did they all come from? Are they from other parts of the world or are they all from here? But how could they be from here?

You heard stories, of course. Stories of the Fair Folk, of little people that lived behind the world. Stories of old gods that had never learned how to die. But Marra had never imagined that there might be so many or that they might be *right here,* on the other side of a tree root, not far away under the hills.

Even the blistered land had not prepared her for that.

"Hmm," said the dust-wife. She had stopped at a table that held a little wooden tray divided into squares. In each square lay a moth, apparently dead. "Hmm. That one." She pointed.

"Shows you what you need," said the woman behind the table, sounding bored. She was old and wrinkled, with thin gray braids coiled around her head. "You sure you don't want the one that shows you your heart's desire? It's much better."

"Also a lot more expensive, I suspect."

The woman grinned. She had no teeth. Instead her tongue was banded with red and black and had a snake's golden eyes. "Five years of your life. But you get the rest to spend with your heart's desire, so it's worth the price."

"I'll stick to needs, thank you." The dust-wife tapped the moth. It flicked its wings, startling Marra. It was white, but there were broken black lines all over, like writing.

"Ugh. Six weeks of your life."

"Six days."

"One month."

"One week."

"A fortnight, and that's my final offer. And don't blame me when it lands on a bucket because what you need is to drink more water."

"A fortnight's fair." The dust-wife beckoned Marra. "Two weeks of your life, child."

"Uh," said Marra. "What?"

"That's the price in this place, unless you've something to barter."

"What if I'm going to die in a week?"

"Doesn't work like that. It's off the time you *could* live. If you get hit by a beer wagon tomorrow, everyone still gets paid."

Marra felt a shiver crawl down her spine and fought it back. *You wouldn't give up two weeks of your life for your sister? To save her from losing all the weeks of hers?* "All right."

"Half a moment," said the snake-tongued woman. She pulled out a silver abacus and moved the beads back and forth. "There. Fortnight." The dust-wife looked over and nodded approval.

The abacus had a little dish at the bottom filled with what looked like plant stems. The woman picked one up and Marra saw that it was a caterpillar. "Hold out your hand."

Marra held her hand out worriedly. Would it hurt? What did losing two weeks of your life feel like?

The snake-tongued woman dropped the caterpillar into her palm. It unrolled itself and crawled over the side of her hand. Marra noticed, unsurprised, that her hand was trembling.

The caterpillar attached a thread of silk to her thumbnail and let itself down. It curled itself up and began a rapid wiggle, spinning silk across itself. Marra stood frozen, watching it build a cocoon far faster than any normal caterpillar she had ever seen.

In less than a minute, it was wrapped up and had turned a bright shade of green. "Ah . . . I . . . What am I supposed to do?" she whispered to the dust-wife.

"Won't be long," said the dust-wife, watching the caterpillar. Bonedog realized that Marra wasn't moving and sat on her foot, pelvis digging into her ankle.

The cocoon split open. A crumple-winged moth emerged, velvety brown in color, stretching wet wings. "There we go," said the snake-tongued woman. She caught Marra's wrist and pulled it toward her, plucking both moth and spent cocoon from her hand. The moth went into one of the little wooden boxes, and then she popped the empty cocoon into her mouth. Marra caught a glimpse of the snake tongue opening, and she turned away, feeling vaguely queasy.

"Take your moth," said the dust-wife, pointing to the white one still in the tray. Marra reached out and fumbled the white moth free. "Now, blow on it and tell it to find you what you need."

Marra had an increasing sense that she was in a dream, even more so than she had in the blistered lands. Only Bonedog's solid, uncomfortable weight convinced her that it was all really happening.

She lifted the moth level with her face. It was very fuzzy and had big black eyes. *Don't think of it like an insect. Think of it like a . . . a mouse. A mouse with feathers for ears.*

She blew across the moth's back. "Please," she whispered to the moth, "find me what I need to help my sister."

Its wings shivered. For a moment the black lines seemed to rearrange themselves, forming letters, words, sentences. Then it spread its wings and flew.

The brown hen took a snap as the moth went by but missed as the dust-wife flicked the staff aside. "Shame!" she said to the hen. The hen looked unrepentant.

"Now what?" asked Marra.

"Now follow that moth!"

* * *

They threaded their way through the goblin market, through the strange sea of people. The moth stayed fluttering a little way overhead, swooping to avoid antlers or banners or wings.

They had moved across two aisles and turned down the third when the crowd shifted around them. The people of the goblin market drew back, leaving a long avenue open between them. Conversation hushed, not in awe but in annoyance. Marra was reminded of the way that crowds moved to avoid a leper with a bell.

The woman who came down the center of the aisle moved as stately as a queen. Marra's impression was that she was very tall, and yet when the woman drew near, Marra could have met her eyes without looking up. Perhaps her apparent height was because of the light.

For she did not glow—not precisely—but she moved through a cloud of light as if it were dust. Her footsteps kicked up motes of brilliance. The light roiled around her feet and trailed behind her, refusing to settle. She carried a severed hand in her right hand. Her left wrist ended in a stump, not bloody, simply there. The motes of light seemed to gather near it, briefly forming fingers, then falling back to the ground again.

"Saint," muttered someone behind Marra in a tone of disgust.

Perhaps Marra and the dust-wife had not pulled back far enough in the crowd. Perhaps it was simply the brown hen, who refused to be intimidated by anyone, who let out a grumpy *errk* and fluffed her neck feathers. The saint turned her head.

Her face was as serene as the statues of the convent. She was not Our Lady of Grackles—Marra was almost certain of that—and yet it seemed perhaps the two might know each other. Did saints communicate? Was there some place that they all went and spoke together, putting their feet up and shaking their heads over mortal foibles?

For a moment the eyes of the saint looked into hers, as deep and wise as a good dog's eyes.

The sisters at the convent had never prepared her for what to do if you met a saint. It was not assumed that the issue would ever come up. Marra sank down to one knee, almost genuflecting, as she looked into the saint's eyes.

Did the serene lips curve up a little? Marra could not say. It took an effort to drag her gaze away. The world was dark and seemed to throb in the corners of her vision, as if she had been staring into a fire. She blinked away tears.

The dust-wife said something that Marra couldn't quite make out and pulled her to her feet as the crowd closed up behind the saint. The brown hen *errk*ed again.

"Where did the moth go?" asked Marra. She rubbed her eyes, trying to clear the dazzlement from them.

"Not sure . . . there! End of the aisle." She plunged ahead. Marra hurried after. The strangeness of the market seemed less somehow after the saint's passage, or perhaps strangeness did not quite measure up to glory.

The moth circled overhead, spun too close to a light—Marra held her breath—and then dropped down into a stall. Marra inched closer to it and saw velvet cloth laid out with dozens of small white objects. Jewels? Ivory? Shells?

Teeth.

Of course it would be teeth, her mind said, while her skin tried to crawl off her body and run away screaming. *It was never not going to be horrible. Teeth. Yes.*

The apparent owner of the stall had brilliant yellow eyes like a lizard. He lounged against one of the poles holding up the awning, watching the crowd. Ivory clicked softly on his chest from a necklace made of teeth.

I can't possibly need a tooth. Where is the moth?

The white moth had landed on the arm of a broad-shouldered man wearing the remains of a coat and tabard. There was a delicate silver collar around his neck, more like lace than metal. He was stacking boxes near the back of the stall, his face expressionless.

Marra didn't know what to do. Did she just go up to the man and say, "Excuse me, I need you"? That seemed like it could be misinterpreted in a great many ways. She tried to catch his eye, but he did not look in her direction, or at anything but his work.

The dust-wife bent over the teeth, making occasional appreciative noises. Eventually the yellow-eyed man drifted over, keeping a wary eye on the chicken. "You looking to buy, mistress?"

"Maybe. Not quite seeing what I need."

"What do you need?"

"I don't know, but I'll know it when I see it." She prodded a particularly large molar, the size of a shoe. "Hmm. Maybe."

"Cyclops. You won't find another like it."

"I will if I check in an elephant's mouth." She gave him a narrow look. "I wasn't birthed yesterday, my lad."

The yellow-eyed man grinned. "Ah, well, can't blame a man for trying."

The dust-wife's expression indicated that she could indeed blame him. She leaned back, eyes sweeping over the stall.

"The big one back there," she said, sounding bored. "Is he sound?"

"Sound enough. Fool enough to sleep in a fairy fort. I pulled him out before something worse got him."

"He available?"

"Might be. Not sure you want him." He leaned back against the pole again. "He's a killer. Had blood on his hands when I found him."

The man had stopped and was looking toward them. His eyes were too shadowed to make out their color.

"What do you want for him?"

Are . . . are they talking about buying him? No, surely not. Even here in the goblin market where all the rules were different, you shouldn't be able to buy people. Even the awful Northern Kingdom with its awful new king didn't let you buy people. That was barbarism.

"Ten years," said the yellow-eyed man.

"Not a chance. He won't last ten years."

Marra spoke up. "Is he a hireling?"

The yellow-eyed man rolled his eyes. "Anybody who sleeps in a fairy fort is fair game. What you do with them once you've got them is your problem. Eat them, wed them, set them free—it's all the same. He moves boxes for me."

The man who had slept in a fairy fort reached a hand up to the silver collar and touched it, as if picking at a scab.

The dust-wife eyed the necklace around the man-seller's neck and said, "Forget years. I'll give you a nun's tooth."

His yellow eyes narrowed, going sharp as needles. "A nun's tooth?"

"Pulled, not dropped," said the dust-wife. "Eh?"

"Reeeeeally . . ." He glanced at Marra.

Marra had a sudden bad feeling. "Um . . ."

"Smell the convent on her," suggested the dust-wife.

"But—"

"Hush," said the dust-wife. And to the seller, "Go on."

The seller approached Marra, nose working. Marra's skin crawled. *My tooth? What? Is he going to snatch one out of my head?*

"Yessss . . ." said the seller, his nostrils flared so wide that Marra could see an edge of pink inside them, like seashells. "Yes, yes! I taste it. Faith and straw. A hint of vespers. Yes! I'll take it. A tooth for him."

"Wait a minute," said Marra, starting to realize that this was really happening and they were talking about her actual teeth. "Wait. You can't—"

The seller turned his head and shouted, "Eh! Toothdancer! Get over here!"

"The moth says we need him," said the dust-wife. "And one of your teeth has been bothering you, hasn't it?"

"Well, yes, but—"

"I thought so. You wince a little when you chew."

"Eh! Toothdancer! Stir your stumps!"

"But you're going to have someone pull my tooth? Right now? Because a bug landed on him?" She flailed her hand at the man who had been moving boxes. He watched her emotionlessly. She wondered if he was under some spell, or if he simply no longer cared. Then she saw the Toothdancer emerge from behind a curtain in back of the stall and stopped worrying about the other man at all.

The Toothdancer looked like a stork or a heron, with a long hard bill and a curved, mobile neck. He wore a tattered black suit, with feathers sticking out of the holes, and his hands were very human. When he turned his head, Marra saw half a man's face below the beak, as if it were a mask, and yet his eyes were clearly a heron's, the color of new-minted coins, and set back from the beak like a bird's.

She gulped.

"This one," said the seller. The dust-wife took hold of Marra's elbow.

"Will it hurt?" whispered Marra, suddenly six years old again, with a baby tooth that pained her.

"No," said the Toothdancer in a kindly voice. He sounded like a friend, not like a monster with a living mask. "I know my work." He tapped her chin with a blunt finger. "Open, please."

Marra opened her mouth and closed her eyes. It was all completely ridiculous, and she didn't want to do it any more than she had when she was six, and yet you had to—that was how life went when a tooth went bad. You opened your mouth . . .

Something pressed against her lips. She opened her eyes, realized that the Toothdancer's beak was actually inside her mouth, and hastily squeezed them closed again.

Tap . . . tap . . . tap . . . The beak was tapping against her teeth, surprisingly delicate, the end much smaller than it looked. *Oh, sweet gods. Lady of Grackles, let this not be happening!*

Tap . . . tap . . .

The dust-wife held her elbow steady. She didn't tell Marra to relax, which was good because she was so far from relaxed that she thought she might scream.

Tap-ta-tap-tap. The Toothdancer had found the bad tooth. Lower molar on the right side. It had been twinging when Marra ate sometimes, and she had taken to chewing on the other side to prevent a bolt of pain from lancing through her jaw.

The beak withdrew. Marra clamped her lips shut, breathing heavily through her nose. She poked frantically with her tongue and found that the offending tooth was still there.

Maybe it's like magic maybe he's just taking a ghost tooth maybe it will be okay—

The Toothdancer took a pennywhistle from his coat pocket and began to play a spritely tune on it, using the human lips that Marra had seen before. She wondered if the beak opened at all, and then she stopped wondering because her teeth had begun to dance.

They twitched in her jaw like living things. She shrieked, not in pain but in horror, her mouth suddenly full of wiggling bone, as if she were in one of those nightmares where all her teeth fell out at once. It was like chewing and squirming and wiggling a loose tooth, wrapped all together, in time to the pennywhistle's tune.

She tried to bite down hard, hoping to still the awful dance, but it was worse, much worse, all the teeth rattling against each other, her skull filling up with the sounds of chattering. *Oh god oh god no no no no NO!*

If most of her teeth were dancing, the one bad molar was kicking. It felt as if it were battering against her cheek and the rest of her teeth, like a bird at a window, slam, slam, slam.

The Toothdancer leaned in closer and played more quickly. Marra wanted to scream a denial, but if she opened her mouth, all her teeth would dance out. *Oh god this was worse than anything worse than the blistered land, that had been outside, and this was inside her skin inside her* face—

With a popping sensation, the bad tooth pulled itself free of her jaw. It landed on her tongue, bouncing like an insect, and began to batter against the backs of her lips. Marra yelped at the sensation of hard, crawling life loose inside her mouth. She tried frantically to spit.

The Toothdancer dropped the pennywhistle, leaned in, and plucked the tooth neatly from the surface of her tongue with his beak. He turned and dropped the tooth, wet and glistening, into the tooth seller's palm.

Then he bowed very politely to Marra, patted her arm, and walked away.

Marra wrapped her arms around her ribs and sank to her knees, gasping. It hadn't hurt. She would have preferred that it hurt. She would prefer that she had never felt the sensation of all her teeth leaping and bounding in their sockets. She touched her tongue to the gap, hesitantly, and tasted blood.

"Oh god," she said hoarsely.

She thought she might start crying, but that would be to show weakness in front of the goblin market. For all she knew, there was a creature who would pull the tears out of her skull like teeth and sell them. She squeezed her eyes closed and thought fixedly about the pit of bones, the wires in her hands, silver looped over silver, building Bonedog, building calm.

An arm went around her, warm and solid. The dust-wife? No, surely not. Who, then?

For a wild instant she thought it was the Toothdancer, who had a kind voice, and the sudden horror of the thought made Marra open her eyes.

The white moth was just visible on his opposite shoulder. He knelt beside her, arm around her shoulders, the muscles in his jaw tense under the line of blue-gray stubble. "Enough," he said to the tooth seller or the dust-wife or both. "Stop this. I'm not worth it."

"Done is done," said the stall owner, licking Marra's tooth. "No taking it back now."

Bonedog had realized that something was wrong and was trying to get to her. The man she had sold a tooth for half turned, throwing his body between them. *No, no, it's all right; he doesn't know . . .* Bonedog must have looked like a monster to him, in this place already full of monsters. "It's all right," she said against the man's shoulder. "The dog is mine. My friend."

She didn't know if she spoke loudly enough, but he must have heard. He moved, one arm still around her, and Bonedog jumped in to wash her face with a nonexistent tongue. Bone and wire claws on her knee pricked through her clothes and she took a deep breath and said, "It's fine, boy. I'm fine."

"Here," said the dust-wife, handing her a tiny square of fabric. "Felted cobweb tobacco. Put that in the hole. It'll keep it from going bad."

She pushed the fabric into the gap in her teeth and nodded.

"Better?" asked the large man holding her. He spoke quietly, almost under his breath. Perhaps he, too, had learned not to show weakness.

"Better," she said.

He got to his feet and helped her up. The corded, effortless strength of his arm might have been alarming under other circumstances, but in the goblin market, she was glad of it.

"You want the collar?" asked the yellow-eyed man.

The dust-wife sniffed haughtily. "Take it off."

"As you wish." He reached toward the man's neck, and Marra watched the man very obviously not flinch away and wondered what not flinching cost him. The yellow-eyed man flicked the collar three times with his thumbnail, and it fell apart into cobwebs and dust.

The man inhaled sharply. The yellow-eyed man said, "Your problem now," and turned back to his wares, fondling Marra's tooth.

The dust-wife walked away and turned a corner. The man waited for Marra to move before he followed. His eyes were brown in the twisting light of the market, but there were still shadows on them.

"There," said the dust-wife. "We'll talk later, young man. Stay close, and we'll get out of here in a few moments yet."

"Are you human?" he asked, looking from the dust-wife to Marra.

Marra nodded. The dust-wife shrugged. "My parents were, anyway. You able to walk out of here under your own power?"

He swallowed. "Yes."

"One more thing we need," said the dust-wife, patting Bonedog's skull. "Then we're done."

"Not another tooth," croaked Marra. The dust-wife shrugged again.

She walked away through the crowd, one hand on Bonedog's collar. Marra moved to follow.

"May I take your arm?" asked the man.

Marra blinked at him. The formality of the gesture seemed to come from a world a long way off, a world where she was a princess instead of a nun. Did he think that she needed his support?

You did just collapse in front of him . . .

Then it occurred to her that he had been a prisoner in the market while she walked free. Perhaps he wanted to be sure that no one tried to imprison him again. "Yes, of course," she said, slipping her arm through his. She tugged him forward, following after the dust-wife.

The dust-wife backtracked down one of the aisles they had passed, and stopped before a stall that seemed to be divided in half. One side groaned under the weight of gems and gold, piled up and carelessly spilling over a silken runner. A bird with feathers made of fire watched over them, in a cage with bars that shone like moonlight.

The other side of the table barely registered to the eye. River stones and dried leaves, on an old burlap feed sack. There was a birdcage there, too, with a little gray finch perched inside it. As Marra watched, the finch opened its beak and sang two small, twittering notes, then pecked at a scatter of seed on the floor of the cage.

She looked at the caged phoenix on the pile of treasure, then back to the finch and the burlap and the stones, and began to realize what sort of stall this might be.

"I need a glamour," said the dust-wife. She picked up a river stone and set it down in the pile of treasure. It acquired facets and blazed like a ruby under her hands. She picked up a coin, stamped with the face of an ancient king, and moved it to the other side of the table, where it was a dried leaf with the edges turning to powder.

The person behind the stall nodded. Their appearance shifted every few seconds—old and young, short and tall, male, female, neither, both. "What do you wish disguised?"

The dust-wife clicked her tongue to Bonedog, tugging him forward.

"Nice work," said the glamour seller, coming out from behind the table. Their appearance settled somewhat, into a nondescript person with enormous donkey's ears. "Yours?"

"Mine," said Marra.

The glamour seller's ears swiveled in her direction and they nodded. "What would you like?"

"Sight and touch," said the dust-wife, "so that bystanders don't notice her dog is lacking in the flesh department." She thought for a moment, then added, "I suppose sound is expensive?"

"Sound's expensive," agreed the glamour seller. "People expect to see or feel certain things. Their minds do half the work. Play with sound and you have to convince the world, too, or else the echoes don't come out right. And don't ask me for something that will fool other dogs. I'm good but not that good."

"If it fools human onlookers, that's enough," said the dust-wife. "What does it cost me?"

The long gray ears flicked. "Is your demon for sale?"

Everyone looked at the brown hen. The hen said, *Errrrrk,* in much the same tone that the Sister Apothecary used to pronounce someone dead.

"No," said the dust-wife. "She's my best layer. Could give you a demon's egg, though."

"Done," said the glamour seller. The dust-wife fished the day's egg out of her pocket, and the glamour seller went back behind the table and began digging through a basket. The contents of the basket looked like so much junk to Marra, but then, so did the contents of the dust-wife's pockets. She poked the hole in her jaw with her tongue and found that the bleeding had stopped and the little square of felt had settled into the empty socket as if it belonged there.

The man at her side stood like a palace guard. He had the same erect posture, the same air of watchfulness. Marra wanted to ask him how he came to be a prisoner in the goblin market and what a fairy fort was, but surely this was not the time, not when they were surrounded by creatures alert for weakness . . . She poked her tongue at the hole again.

The glamour seller took a ball of twine and a handful of snail shells and began measuring Bonedog and muttering.

"Are you all right?" whispered Marra, when she couldn't stand it any longer.

The man looked down at her. "I don't know. Are you planning on killing me?" he asked. He sounded as if he were commenting on the weather.

"No! I need your help, but I wouldn't . . ." It occurred to her suddenly that killing a prince was a very dangerous thing to do, and perhaps the moth had landed on him because someone was going to have to die, and that was what she had needed after all. *Oh gods! That can't be it, can it?* "That is, I don't know if I . . . I . . ." She stared up at him, having run out of words and wanting very much to not have said anything.

One corner of his mouth crooked just slightly. Marra stared at it wonderingly, that anyone could maintain a sense of humor in this dreadful place. He bent his head toward hers. "This is not the time or the place," he murmured. "We can sort everything else later."

"Right," mumbled Marra. "Right. Yes."

"Twine and snail shells, wires and bones," sang the glamour seller, half to themselves, while their ears flicked and swiveled. "There!" The twine was a grid, then a net, then they flung it over Bonedog, who bounced on his feet as if he were being given a treat.

The glamour settled around him and left a smell like burning dust. Marra saw the outlines of flesh, a shadow of fur, and then Bonedog shook himself and he was a great gray dog with a skull like a battering ram and a blaze of white across his chest. His tail was still a narrow, bony whip but there was fur across it. He had immense jowls and when he looked up at Marra, they all sagged into a gigantic smile.

"Oh, Bonedog," she said. He licked her hand and she could feel his tongue, not quite substantial but more than it had been.

"Enough of this place," said the dust-wife. "Everyone have their souls still? Shadows still attached? Then let's go before that changes."

They went up the stairs very slowly. The staircase seemed much longer going up than coming down. Perhaps that was always the way in a fairy world. The man she had ransomed, the man she needed, had his arm locked around hers. They leaned against each other, shoulder against shoulder, two humans in a place where no humans should ever have come. When Marra looked over at him in the sickly firefly light, she could see a silvery terror in his eyes, mastered but very much alive. Bonedog walked beside them, Marra's hand wrapped around the rope collar. She felt the illusion of fur against her fingers, except when she didn't and he briefly felt like bones.

The square at the top of the stairs became deep blue instead of black. It grew closer one agonized step at a time, bisected by the dark figure of the dust-wife. Stars began to appear in it, but the outline seemed restless, as if there were a shadow laid across it that should not have fallen just there.

There is something waiting at the top, Marra thought. *How many teeth will it take to get past? How many years off my life to buy our way free?* She exhaled on a long, shuddery breath and the man beside her half carried her up the next step, until she found her strength again.

It will take as many as it takes.

There was something at the top. She never saw what it was. The dust-wife reached the opening first and a shadow reared up, but the hen threw back her head and crowed like a rooster at dawn.

The shadow fled. The hen settled, making an indignant *errrk*. "I know," said the dust-wife soothingly, "I know. Crowing is always so embarrassing for a lady."

Rrr-rr-rrrk, muttered the hen, shaking out her neck feathers.

They emerged, stumbling, into the starlight. The man at Marra's side gasped in air as if he had never breathed before. "Free," he said. "Am I free of that place?"

"Almost," said the dust-wife. "Not quite yet. We've got one foot in the other world, and it isn't safe to linger." She led them back along the river, toward the tree root. The man still held Marra's elbow. She did not know whether to feel trapped or to be glad of the touch.

The drowned boy was waiting on the other side of the roots, chin-deep in the water. He gargled at them and the dust-wife made a noise of annoyance and gestured at him, swift and rude and backed by magic. The drowned boy sank down into the water and swam away, fast as an otter. "Now," said the dust-wife, leaning on her staff. "Now we're all the way back. Now you're free."

Chapter 9

I am Fenris," said the man. He started to say something more, to add another name or a rank, perhaps, but cut himself short. "Fenris," he repeated instead.

"Marra."

"Fenris," said the dust-wife. She snorted, looking over at Marra. "So you built yourself a dog and found yourself a wolf. If a fox shows up looking for you, we'll have a proper fairy tale and I'll start to worry."

"Why?" asked Marra. "If I'm in a fairy tale, I might actually have a chance."

"Fairy tales," said the dust-wife heavily, "are very hard on bystanders. Particularly old women. I'd rather not dance myself to death in iron shoes, if it's all the same to you."

"Perhaps you're the fox," said Marra.

"Ha!" The dust-wife's laugh really did have a bit of a fox's bark to it. "I deserved that."

"Do you have a name, Lady Fox?" asked Fenris. Marra could not tell if he was amused or irked by the conversation.

"Yes," said the dust-wife.

The silence stretched out. Marra picked at a thread of the nettle cloak, waiting.

If there was a battle of wills, the dust-wife won. Fenris's laugh was not terribly unlike the dust-wife's, the short, self-deprecating sound of a man who could still recognize absurdity. "What do you wish me to call you, then, ma'am?"

"*Ma'am* will work very well indeed. I am a dust-wife."

"Ah." He nodded. "One of those who live among the dead? We do not have them in my country, but we know of them."

The silence grew again. Marra wondered what he was thinking and what he made of them. *A shy nun and an old woman who communes with the dead. I don't know if I even know what I think of us . . .*

He's a killer, the yellow-eyed man had said. The thought was alarming. Fenris was large enough to break her in half with his bare hands, and however imperious the dust-wife was, she was still fundamentally an old woman with a chicken. Did he think he was still a prisoner? They'd ransomed him from the tooth seller, but they hadn't exactly set him free, had they? She'd gabbled something about needing him in the market. If he decided to escape his supposed captivity, their only defense would be a dog who was currently bouncing in the water to make it splash.

"You don't have to stay with us," she said.

Fenris looked over at her, his eyes unreadable. "Beg pardon?"

"I mean . . ." *No, don't explain about the moth—the moth is too complicated and sounds ridiculous if you say it out loud.* "Uh, there was magic that took us to a thing we needed. And it picked you. But you aren't a prisoner anymore."

"Magic said that you needed me?" He was smiling now, but it was a smile like his laugh, not so much humorous as incredulous at the shape of the world.

"Don't get any ideas," said the dust-wife. "Might turn out that our fate is sealed inside a jar and we need someone to loosen the lid."

His laugh that time had genuine humor in it, which seemed to surprise Fenris as much as it surprised Marra.

"Do we have time for me to wash?" he asked, as they left the river. "It has been a long time . . ."

The dust-wife shook her head. "Not here. The dead are restless and won't settle for a day or two. We'll find you a pond where no one's drowned."

"Well, I do like not drowning."

It took them perhaps half an hour. Even though Marra felt as if an age of the earth had passed in the goblin market, the moon had barely moved in the sky. It splashed a white reflection across a stock pond. Several sleeping cows stood on the other side of a fence, black shapes on the moonlit grass.

"How did you end up in the goblin market?" asked Marra, as Fenris sat down by the edge of the pond and began to unlace his boots.

"I was a fool," said Fenris. "I slept in a fairy fort. I knew better, but I . . ." He looked away.

"What's a fairy fort?" asked Marra.

"A ring of earth. Trees grow up the sides, but the centers are usually clear. Ruins, some say, of an old people. Dwellings of the hidden ones. Uncanny places. I should not have been there."

"You were on the run from something," said the dust-wife crisply, "or you were trying to kill yourself but didn't have the nerve to hold the knife. You're from Hardack, by your accent, and no Hardishman would sleep in a fairy fort, not dead drunk with two broken legs."

Fenris's lips twitched. He inclined his head to the dust-wife. "As you say."

"Well?" The dust-wife plunked herself down. The brown hen regarded Fenris with a baleful eye. "Which was it?"

"Both," said Fenris. He rubbed his forehead. "I am . . . was . . . a knight. In Hardack, as you say. I served the Fathers, not any particular clan. The Fathers rule the clans, but their rule is not absolute. Those who serve them work as diplomats as much as enforcers."

"And?" said the dust-wife, merciless.

"And I was a fool." He said it with no particular intonation, less flagellation than fact. "I did not recognize what was under my nose, and the day came that I had to kill a man because of it. A clan lord."

Marra pricked up her ears, suddenly intent. Was a clan lord as well protected as a prince?

"There was nothing I could do, within the law," Fenris said. "A lord's word is law in the clan's keep. The Fathers could censure him, but they could do no more. So I could let him walk free with blood on his hands, or deal justice with blood on mine." He shrugged. "I murdered three men who had committed no crime except defending their liege, and killed the lord, and left my sword atop him so that they would know who did the deed. And then I walked away and spent the night in a fairy fort."

"Deliberately," said the dust-wife thoughtfully. "You wanted to die, but not by human hands."

Fenris gave her a quick, wry glance. "For all that we say that we are servants of the Fathers, everyone knows what clan we hail from originally. I am a criminal, but whoever killed me would make an enemy of my clan. But if I was not killed, then the clan of the lord I had killed would lose face as long as I walked free." He tossed a pebble into the water. "It was not their fault that their lord was a monster. They suffered under his hands more than any of the rest of us."

"And Hardishmen consider suicide shameful," said the dust-wife.

Fenris shrugged. "I do not much care for my honor, but to fall on my sword would be to say that I believed what I had done was wrong." He sighed, and a little emotion crept at last into his voice. It sounded like weariness. "So here I am. I was in the goblin market for a long time and I am very tired."

* * *

Marra looked toward the pond. Fenris had requested a little privacy to bathe. She wondered if he was really doing so, or if he was running off into the woods to put as much distance between them as he could.

I did not tie the bone dog, and he came back. She rubbed Bonedog's skull, feeling the ghost of fur under her fingers as they pushed through the glamour.

"That was a sad story," she said aloud. "Poor man."

"If it's true, yes," said the dust-wife.

"You don't believe him?"

"Mm." The dust-wife shrugged. "He doesn't feel like a liar, but that only means he believes himself. I imagine most of it's true, more or less. But there's men that would kill a rival and convince themselves they'd done it for noble reasons." She laced her fingers behind her head, lying back on her bedroll. "Everybody makes up a story about their sins. Sometimes to make them less, sometimes to make them the worst thing a mortal's ever done. Really depends on the person. I'd wager this one's more martyr than apologist, but you never can tell."

"Do you think he'll try to leave?"

The dust-wife shrugged again. "If he comes back tonight, I doubt it. But if he has any sense, he'll take his freedom and go and we'll never see him again."

Marra bit her lip. "The moth said we needed him."

"We needed him *then,* yes." The dust-wife tilted her head. "It is possible that he has already done what he needed to do."

"What?" Marra frowned. "That was an hour ago!"

"Yes. And perhaps we would have been attacked in the goblin market if we had not had a large bodyguard walking with us, and his purpose is over and done."

Marra blinked. "Do you . . . do you think that's likely?"

The dust-wife shrugged yet again.

"But if it isn't, we still need him!"

"Indeed. But just because you need someone doesn't mean that they are under any obligation to provide. He may leave to take his chances elsewhere."

"I have not left," said Fenris from the shadows. Marra jumped. How could a man walk so silently? And how much had he heard?

She looked up, and Fenris walked out of the shadows, his tread slow and heavy as a draft horse. "I have little enough sense, Lady Fox," he said. Again that bemused smile. He turned his gaze to Marra. "We ransom prisoners often in my land, and usually it is only with gold. But you have bought my freedom with your own blood and bone. What little honor I have left is yours, and if I can be of service, I will."

* * *

Breakfast the next morning was dry bread without even one third of an egg apiece. Fenris snapped his up in three bites but did not complain about the scanty rations. Marra wondered how on earth they were all going to feed themselves on the way to the Northern Kingdom.

Fenris walked much more quickly than either of them at first, a ground-eating stride that would probably have him in the Northern Kingdom before Marra and the dust-wife had even left the Southern. He had to stop and check himself several times, almost apologetically.

Marra was having a difficult time herself. She had become used to ducking away from travelers, to making sure that Bonedog was out of sight. The first time that a farm wagon passed them, she grabbed his collar and almost dove into a hedgerow before she remembered.

The wagon driver did stare at them, but not at Bonedog. Instead he was looking at the hen on top of the dust-wife's staff and grinning hugely. "How'd you teach her to do that?" he called.

"Teach her, nothing," said the dust-wife. "Couldn't get her to stop." The driver laughed loudly and tapped his cap, then drove on, while Marra tried to calm her racing heart.

"Easy," murmured Fenris.

It was on the tip of Marra's tongue to be annoyed, but then she looked over at him and realized that he was talking to himself as much as to her.

How long was he in the goblin market? Does this seem strange to him as well?

She turned it over in her mind for a few moments, and then she simply asked.

"Too long." Fenris looked up at the sky, which had lost the pale gray-gold notes of dawn and was turning to blue. "It was hard to keep track of the days. They say that people who go into a fairy fort will dance for a night and come back to find that years have passed. I don't know if that's true. I don't know if the goblin market is always running. It seemed like I was always there in the stall, but sometimes I'd sleep and it felt like a long, long time had passed. And sometimes it was . . . different."

"Different how?" asked the dust-wife sharply.

"Colder. Darker. Different . . . things."

"Things? Do you mean people?" asked the dust-wife.

"I mean that when my captor sold a tooth, the *thing* he sold it to looked like a woman, right up until it bit the tooth in half like an apple." His voice was very calm, and he did not look at either of them as he spoke. "Then it pounced on the first person that walked by and left them dead on the floor of the market. And that yellow-eyed bastard only complained about the mess and called someone to haul the body away."

For the first time that Marra could remember, the dust-wife looked very slightly abashed. "Ah. Dark of the moon. The goblin market is at its worst then."

"I'm sorry," said Marra.

Fenris looked at her then. His eyes were bleak, but he forced half a smile. "I was, too. For all of us. There were a few other humans, I think, working in other stalls. It's hard to say. We would nod to each other, but we did not get a chance to speak." He drew a deep breath and straightened his back. "Well. If that was the dark of the moon, then I suppose I was there for three months. I would have guessed it was more like a few weeks. The days seemed very long, but not like that."

"What did you do?" asked Marra.

He shrugged. "Thought, mostly. Turned over all the ways that I had failed, and all the places I could have turned aside from my path. Thought about escaping." He shook his head. "I wasn't able to talk to anyone else but the Toothdancer. He was not so bad, for all his looks. But it was a cruel place." He exhaled slowly through his nose. "And I, being a selfish bastard, thought only of getting free. Perhaps I should have told you to take someone else in my place. I deserved my captivity."

"You're the one we needed. Or that the moth said we needed."

He shrugged again.

"Perhaps when this is all over," said Marra recklessly, "perhaps we could go back. Find the others there."

The look he gave her this time was surprise. "Will you sacrifice a tooth for each of them, then?"

Her skin crawled at the thought, but what was a tooth compared to someone's life? "If I have to."

The silence went on too long, and then he offered her his hand, not to hold but to shake. Marra did. His fingers were calloused against her skin.

"So," said Fenris. "Now that we have pledged to one another's hopeless quests, may I ask where we are going on yours?"

"The Northern Kingdom," said Marra.

"I have not been there," Fenris said. "You must warn me if there are any customs that I do not know that will lead us all into difficulty."

"I don't think there are any," said Marra. She racked her brain, trying to think of anything useful. "But I don't know if I'd know. I grew up very near there, so my people would do the same thing, I suppose. Um. Don't hit anyone in the face with a glove?"

Fenris's expression was indescribable. "Is this a thing your people do often?"

"No, not unless we want to fight duels. Which we don't. I mean, I don't."

"Might save time," said the dust-wife. "We send him to duel the prince and get it over with."

Marra considered this. Fenris was a little older than the prince but a great deal larger. Did that matter? "Hmm . . ."

"A prince, eh?" Fenris glanced at her for acknowledgment. "And you want him dead?"

"Is that a problem?" *What if he leaves and tells the prince? No, we didn't say a name, and he's never even been to the Northern Kingdom. He can't know it's Vorling, and anyway, Vorling's the king now . . .*

"Does he deserve to die?" asked Fenris, as if they were talking about the weather.

"Very much so."

"Then it's not a problem. Do your rulers accept challenges from strangers, though?"

"No . . ." said Marra. Of course it wouldn't be that easy. "No, I'm pretty sure they don't."

"Good. It's a foolish way to choose rulers, even if it does make things less convenient for us now."

"They allow it in Hardack, as I recall," said the dust-wife.

"They do," said Fenris. "It's foolish there, too. You get a competent, judicial man who knows the names of each of his vassals, who can balance the needs of the clan against the needs of individuals . . . and then you get a brute whose only skill is swinging an axe. And like as not, the man with the axe wins, and then it's his boot on the clan's neck until someone sends to the Fathers to sort matters out, which half the time we can't."

"I'm beginning to suspect you've dealt with this before," said Marra.

"However did you guess?" He gave her a wry glance. "Yes. I've seen four clans ruined by it. One saved as well, but we could have found other ways. What did this prince do?"

The question was delivered in the exact same tone as the rest, and it caught her by surprise, like a blow. She missed a step and Fenris moved to catch her, then stepped back when she caught herself on her own.

"He killed my sister," she said. "And my other sister . . . his now wife . . . he . . ." Her throat tried to close up again and she forced the words out. "He hurts her. He leaves marks and she . . . she stays pregnant so that he will not beat her, but she will die of it eventually. Then he'll take another wife and do it to her again."

Fenris nodded, as if what she had said was perfectly comprehensible, even though she could barely comprehend it herself. If the fact that a nun was kin to a prince's wife surprised him, he gave no sign. "I understand. Men like that never stop. If they can be isolated or thrown at the enemy, it is for the best, and then the clan gets some good of them in the end. But often they cannot be, and then we must find other solutions."

"That's what we're trying to do," said Marra. "Other solutions. Whatever that may be."

"It's a fool's errand and we'll probably all die," said the dust-wife.

"Oh, well then," said Fenris. "I always enjoy those."

"What now?" Marra asked the dust-wife. "You had the ideas before. Or do we simply walk north until we get there?"

The dust-wife scratched her hen's keel bone thoughtfully. The bird looked annoyed, but then, it always did. "I can almost see my way forward," she said. "If it were only mortals we faced, then you and I and your large friend there might be enough. But the godmother is where everything falls down."

"The prince's fairy godmother?"

The dust-wife nodded. "They've had the same one for a long time. Bound to the royal family and kept alive long past when a sensible person would die. Her protection will lie over the prince." She gnawed on her lower lip. "The dead I may command, but that is a different power."

"Stronger?" asked Marra.

"Different." The dust-wife paused, then smiled ruefully. "Probably stronger. I speak with the dead and for the dead. Our two powers have nothing to say to one another. We might pass each other in the street without speaking or she might blast me into nothingness."

"I suppose you can't blast her into nothingness first?" asked Fenris.

"I've never tried," admitted the dust-wife, "but it doesn't seem very likely."

Marra sighed. "So what do we need to fight a power like that? My fairy godmother was nearly useless."

The dust-wife raised an eyebrow. "You had a fairy godmother?"

"Yes, of course. Princesses, you know . . ."

"Not all of them," said the dust-wife, "not even most of them, come to that. And the ones who do tend to be in much larger kingdoms, not little nations poised between dangerous neighbors. Power calls to power."

Marra snorted. "Well, she wasn't worth much, so you're not far wrong."

"Oh?" said the dust-wife.

"She blessed us all with good health," said Marra grimly. "And

Damia she said would marry a prince. Which wasn't much of a blessing, given he killed her."

"Health's not so little a thing," said the dust-wife. "Compared to the alternative, anyway."

Marra's lip curled. "She might have wished us *safe*," she growled. "Or at least that we wouldn't marry someone who'd murder us."

"She might have," said the dust-wife. "But parents object to people making pronouncements like that at christenings, for some odd reason."

"You'd think they'd be grateful."

"No accounting for human nature."

Marra did not know Fenris well enough to read his expressions, but she would have sworn that he wanted to say something. He kept glancing at the dust-wife. A line formed between his eyes with each glance, growing deeper, until finally he apparently gave up and said, "Lady Fox?"

The dust-wife snorted. "Yes?"

"You claim to speak with the dead?"

"I don't claim it," said the dust-wife calmly. "I do it. Although most days it's less speaking and more listening. People who won't shut up in life rarely shut up in death."

Fenris shook his head. After a moment he said, picking his words carefully, "I do not know that I believe in ghosts."

"Yet you believe in fairies," said the dust-wife, sounding amused rather than offended. "Enough that you offered yourself to a fairy fort."

"And now I suppose that I should say that is different," said Fenris. "But the truth is that I did not believe in fairies, either. No one I know does." He rubbed a hand through his hair, and Marra saw threads of white salted through the dark length.

"You did not believe in fairies, but you were afraid of a fairy fort?" said Marra, puzzled.

"Well . . . yes." Fenris gave her another of his bemused how-am-I-here smiles. "We do not believe, but you still wouldn't cut trees from a fairy mound or spend the night in one. Just in case there is something there, whether you believe in it or not."

"There you are, then," said the dust-wife. "The dead are there, whether you believe in them or not."

"Mm."

Marra felt an urge to jump in and try to smooth the conversation over, but she did not know how she would manage that. She had never liked disagreements, but they both seemed amused, anyway, rather than heated. She studied Fenris under her lashes, trying not to be too obvious.

In daylight, he was even larger than she had thought in the goblin market. Broad shoulders, barrel chest. Even if he was older than the prince and had thickened around the middle with age, no one would mistake him for anything but a warrior. His hands were covered in dozens of small, healed scars and his forearms were corded with muscle. You did not get muscle like that simply from lifting boxes. *If he wanted to, he could probably throttle me one-handed.* Marra licked suddenly dry lips. *The spell said we needed him. Surely we couldn't need someone who was going to try to kill us. Unless the world is very strange indeed, and maybe I should be dead and the dust-wife should raise me up and send me after Vorling as a vengeful shade.*

This seemed like a lot.

The dust-wife clearly had no fear of Fenris, even if he was twice her size. "You do not believe in ghosts, Hardishman," she said, "yet would you desecrate a grave?"

Fenris's eyes went wide in clear dismay. "No! Of course not."

"Well then."

They walked along in silence for nearly half an hour. Bonedog nosed at something in a hedge and snapped his jaws closed. Whatever it was fell out through the bottom of his jaw and ran off into the grass. He came back, grinning hugely, very proud of himself.

Finally Fenris broke the silence, saying, "You may be right, Lady Fox. But I find that I feel differently about the fairy forts than a grave. Even when I did not believe, the forts were . . . uncanny. There was always a little dread, under the surface. Dread of the unknown.

But when I think of desecrating a grave, I do not feel dread but re-vulsion. I am not afraid of what lies in the grave, but it would be dishonorable. Disgusting, even. I do not fear retribution; I fear what sort of person I would become by doing it."

The dust-wife slowed then and gave Fenris a sharp, appraising look. The brown hen gave an indignant squawk and rocked on top of the staff.

One of her rare smiles crooked her lips. "You are still wrong, Hardishman," she said. "But you are wrong in an interesting way."

Fenris bowed his head, a knight accepting praise from a queen, and Bonedog wagged his tail and barked silently at them both.

Chapter 10

Traveling on the road with Fenris was different than traveling solely with the dust-wife. Different and also, Marra had to admit, easier.

He was clearly used to camping roughly. He could build a fire while Marra was still fumbling with flint, and keep it going longer. He had no gear of his own after his time in the goblin market, so the dust-wife sacrificed a metal measuring cup and Marra handed over the smaller of her two knives so he could eat and drink.

After two days, Marra no longer seriously believed that Fenris would turn on them. He was calm and judicious and the dust-wife needled him more or less constantly, which he took in good humor. Occasionally Marra would share a glance with him, a bemused one that said, *Can you believe that two sensible people such as us are in this situation?*

The look warmed her. She had not shared that look of fellow feeling since she had left the Sister Apothecary at the monastery.

Nevertheless, there were times when he stood up too quickly, or loomed too large, and some shadow on her mind whispered that no one had thought Vorling would turn on his wives, either. *Am I being too cautious? Or not nearly cautious enough?* And she remembered the farmer who had tried to kill her, the one who likely thought that he was a decent man but had seen only a monster from the blistered land, and she would put a few more steps between them and try not to make it too obvious.

If he noticed, he gave no sign.

He did eat more than the dust-wife and Marra put together. She could tell that he was trying not to, but she could also hear his stomach growling. They stopped at farmhouses whenever they could. One night all they had was tea, but the next afternoon Bonedog rousted a rabbit and Fenris cleaned and spitted it and they ate better than they had in days.

As they went farther north, travel became easier. Everyone needed firewood split and Fenris could use an axe with the ease of long practice. They went up to doors and asked if he could chop wood in return for a bit of food for the road, and generally people were happy to see them. Occasionally they'd even point to someone farther along the road that would also need work. Fenris's stomach stopped growling, and they no longer had nights where there was nothing but tea.

With the north, however, came cold. Since Fenris had no gear, he had no blankets, either. They slept in barns when they could, but that was not always possible. Marra woke one morning to find frost on the ground and Fenris crouched so close to the fire that his beard was in danger of going up in flame.

"Uh," she said that night. "It's cold. If you'd like to share my blanket . . ."

The dust-wife snorted. Fenris's eyebrows went up. Marra wondered if that was a euphemism in Hardack, too. "Not like that," she said hastily. "I mean, if you're cold. It's cold. That is to say, you can have part of mine. I'm not suggesting anything more than that."

The dust-wife was having a coughing fit. Fenris, however, bowed his head gravely to her and said, "It is probably not the path of honor to deprive a young woman of half her blanket, but my bones are old enough that I thank you."

"I'm not that young," said Marra.

"And don't even talk to me about old bones until you're over seventy, youngster," said the dust-wife.

Fenris gave her a mild look. "That's about thirty years hence, at which point you will undoubtedly tell me that I cannot complain until I am over a hundred."

The brown hen cackled and the dust-wife thumped the staff until the bird flapped. "Don't get smart," she muttered, although whether she meant the hen or Fenris, she didn't say, and no one tried to find out.

Marra unwrapped her bedroll. The dust-wife had given it to her, one long blanket, enough to wrap one person comfortably, even if, like Marra, she tended to stretch out in her sleep.

It was very small for two. They lay down back-to-back, the blanket over both of them, although Marra was quite certain that Fenris was giving her the lion's share. She could feel his back against hers like a wall, though they were both wearing too many layers for her to catch his breathing.

Bonedog usually slept humped over her feet, his rib bones gouging into her ankle. Finding two sets of feet, he did not seem to know what to do. He circled, whined briefly, and then draped himself over her shins. The glamour tried to soften the hard points of his pelvis but failed.

Marra could not seem to get comfortable, either. It was hard enough to sleep on the ground, but had the ground been this hard last night? Was that a rock under her? Her arms were pulled inside her robes for warmth, but had the sleeves always been so constricting?

She shifted position, trying to get comfortable, then wondered if she was waking Fenris up, or if he was still awake and she was annoying him. She didn't squirm this much when there wasn't another person there, did she? Or did she, but she didn't worry about it and didn't notice she was doing it?

How many years had it been since she'd slept near another human being? She tried to remember. In smaller houses, with fewer beds, people bundled up two and three to a bed, but princesses slept alone.

When she had been very young, she had sometimes crept from her bed to Damia's. *I had a bad dream*, she would say. Her older sister had been very patient, had pulled the blankets aside and helped her climb up onto the tall bed. Marra remembered it all with sudden vividness, the scent of dried lavender under the pillow and the crispness of the sheets. She hadn't thought of that in years.

I can't remember Damia's face, she thought, gazing dry-eyed into the dark, *but I remember the lavender.*

Her back was beginning to warm up. Unfortunately one side of her sinuses was starting to clog. Normally she would have rolled over, but if she did that, she'd have her face squashed into Fenris's spine. She wished she could sleep on her back, but it always made her feel short of breath. (Women in her family did not sleep on their stomachs after puberty. She hadn't even tried since she was fourteen.)

She fidgeted again, located a rock under her hip, and tried to get it out of the way without squirming too much. Bonedog got up, circled three times, and collapsed again in exactly the same position.

Fenris is probably regretting agreeing to this. He is probably thinking he got better sleep with his face an inch from the coals.

It was foolish to even try . . . she thought, and then it was morning and the warmth against her back was gone and the brown hen was clucking irritably for her breakfast.

* * *

The day they crossed back into Marra's own kingdom felt strange, because it didn't feel like anything at all.

The borders were porous and no one particularly cared, and they were on a back road that lacked even a guard post. There was a faded wooden marker with an approximation of the royal crest burned into it, recognizable even if the dragon looked more like a snake and the hare looked like a blobby dog. Marra paused at the line, then stepped over as if stepping into cold water.

I should feel something, she thought. *This is my land. I'm a daughter of the royal house.*

She didn't.

She'd been asleep on the coach when she had crossed the other way, and she'd been so anxious about finding the dust-wife that she hadn't given it much thought. But this time she knew where she was and she was walking into her own kingdom and it seemed as if she should feel . . . something.

"Problem?" asked Fenris.

"I live here," said Marra. She nudged the dirt with her boot. "I'm home, I guess. Except it doesn't feel like much of anything."

"Ah."

"The poet Tarus said that when he came home, the land itself sang under his feet, and his heart sang with it."

"That may be unique to poets." Fenris started to rest his hand on a nonexistent sword hilt, caught himself, and shoved his hands in his pockets instead. "I came back from my first campaign and I'd been in my own clan's lands for half an hour before I noticed."

She glanced up at his face, surprised.

"I was cold and wet and very tired," he said. "When I did feel something, it was because I realized we were only about twenty minutes from the keep and I might get warm again." He shrugged. "And then again, other times I have come home and felt as if I had finally woken up after a long illness. I suspect these things say more about us than they do about the land itself."

Marra was watching his face, and so she saw the sudden flash of pain across it, quickly stifled, the deepening of the lines between his eyebrows.

"Will you be able to go back to your clan's lands again?" she asked.

"No." He lifted his head, looking around them. This part of the countryside did not go red and orange with autumn, only dun and yellow. Wind rustled through the dry stems of broom straw at the edges of the road. "No. I can go anywhere in the wide world that I wish, but the borders of Hardack are closed to me."

"There is no appeal?" asked Marra. "You can't . . . um . . . wait for someone to die? Or forget?"

His smile was acknowledgment that she was trying, not happiness—a quick flicker, then gone. "No. My return would start a senseless war of vengeance. I will not sentence so many people to die merely because I am homesick."

"I'm sorry."

"As am I." The flicker of a smile lasted longer this time. "But I am told that this is a fool's errand and we will all probably die, so I do not let it trouble me overmuch."

They trudged onward, into her kingdom, Bonedog weaving in and out between them. Marra thought of all the stories of exiles returning home, and wondered how many, like Fenris, simply never returned at all because the price was too high.

And what will I do, if we succeed? Will I go back to my little room at the convent and hope to be left alone again?

It was because of Prince Vorling that she had never married. He did not want any competing claims to the little kingdom's throne. If he was dead, would that change?

Lady of Grackles, please, no. Let me stay insignificant. Let me be a weaver and a midwife, not a princess.

She took a deep breath, then set the thought aside. *This is still a fool's errand, and probably we will all die.* A familiar thought. It was strange to take such comfort in it.

"Marra?" The dust-wife looked over at her. "Where does your godmother live?"

"My godmother?" Marra frowned. "I don't know. No, wait . . ." She rubbed her forehead, trying to dredge up old memories. Had her mother said something once? Nothing important. The godmother had not been important, had just been one more actor in the drama of childbirth. But they had gone out in a carriage years ago, passing through the countryside on the way to somewhere else, and the queen had said something about the godmother living over that way . . .

"I think near Trexel," she said finally. "We went out for hawking and Trexel is where they have goshawks."

"You're a falconer?" asked Fenris.

"Not even remotely," said Marra. "But there's an absurd tradition that only the royal family is allowed to hunt with goshawks, so we have to go out and there's a whole ridiculous ceremony where the falconers gift you the birds and then you ask them to hold the bird in trust, so that they can hunt with them. There's probably still a bird or two out there that are technically my property, but what am I going to do with one?" She remembered the ceremony more clearly now, the pale bird with its mad red eyes and the heavy glove weighing down her arm. "So the falconers get to fly goshawks and put food on the table for the house that trains them—I've forgotten the name, one of the distaff branches—but if anyone asks, the birds belong to the royal house."

The dust-wife had paused while the hen climbed down her arm and made her way to the pack to lay her daily egg, but snorted at this. "Not the worst system I've ever heard of. The godmother lived near there?"

"I think so." Marra had a vague memory of her mother trying to entertain her and her sister, pointing out the window and saying, "Your fairy godmother lives over that way. Isn't that interesting?"

"Then let us make for Trexel," said the dust-wife.

Marra grimaced. She didn't want to see the woman who had sent her sisters out in the world so ill prepared. *But if I must, I suppose I can demand to know why she wasted such a chance. She could have stopped all of this long before it happened. Why didn't she?*

"Yes," said Marra, feeling anger stir in the pit of her stomach, anger that for once had little to do with Vorling. "Yes, let's."

* * *

It was one of life's ironies, thought Marra, that they had left the Southern Kingdom unmolested, only to be attacked as soon as they returned to her own lands.

Marra and the dust-wife were sitting by a well in a little gray town on a little gray road, surrounded by little gray fields. There was nothing to make anyone think it was dangerous. Fenris had negotiated a meal with the innkeeper in return for splitting yet more firewood. Marra was sitting on the edge of the well, thinking nothing in particular, when a shadow fell over her feet.

"The hell are you supposed to be?" said a thick, wet voice.

Marra jerked upright, panic firing her nerves. She had to grab for the stone to keep from pitching backward into the well.

The owner of the voice was not looking at her. He was a big, lanky, rawboned man and he was swaying slightly. *Day-drunk*, thought Marra. *Oh, Lady of Grackles.*

He was looming over the dust-wife.

The dust-wife was deeply unimpressed. Under normal circumstances, Marra would have applauded her calm, but she'd encountered a few drunks in her time with the Sister Apothecary and very few of them liked to be ignored. It made them angrier. The Sister Apothecary had been good at talking them down, usually by saying that there was a birth going on and suggesting they go have a toast to celebrate. Unfortunately that didn't seem like it would apply here.

"You a witch?" asked the drunk, stabbing a finger at the dust-wife. "That your *familiar*?" He snickered.

Marra looked around wildly. Where was Fenris? Behind the inn, probably, chopping wood. *Dammit.* Two or three bystanders had stopped and were watching, but no one was intervening.

"Go back to the bottle, man," said the dust-wife. "Leave an old woman alone."

He made a grab for the brown hen. He was in no danger of succeeding, but the dust-wife stepped back anyway. Marra was very sure that the dust-wife could protect herself, and also that if she did, they might have to leave the village in a hurry.

Do something! Stop this! Think! *How are you going to fight a prince if you can't even handle one drunk?*

"There's many a man who'll not think twice to mistreat a woman but who lives in fear of a habit and a holy symbol." Remembering these words, Marra stepped in front of the dust-wife, running her fingers down the cord that held the carved grackle feather. "We mean no harm, my son," she said, trying to sound like the abbess.

The drunk blinked at her. "The hell are you?"

"I serve Our Lady of Grackles." She sent a silent prayer to the Lady to add it to her tab for these frequent impersonations.

Glory be, he took a step back. Marra had a moment to think that she'd pulled it off, that it was all going to work, and then Bonedog began to bark at him.

Perhaps if he had a voice like a normal dog, it might not have mattered. But the working throat and snapping jaws of a silent bark caught the man's attention and he aimed a kick at Bonedog, with predictable results.

"Ow! Goddamn beast bit me!"

Oh hell. She snatched for Bonedog's collar and took a step back.

"It bit me!" he shouted to the growing crowd. "You all saw it!"

From what Marra could see, Bonedog had barely scraped the man's boot leather. She took another step back, dragging the dog with her. The dust-wife muttered something under her breath and dipped a hand into a pocket. Marra hoped she was grabbing something that would calm the man down, not something that would strike him dead and leave them with a corpse to explain.

A shadow fell between them.

"Excuse me," said Fenris.

Relief flooded Marra. At least if they had to make a break for it, they wouldn't get separated. And possibly the drunk would listen to another man, if not a nun.

The drunk turned. He had to look up to meet Fenris's eyes. "This isn't your problem, old man," he said.

"Friend," said Fenris in a just-between-us voice, "you're frightening the nuns. Let them go on their way in peace. The gods look out for them and so should we, eh?"

"Their dog bit me," muttered the drunk man.

"Ah well, even nuns have protectors, eh? Come now. I'm new in town, and you look like the sort of man who can tell me where I might find something . . ."

Fenris had a sort of matter-of-fact air that made it seem like the easiest thing in the world to go along. The drunk allowed himself to be escorted to the inn door, telling Fenris very seriously about blacksmiths and horse collars, and it should have worked, except that a bystander snickered and said, "Running from a nun, eh?"

"Oh hell," said the dust-wife.

The drunk wheeled around. Everything happened very fast and all at once and Marra had to grab for Bonedog's collar and then the drunk man was *right there* and something glittered in his hands and somebody shouted and Marra yelled, "Fenris, he has a knife!" and then, almost apologetically, Fenris stepped in close and punched the drunk in the head twice.

The man shook his head as if to clear it and Fenris punched him again. This time he fell down.

"And now I believe we should be going," said Fenris. "Quickly."

The three of them did not quite run out of the town, but they weren't slow. Bonedog wanted to go back and bite the man and Marra's shoulders ached from holding him.

When, after about twenty minutes, no one appeared to be chasing them, she relaxed enough to feel some other emotion, and it felt too much like anger for her liking. "Fenris!"

"Yes?"

"You could have died!" hissed Marra. "He had a knife!"

"But you would have gotten away," said Fenris.

"But—" Marra gaped at him, not sure if she wanted to throw herself into his arms or shake him until his teeth rattled. "But you would have been dead!"

He shrugged.

Marra took a deep breath. Why was she angry? It didn't make any sense to be angry, except that she'd been afraid and the fear didn't know what to do with itself. *It was just a drunk. You're fighting a prince. You'll face worse dangers than this.*

"Enough," said the dust-wife. "No one is dead, and let us get out of here while that's still true."

Chapter 11

It was easy to find the godmother, once they got to Trexel. Marra had visions of the dust-wife using magic or asking the dead, but what she actually did was lean over a fence and say, to a woman with three children and a harried expression, "Is there a godmother who blesses children about?"

The woman's face briefly turned cheerful. "Oh yes— Don't put that in your mouth! The godmother. She's very kind— I swear to the saints, Owen, I will take you to market and sell you for a three-legged goat!—Five miles down the road, turn where it crosses the stream and go along the bank until— Owen, I've had about enough!—You'll find a little house with a garden and a signpost out front. The sign's fallen down, but the post is still there. There's usually trumpet flower up the post and I don't think we've had a hard enough frost yet— *Owen! You leave that cat alone!*"

These directions proved quite good, unlike Owen. They found the garden, the house, and a post with a wooden crosspiece and two rusted iron links that had probably held a sign at some point. The trumpet flower had gone up the pole and flowered extravagantly scarlet.

"Hello?" said Marra's fairy godmother, looking up from her work in the garden. Marra knew her at once, though she had not seen her since she was in the cradle. Something inside her snapped toward the woman, like an iron filing snapping to a magnet. *Her. There. That's the one.*

The garden was just slightly out of control. It was nothing that a week or two of work couldn't fix, but the weeds were flourishing around the base of the plants and Marra could see the dried stems of last season's beans still twined around the poles, despite the new growth covering them. None of the preparations for winter had been made, although the first frost would hit any day now. *A little too much for one person.*

Her godmother had the kind but faintly anxious look of someone who was permanently in just a little over her head. She smiled at Marra, a smile with a little worry at the edges, and started to say, "How can I hel—" and then a line formed between her eyes and in midsentence, she switched to "Oh! You're one of mine, aren't you?"

She dropped the stake that she had been trying, without success, to slide into the already rampant tomatoes. She was round and flushed and there were sweat drops on her forehead. As Marra watched the woman push to her feet, wiping at her face and leaving a streak of dirt across her cheek, it was hard not to compare her to the ancient aquiline majesty of Prince Vorling's godmother. It was not a kind comparison. Marra felt a pang of something like despair.

"I can always tell," said the godmother happily. "I'm Agnes!" She reached out to take Marra's hand with her own. There was dirt on her fingers and a dead tomato leaf adhered to her hair. "It's so good to see one of mine all grown up!"

She hasn't got the faintest idea who I am, does she?

"I'm Marra." The dust-wife stepped through the garden gate, with Bonedog and Fenris hard on her heels. "*Princess* Marra."

The dust-wife walked forward. There was a run in the corner of the garden with a half dozen hens. The brown hen looked down at them imperiously, then away, profoundly uninterested in her fellows.

Agnes's mouth fell open. "Oh," she said in a much different voice. "Oh. You're . . . oh." She looked down at Bonedog, and her eyes widened. "Oh." She wiped her hands on her skirt, leaving stains. "I see. You . . . ah. You should come in. Maybe tea?"

"Tea would be a kindness," said the dust-wife, inclining her head.

They all followed the godmother into the cottage. It was cluttered but not dirty, the windows large and streaming with light. Agnes hurried to put the kettle on.

The uselessness of it all struck Marra like a blow. This was the woman who had given them all a gift of health and said that Damia would marry a prince. And meanwhile Vorling's godmother kept the entire kingdom wrapped in immortal magic, warding off enemy curses and usurpers to the throne. "We should go," said Marra in an undertone. "She won't be able to help us."

The dust-wife gave her a quelling look. Agnes, who must have heard, continued making tea. "It's good tea," she said. "The horse trader brings it, you know, when he's gone to sell a string of yearlings. I blessed his youngest and he brings me tea every time. I tell him he doesn't need to, but it's such good tea, and he's such a sweet man to do it."

"What did you bless her with?" asked the dust-wife.

"Health, of course. I always give them—"

"*Health!*" exploded Marra. She had not thought that she could feel rage toward this small, foolish woman but there it was, coiled around her heart, and suddenly it had found an outlet. "You gave Damia health and marriage to a prince and she was healthy enough, yes, right up until the day the prince killed her! And Kania is healthy now, too, and so she survives the beatings he gives her and the pregnancies she's forced to bear one after another. Health! What were you *thinking*?"

The fairy godmother stopped moving. Her hands locked over the edge of the little washbasin and her back sagged. After a moment she reached slowly for the tea.

The cottage was utterly silent as she made the tea and brought the teapot slowly to the table. She put out mismatched mugs. Her eyes were full of tears, and Marra began to feel ashamed of herself, as angry as she still was. Agnes's hands were shaking. The dust-wife took the teapot away from her and poured it.

"I always give them health," said Agnes, wrapping her fingers around her mug. "It's a good gift. You lose so many children to fevers, you know, every year. Not one of mine ever died of fever."

A suspicion began to form in Marra's mind, but the dust-wife got there first. "Health is the only gift you can give, isn't it?"

Agnes nodded. "The only one that anyone would want."

"But you said that Damia would marry a prince . . ." Marra let her voice trail off.

"It seemed like a safe bet," said Agnes, gazing into her mug. "She was the oldest daughter of the king and queen. I thought it was likely she would." She wiped the back of her hand across her eyes. Her voice shook. "Health's a *good* gift."

"It is a very good gift," said the dust-wife in a voice that left no room for doubt. "You have saved many lives."

The godmother smiled a little, and another tear fell and landed, unheeded, on the table.

Marra began to feel like a monster.

This isn't some great power who could have saved you. She did her best. And you've never been really ill in your life, have you? You recovered from that fever. And if it weren't for her, perhaps Kania would not still be alive to save.

"I'm sorry," she said. She was still angry, at the universe if not at Agnes, and it came out clipped. She tried again. "I shouldn't blame you. I didn't realize . . ." She gestured aimlessly.

"It's all right," said Agnes. She reached out and patted the air near Marra. "I didn't know that your sisters . . ." Another tear slid down her face. "I'm so sorry, my dear. I wish I could have given them something better. I would have, if I could." She smiled, though her lips were trembling.

"I mean no offense," said Fenris, speaking for the first time. His voice sounded like a growl of thunder in the small space, after the voices of the women. "But why would a godmother with such a specific talent—however useful—be chosen to stand for the royal family of the kingdom?"

Marra admired his diplomacy. When he had said that he was a warrior and a diplomat, she'd given more weight to the part with swords than words.

"Ah," said Agnes. She wiped at her eyes again. "Did no one tell you, Marra?"

"Tell me what?"

"The reason I'm the royal godmother." Her smile this time was stronger, if self-deprecating. "I'm your great-aunt Agnes."

* * *

Of course we would be related, thought Marra wearily. *Of course the godmother who is terribly outmatched would be family. All of us are small and in too far over our heads. Perhaps it's simply in our blood.* It did make a kind of sense, though. Why the Harbor Kingdom would have a fairy godmother at all. *Power calls to power*, the dust-wife had said. *And we have so little power that all we could call up was a relative, and not even a powerful one.*

"I didn't think there was any magic in the royal family," said Marra.

"Oh, there isn't. And my father—your great-grandfather—the king," said Agnes, "for the most part was very faithful. That's what made it so odd, you see. He was out hunting one day and met a woman and she enchanted him. They'd made love twice already before he realized that she had cow hooves and tore himself away. Eleven months later, she came to the palace. It was . . . oh, not a scandal, exactly. She was very discreet."

Unprompted, the dust-wife poured more tea into Agnes's mug, who took another swallow, her voice growing stronger. "Obviously your grandmother knew. But the woman came with the cow's hooves obvious, so she didn't blame the king for it, because she knew he had to have been enchanted. I think he would probably have had me killed, to try and make it up to her somehow, but she said that I was part of the family, even if I was a bastard, and nobody was killing anybody." Agnes took another sip of tea. "Not at the palace, of course. The king's old nurse had retired in comfort, and I was sent to her. I don't have cow hooves myself." She grinned, a brief flash across her round face. "I'm sure all of you are suddenly wondering what's inside my shoes! No hooves. But there's enough fairy blood in me that I was a godmother." She sighed, the grin fading. "I've always wondered if my mother would have kept me, if I was more powerful. I suspect she had a plan, and probably I wasn't right for it after all. But I don't want you to think anyone was ever unkind to me! Not at all. And of course when I could be a godmother, the queen insisted I come out and do the blessings. I think it was her way of trying to acknowledge me as part of the family, you know. She was very gracious. She didn't have to be, but she was."

Marra looked at the earnest, hopeful face of the godmother and felt as if she had been unspeakably cruel.

Why did I think she must have slighted me? Why didn't it occur to me that she might just be doing the best she could?

She answered her own question almost immediately. Because of Prince Vorling. Because the one godmother she had seen as an adult was a terrifying power, so she had assumed that all godmothers fit the same mold. *Vorling and his kingdom get proof against malign magic, and we have a witch who is simply grateful that she wasn't murdered by her own father and received the barest acknowledgment from her family. Saint's teeth.*

The anger that had simmered inside her shifted and found a different target. How dare they dump Agnes in the middle of nowhere? If she had not had so much else to deal with, she would have brought her great-aunt to the palace herself and demanded that she be treated like family.

Which means . . . what? That she is dragged off to live in a palace she does not know? That she is watched by courtiers every moment? That she has no privacy to herself?

That she gets married off to a monster to forge an alliance?

Marra put her head in her hands and heard herself give a brief, choking laugh. Over her head, she could hear the dust-wife quietly explaining what they planned to do to Vorling, and the godmother saying, "Oh. Oh my!"

Someone squeezed her shoulder. Fenris. His hand was warm and she leaned toward it a little, drawing strength from the grip. Perhaps she could ask him about how to help Agnes. He had experience with diplomacy the way that she did not. She was almost a nun and barely a princess and she had never felt the lack more keenly than these last few weeks.

Bonedog rolled over and wiggled on his back. Agnes looked at him thoughtfully. "He's magic, isn't he?" she asked. "I don't mean like a familiar. I don't quite know what I mean. But something."

"There's a glamour on him," said the dust-wife. "Look sideways a bit."

Agnes frowned. "I don't . . . wait . . ." She turned her head and squinted, then said, "Oh! He's all bones, poor thing!"

"I don't think it bothers him much," said Marra.

"Well, he's a dog. They don't have an idea how the world's supposed to be, so it doesn't bother them when it isn't." Agnes frowned. "Except herding dogs, I think. They have a pretty clear idea in their heads, so they're always nipping and worrying and trying to get it to fit. Of course, there's people like that, too."

"A great many of them," rumbled Fenris. "They are either excellent organizers or terrible zealots. There doesn't seem to be a great deal of middle ground."

"Right." Agnes nodded. "All right. Well, I see there's no hope for it. I'll come with you, then, shall I?"

Marra stared at her.

"Kania's my niece," said Agnes. "And her child is my grand-niece. Or grand-nephew." She rubbed her face. "Or perhaps it's my great-grand-niece and my great-grand-nephew. I can never keep track. But anyway, they're in danger, so I'll come."

No, thought Marra. *No, this is absurd. She'll die.*

. . . Haven't you been saying this is a fool's errand and you'll all die?

Yes, but I didn't mean . . . not like . . .

"Good," said the dust-wife. "I'm glad to have a godmother along. There's magic and then there's magic and there's the dead and then the living and I'm only skilled with one."

"I don't know how skilled I am," said Agnes. "But I'll do my very best to help."

"But . . ." Marra felt as if she should put a stop to this, but she didn't know how to say, *Agnes is useless—can't you see?*

As useless as a princess who only knows embroidery?

She stared into her tea.

Marra knew just how useless she felt, and yet somehow she had pulled together the dust-wife and Bonedog and Fenris. Perhaps . . . perhaps this was more of the same. Her hand crept to the carved grackle feather. Perhaps the saint was leading her.

"All right," she said, not looking at Agnes. "All right. Thank you."

"Five of us," said Fenris, looking over at the others approvingly. Marra leaned down and scratched Bonedog's spine until his jaws clattered with pleasure. "Five is a fist. Five is a hand on the enemy's throat."

"I suppose that makes us each fingers," said Marra. She curled her own around Bonedog's spine, taking comfort from the hard ridges. "You're the thumb," she told the dog. Bonedog wagged his tail.

*   *   *

They slept that night on the godmother's floor, near the hearth. Agnes took down blankets and so Fenris had his own and they no longer had to sleep back-to-back.

It should have been a relief. She had her own blankets again and no longer had to worry about keeping him awake with her fidgeting.

Of course, I am contrary as ever and nothing goes easily.

Her back felt cold and unprotected. She felt as if something might grab her. Her mind conjured all manner of demons in the dark: the drowned boy, the Toothdancer, all reaching out to grab her.

You are being ridiculous. You are much safer in here than you ever were on the road. And you shared a blanket less than a fortnight. You haven't had time to get used to sleeping next to someone. This is absurd.

Anyway, he's . . .

He's what?

Bonedog rolled over on his back, wired paws paddling at the air. She could hear the even sound of Fenris breathing.

Grow up, Marra. You're trying to save your sister and kill a monster. This is not the time to feel anything else. You're too busy.

There was a large basket to one side of the hearth, full of yarn.

Marra shifted around, scooting the blankets until she could set her back to it. Immediately she felt better.

There. You see? It's not him after all. It's just being nervous. It doesn't mean anything. He's only a companion on the way. That's all . . .

The relief that she felt was too great to be anything but a lie, but Marra took comfort from it nonetheless and drifted to sleep, listening to the sound of Fenris breathe.

Chapter 12

Intellectually, Marra knew that there had never been any chance of getting an early start. *And I shouldn't worry about it. One more day, more or less, is not going to change anything. If I wanted to be done sooner, I should have started sooner.*

Nevertheless, she felt a pang as the sun crawled up the sky and noon passed with no sign of getting on the road at all. Agnes had cooked an enormous breakfast to use up all the food in the larder, then had packed, unpacked, repacked, and was about to start on a third round when Fenris gently stepped in and offered to carry the extra.

"Are you certain?" asked Agnes, blinking up at him.

"Yes, of course. Though I will beg a blanket or two from you as well, for the road." Which sent Agnes off in a flutter to locate blankets for him, leaving her gear strewn across the kitchen table.

"She seems . . . easily distracted," said Marra, determined not to say anything harsher after she had made such an ass of herself the day before.

The dust-wife also looked distracted, gazing after Agnes. A line had formed between her eyes.

"Something wrong?" Marra asked.

"Mmmm." The dust-wife shook her head. "Wrong, no. Interesting. I'll sort it out, I expect."

Marra wrinkled her nose. "*Interesting* interesting, or *dangerous* interesting?"

The dust-wife peered down the hall. Agnes's voice floated back to them. "Oh dear, this one has a hole in it . . ."

"Interesting," said the dust-wife finally. "I can't tell you more than that yet."

* * *

Eventually they did get on the road. Marra thought, somewhat despairingly, that they'd be lucky to make five miles before they had to stop, but she kept her mouth shut. At least they were moving. *And anyway, you just uprooted the woman's entire life and yelled at her about being a lousy godmother. Half a day isn't much at all.* She flushed and stared at the road in front of her, embarrassed by her own frustration.

It's because you're too much alike. What did the abbess used to say? That our own flaws infuriate us in other people? How long did it take you to leave the convent?

Blissfully unaware of Marra's thoughts, Agnes was walking alongside the dust-wife. Occasionally the godmother reached up to chuck the brown hen under the chin. The hen seemed deeply appalled but was apparently too surprised to resist.

"How does one become a godmother, then?" asked the dust-wife. "Is there training?"

"Oh dear. I wish there was! Maybe there is, if you know the right people. But I didn't. Don't." Agnes waved her hands. "I knew that a godmother was a thing that people like me could be, you understand. So I practiced."

"How does one practice something like that?" asked the dust-wife.

"On kittens, mostly," Agnes said. "I think I blessed every barn cat from the time I was nine or ten on. Ducklings, too. And once I ran out of those, mice." She bit her lower lip. "I tried everything I could think of. That they would live for many years, that they would find love, that they would never know hunger. Nothing took. You can feel it when it takes, you understand—it's like stamping your foot down and then you see the footprint. I can see the print after the blessing. Marra's still got it. And Fenris . . ." She screwed up her face thoughtfully. "There was a godmother at your christening, wasn't there?"

"We don't call them that in Hardack," said Fenris, "but I believe our erl-wives perform the same function. Can you see it?"

"Oh yes. You will live with honor and never waver. Your shield will not break."

Something about the solemnity of the words, delivered in Agnes's thin but cheerful voice, made Marra want to laugh. Fenris smiled broadly. "That is correct," he said. "And my shields never broke in battle, either. Mind you, I dropped a fair number of them over the years . . ."

"What about curses?" the dust-wife asked. "There are many stories about the wicked fairy at the christening."

Agnes shook her head. "I'm not sure," she admitted. "I always wondered if maybe those godmothers could only give bad gifts. And then you have to wonder if maybe there are lots of godmothers out there who don't do anything because the only gifts they could give would be curses."

"Have you ever tried to curse?" asked the dust-wife.

Agnes ducked her head, failing to hide a guilty expression. The dust-wife pounced like a chicken on a worm. "You did. And you found you could, couldn't you?"

"I shouldn't have," whispered Agnes. "It was on a mouse. I . . . I said it would die before its seventeenth birthday. I'd read a story with a princess who was cursed and . . . well, I shouldn't have, but I did. And it took. I felt it. It was like a black stain on that poor little thing's future." She dabbed at her eyes. "I tried to tell myself that mice hardly ever live past two anyway. Most of them don't live anywhere near that long. But what if it *would* have been a particularly long-lived mouse and I cursed it?"

Sweet Lady of Grackles, thought Marra. *She's genuinely upset that she might have stopped a mouse from becoming ancient. Because of course she is.*

"You said before that health was the only gift you could give that anyone would want," said the dust-wife. "Were there other gifts? Ones that you think no one would want?"

Agnes, wilting beneath the inquisition, hung her head. "Yes. Keen whiskers. I'm good at keen whiskers. It isn't much good for anything but kittens and mice, though. You can't give a human baby keen whiskers. It wouldn't work—or what if it *did*?"

Marra pictured a child in the cradle suddenly growing a full set of cat whiskers and put her hand over her mouth.

"Now, that would be an interesting experiment," said the dust-wife.

"No," said Agnes, with surprising firmness. "No, I wouldn't do it. It's not fair to the child. It's not *decent*."

"I suppose." The dust-wife didn't sound entirely convinced. "Any others you managed?"

"Well, I blessed a whole litter of mice that cats wouldn't eat them. But I don't think that's very useful for a child, either. And then once I said a kitten would have many fine sons."

All three of them looked at her sharply. Bonedog, sensing something, whined.

"I'd just been reading a book, you see, and it had a king and a queen and she bore him . . . I was *twelve*! I didn't think!"

"What happened?" asked Marra. In her head, her mother's words echoed around and around, like a coin in a begging bowl. *We shall hope the next child is a son. Kania is riding a dragon, and all of us in the kingdom are riding along with her . . . hope the next child is a son, hope the next child is a son . . .*

"It was awful," said Agnes. "She had six litters and every kitten was a tom. The barn was overrun. Nothing but fighting and pissing everywhere, and yowling when they weren't pissing."

"Just like the barracks," said Fenris nostalgically.

"Interesting," said the dust-wife slowly. "So you are rather more versatile than you claim, but health is the only gift that you're willing to give."

"Health can't go wrong," said Agnes. "Most of the rest can. If you bless a mouse that they'll always be happy, they run right out in front of a cat and get happily eaten. But health always works. No one regrets being healthy."

"What did the prince's godmother say?" asked the dust-wife, turning to Marra. "Her exact words?"

Marra wracked her brain, drawing up the image of the ancient godmother, the stained-glass skin stretched over bone. "'I shall serve her as I have served all her line, my life bound to theirs. No foreign magic shall harm them. No enemy shall topple their throne. As it has been for all the children of the royal house, so shall it be for her, as long as I draw breath.'"

Agnes sighed. "That's a good one," she said. "A big one. I couldn't do that."

"That's what we're up against," said Marra. "Vorling can't be harmed by foreign magic. Supposedly the Northern Kingdom's enemies are always throwing spells at them, but they don't take." She remembered the king, aged and infirm before he had turned fifty. "But it burns them out. I wish it would burn Vorling out faster."

"Can his guards be harmed by magic?" asked Fenris.

"Eh?"

"Well, if Lady Fox here can arrange to put his guards to sleep, I can just stab him."

The dust-wife snorted. Agnes's eyes were very round.

"What?" said Fenris. "Simple plans are best."

"You're not wrong, but I doubt I can put an entire palace to sleep," said the dust-wife. "Particularly since I've never put even one person to sleep. I have a great many talents, including raising the dead, but if you want lullabies, that's someone else."

"Can you distract them somehow? At least long enough for me to stab him?"

"Probably not long enough for you to get away again, no."

Fenris raised his eyebrows. "That's not really a requirement, is it?"

"Yes," said Marra, annoyed. "It *is*."

"Fine, fine." He lifted his hands. "No death-and-glory final stands unless we have no other options. Hmm. Can you raise up an army of the dead to fight the guards?"

The dust-wife rolled her eyes. "Armies of the dead *seem* like a good idea," she said. "Until you're standing in front of a thousand blind, withered husks who only know how to kill and kill and keep on killing. We might as well just drop plague corpses in the town well at that point."

"I would have to object to that," admitted Fenris. "All right. No armies of the dead, then."

"*Could* you do that?" asked Marra tentatively.

The dust-wife shrugged. "I don't know. It's never really come up."

"Yes, but if it did, would you know how?"

Feathers and movement announced the brown hen's emergence from the pack. The chicken walked up the dust-wife's arm and settled back on the staff, her comb at a decidedly jaunty angle.

"I know how I'd start," said the dust-wife finally. "Some things I expect you don't know until you're doing them. But it's been done before." She leveled a glare at Marra. "But don't get any ideas. We're here for a straightforward regicide, not to level the city."

"Yes, ma'am," said Marra meekly, and dropped her head.

* * *

They stayed that night in a barn, courtesy of Fenris's firewood-splitting skills. The farmer even threw in a meal of salted potatoes and gave them apples for the road.

"I promise I did not bring you along to make you split firewood," said Marra.

Fenris laughed. The two older women had gone inside to sleep, and it was only the two of them and a very small fire, well away from the barn.

"It's all right," he said. "I've done many things that were terribly important, lives hanging in the balance and so on and so forth. There is something pleasant about chopping wood. If I miss a stroke, nothing awful happens. If a piece of wood is not quite right, it will still burn. If I stack it and it isn't perfect, clans will not fall."

"It sounds very difficult."

"Mm. Sometimes." He fixed her with a thoughtful look, and it occurred to her that his eyes were the color of sun-warmed earth, and she did not quite know what to do about it. "But you know, don't you? You are the daughter and the sister of queens, so there must have been many times in your life when things hung on your actions."

Marra inhaled sharply. Fenris poked at the fire with a stick. "I'm sorry," he said. "I did not mean to distress you."

"No. No, it's not your fault. I . . . yes. I have too much power for who I am. My mother sent me away, finally, and I know it was partly because I was not . . . not good at these things. But none of it is *my* power. It is only other people, moving me on a game board. It was a relief when I went to the convent. When I have to come out, for the christenings or the funerals . . ." She wrapped the nettle cloak more tightly around herself. "It's why I like needlework," she added.

Fenris lifted an eyebrow.

"Like splitting wood. Like you said. Embroidery doesn't *do* anything. It isn't anything but what it is, and I don't have to worry that I'm doing something terribly wrong and my tutors will get sent away or that I slighted someone important and they'll want to close down trade with my kingdom. I can just make pictures and patterns, and if I make a mistake, I can tear it out again and no one dies." She took a deep breath. "It doesn't matter that I'm a princess. The thread doesn't care."

She was looking at the fire and did not expect the hand that came out of the dark and took hers and squeezed.

"And yet here we are," he said. His thumb lay like a warm bar across her palm. His hands were very large compared to hers, and the calluses from the sword and the axe were much thicker than the ones she had developed from shoveling stables. "Freed of all our duties, we charge headlong to take on another responsibility."

"I have to save my sister," said Marra. "I lost one already." She laughed and heard the bitterness in it. "Kania doesn't even like me very much, I don't think. But I still have to do it."

"And very likely we will not survive." He rubbed her palm absently. She wouldn't swear that he even knew he was doing it.

"We will," she said. She caught his hand in both of hers, gripping hard enough to hurt. "Fenris, we *will* survive."

He gave a half smile and a small nod. She could tell that he was humoring her, and she recalled the look in his eyes when she had yelled at him that he might die when that drunk had pulled a knife. *He doesn't want to die, I don't believe he does, but . . . it's like he expects to. Like it's inevitable.*

Like he doesn't mind.

"Suppose we do survive. What happens then?"

"I don't know." Marra looked at the fire. "I suppose I go back to my convent and work on my embroidery."

"Mm." He squeezed her hand again, then released her and began to put out the fire. "Well, if you find that your convent needs someone to split firewood, it happens that I know a fellow . . ."

* * *

Two days later, they reached the capital of the Northern Kingdom.

She had been keeping her head down, hoping not to be recognized, and mostly watching the dust-wife's feet. When they topped a small rise and the dust-wife stopped, Marra looked up for the first time in what felt like hours.

The prince's city shone savagely before her, high walls leading in an endless spiral to the Northern palace. People streamed through the gates, vanishing into the maw of the city, and all she could think was that there were so many people, hundreds, thousands, all of them living in the prince's city and loyal to him and what was she? What were five against so many? What could they do?

It is too much, she thought bleakly. *We have grand plans, but in reality? Most likely we'll get into the city, and look up at the palace, and talk and plan and talk some more, and eventually realize there's nothing we can actually do, and leave again. That's the way it happens outside of the stories.*

The weight of this thought was suddenly very real, more than a feeling, a physical burden, heavy in her stomach and tight in her chest, and before she realized, she staggered unsteadily to the side of the road and went to her knees, out of the way of the crowd of traders and pilgrims. None of them looked at her. A dusty, weeping woman meant nothing, not with the sight of the city so bright and cold and hard before them.

It was Bonedog who noticed first. He put his paws on her shoulders and licked her face frantically. There was enough of the glamour for his tongue to feel wet, but he could not actually touch her tears.

"Good boy," Marra whispered. "Good dog." He was a good dog. Even if his master failed to save her sister or her kingdom, she had done one good thing—giving Bonedog a second chance.

Then Fenris was beside her, putting his arm around her as he had in the goblin market. He half lifted her, his great strength no longer shocking, and moved her farther out of the way of the crowd.

Fenris. Yes. There are good men in the world, and I have met one. And he is my friend, whatever else happens.

"Easy," said Fenris. "Easy. Are you hurt?"

It was such a decent, obvious, ridiculous question that she found herself laughing, the quiet, gulping laughter that comes with tears. "No," she said. "No, I just . . ." She waved her hand toward the city. "We'll never do this, will we? This is all completely absurd. We can't do this. It's impossible."

"You wove a cloak with nettle thread," said the dust-wife, standing over her, "and built your own dog out of bones, and *now* you are concerned about what is impossible?" She shook herself and all the jars and bottles in her pockets rattled like a porcupine's quills.

Marra began to feel embarrassed, not just for having dragged the others with her on this absurd mission, but also for having had the poor taste to have a breakdown in the middle of the road. "I'm sorry," she said. Fenris helped her to her feet. His hand against her back was warm and strong. Bonedog lashed her shins with his tail.

"Oh, my dear," said Agnes, sliding her arm through Marra's. "It's all right. It's all just a little overwhelming, isn't it?" She found a slightly crumpled handkerchief and passed it over to Marra. "You've done so much and here we are and now it feels like there's so much left to do, doesn't it?"

Marra accepted the handkerchief. If she'd had more energy, she'd be alarmed at how well the woman had read her. Yes. It did feel exactly like that. She had done so much and was so tired and how could it only be the beginning?

She wiped at her eyes and, arm in arm with her godmother, she passed through the gates that guarded the city of the prince they had come to kill.

Chapter 13

W ell," said the dust-wife. "Now what?"

All three of them looked at Marra, who looked away, at the narrow street, the buildings close overhead. They had made it through the gate unnoticed. No one cared. No one had pointed at her and shouted, "Princess!" or "Runaway!" And now they were inside, standing in a small alley off the main street, and there was the next thing to do.

Bonedog came and sat on her foot. She closed her fingers around his collar and thought, *My dog trusts me,* and then, *My dog is witless and also dead,* but things loosened a little in her chest nevertheless.

"We'll have to find somewhere to stay," she said. "I don't have much money left. But I can't . . . I don't think I should just . . ." She waved her hand vaguely toward the top of the hill and the shining white palace. *Yes, that would go well. I just waltz in unannounced and then the prince turns up dead. I don't see any way that would end with the Northern Kingdom declaring war on my homeland and grinding us all into dust.*

"I suppose we'll have to figure out how to get up to the palace without being noticed," she said, looking down at Bonedog, whose illusionary tongue was lolling out. "And then . . . er . . . well. I don't think we're going to do this tonight, are we?"

She looked back at her trio of—followers? Weapons? Friends? She had been so narrowly focused for so long that she had not thought very much about what to do once she arrived at the city, except that she should stay out of Prince Vorling's sight.

"Definitely not," said the dust-wife.

"Where should we stay?" asked Fenris.

"Um . . ." Marra shook her head. "I've never been here. Down here, I mean. I was always up there."

Fortunately he took this in stride. "Then we will have to learn if there is a curfew and what parts of the city to avoid. I do know that any inn near the front gate is likely going to prey terribly on travelers, so we would be wise to seek accommodations elsewhere."

"Er . . ." Agnes cleared her throat. It was a very small noise, nearly lost in the sound of movement past the mouth of the alley, but everyone turned to look at her nonetheless. It had been a hopeful sound.

"Oh dear," she said, twining her fingers together. "I had a thought. It's not much, but you know how you talked about the moth? The moth that found what you need? I was thinking . . . Well, it seems unlikely. But I might be able to do something like that."

The dust-wife leaned forward, eyes intent. "What do you need?"

"A baby," said Agnes.

"I'm not kidnapping children," said Fenris. "I realize we're working for a higher cause here, but I have to draw the line."

"Oh, goodness no!" Agnes waved her hands, agitated, like a bird trapped against a wall. "No, no! Not a human child! No, of course not! Just a baby something. Anything. And we can bring it back to its mother afterward."

The dust-wife rubbed her forehead. On her staff, the hen cackled.

"What about a chick?" asked Marra, gazing up at the hen. "Would that work?"

"Oh yes," said Agnes. "That would be perfect!"

Buying a live chick in a strange city was surprisingly easy, although Marra imagined it would have been very difficult indeed if it were just her. *I'd have to get my nerve up to talk to a stranger and ask them if anyone sold chickens and where, and if they didn't know, I'd have to ask the next person . . .*

Fenris, apparently untroubled by such complicated matters, simply walked out of the alley and addressed the first local he saw, a man selling pickles out of a large barrel on a cart. "You, sir! Do you know where I might find a place selling live fowls?"

"You sure you don't want a pickle instead? Much less trouble than fowl."

"Sadly, I do not. Not even such fine pickles." Fenris put a hand over his heart, somehow managing to indicate a profound sense of loss at his inability to eat the pickle in question. "But I've need of live fowl at once."

Marra didn't know how he did it, but two minutes later, Fenris was in possession of directions to the market and the location of the least crooked poultry seller in the place. Five minutes after that, they were standing in front of a stall full of assorted chickens. Full-grown hens sat in cages, clucking to each other, and there was an entire box filled with small, fluffy chicks.

The dust-wife's hen drew herself up very tall and glared down at her imprisoned sisters with something very like scorn.

"We need to buy a chick," said the dust-wife.

The chicken seller was a large man with even larger eyebrows. He gazed up at the hen on her perch and raised one eyebrow very slowly. "The crate," he said.

Agnes leaned over the edge of the crate and cooed at the chicks. "Oh, they're always so adorable at this age . . ."

"Focus," said the dust-wife.

"Oh yes, of course. I suppose we'll have to keep it, won't we? He won't just let us borrow a chicken . . ."

The chicken seller did not look like a man who routinely let customers borrow chickens.

Marra shoved her hands in her pockets and tried to look like someone who was possibly a nun and definitely not the queen's runaway sister. After a minute or two, though, it became obvious that she didn't need to bother. The chicken seller gazed at Agnes, who was picking up each chick and whispering to it, then slowly turned to Fenris. He didn't say anything, but his eyebrows were eloquent.

"She's very particular about her chickens," said Fenris. "Very particular."

"It's not taking," Agnes whispered to the dust-wife, just loud enough for Marra to make out the words. "It won't take. Oh, it was a silly idea. I don't know why I thought it would ever work . . ."

"Keep trying," ordered the dust-wife.

The chicken seller looked back at Agnes, then to Fenris again. His eyebrows inched higher up his skull.

Fenris remained absolutely deadpan, as if it were perfectly normal for women to whisper to chicks before buying them. Marra didn't dare look at Agnes, because if she did, she was going to burst into hysterical laughter.

"*Fine*," said Agnes in the tone of someone reaching her limits. Marra's ears popped. "There!"

"*That* took," observed the dust-wife dispassionately.

"Not well at all and I have to keep . . . I'm pushing it . . . It doesn't want to stick; it's like jelly sliding down a bowl!"

"Keep pushing," said the dust-wife. "Keep blessing it over and over if you have to."

"Oh dear . . ."

Marra darted a glance at the chick in question. It was a dark, fuzzy little lump with a bright yellow bill and, for a chicken, a remarkably phlegmatic expression.

The chicken seller's eyebrows did a complex dance across his forehead. He named a price that was frankly ridiculous for a day-old chick.

"Don't be absurd," said Marra, stung out of her silence. "It's a chicken, not a phoenix."

The chicken seller's eyes drifted back over to Agnes, followed by his eyebrows.

"The sooner we pay," rumbled Fenris, "the sooner we will go away."

The price mysteriously plummeted.

Agnes fumbled with her belt pouch and handed over a coin, cupping the chick against her bosom with one hand. "Who's a good chicken?" she said, looking down.

They left the chicken seller and his dancing eyebrows behind and made it into a nearby courtyard without Marra losing her composure completely.

"What did you do?" asked the dust-wife. "There's magic on it, but I can't read it."

"I told it that it would find us somewhere safe," said Agnes. "Like the moth that found what you need. I don't know if it'll work. Maybe it could only take us someplace that it would feel safe or that was safe for chickens. But it's there—I just have to keep pushing . . ."

"That's a curse," said the dust-wife. "That's why it finally took."

"No!" Agnes looked upset, cradling the chicken. "It's not! It's . . . Okay, it's not exactly a blessing, but it's not really a curse. Nothing bad will happen."

"Well, let's see if it works," said the dust-wife. "Go on."

"Okay," said Agnes. "Go on, little chick! Find us a safe place!" She set the chick down on the ground and made flapping motions.

The chick looked around, then cheeped and began to run down the alley with Agnes and the dust-wife in hot pursuit.

"See, this would take much longer with a baby," said Fenris.

Marra jammed her elbow into his side, which was rather like elbowing a stone wall. He grunted, possibly to be polite.

They followed the chick to a staircase, which it could not climb on its own. Agnes swooped it up in her hands. The chick cheeped.

"Magic's fading again," said the dust-wife.

"Oh . . . Well—" Agnes looked around as if she were doing something illicit, then something happened and Agnes looked at least a foot taller and the alley was suddenly full of shadows and her eyes flashed and she said, "You will find us a safe place to stay or . . ." in a voice like the tolling of a great bronze bell.

Cheep, said the chicken. The shadows fled. Marra's ears popped again. Bonedog let out a threadlike whine and put his nose behind Marra's knee.

Agnes started up the steps, holding the chick. It seemed content to ride until they reached the second landing, and then it began to struggle. Agnes set it down and chased after it again, followed by the dust-wife, Marra, and Fenris. Bonedog, who would ordinarily enjoy a good run after a small animal, did not seem inclined to leave Marra's side.

The chick led them, after a few false starts, to a narrow alley that opened into a cul-de-sac. It reached the steps of the building at the farthest end and began to bounce determinedly against them.

"Well," said Agnes, scooping up the chick in her hands. "Is this a rooming house, do you think?"

All four of them looked up at the house. It was small and shabby but very clean, with the kind of cleanliness that spoke of poverty. Marra had seen babies delivered in homes like these and could practically hear a voice saying, "We may be poor, but we're *not* dirty!"

There was a girl sitting on the steps of one of the buildings nearby. She, too, was neat and clean, though her clothes were much too thin and so was she. She looked over at them solemnly. "Are you going to Miss Margaret's?"

"Possibly," said Agnes. "Does she own the house at the end?"

The girl nodded.

"Does she ever take boarders?"

Another, slower nod. The girl thought this over for a moment, then said, "Most people don't stay, though. Only locals. There's no harm in her, Da says, but people don't like it."

"What don't they like?" asked Marra.

The girl frowned. The brown hen shifted her feet and let out a low, worried *errrrk*.

"*Him*," said the girl, eyeing the hen doubtfully. "You'll see him. It's no secret. He can be awful. She's nice, though, Miss Margaret. I run her errands sometimes."

Fenris and Marra traded a brief glance. "A husband, do you think?" whispered Marra.

"Or a brother or a father. Hard to say."

"Dangerous?"

Fenris shrugged. Marra remembered him handling the drunk at the well and felt a stab of envy for anyone who could go through life so unconcerned about possible physical violence.

"Thank you," said Agnes to the girl. She put the chick under her arm and walked to the door of the boardinghouse.

Marra was close enough behind her to hear the godmother whisper to the chick. "Is this right? Are you sure?" The chick peeped. "Was that a yes?"

"That means your chicken is hungry," said the dust-wife dryly.

"Oh dear . . ."

Fenris reached past her while Agnes tried to settle the chicken, and knocked on the door.

They waited for so long that Marra began to doubt whether anyone was coming, and then the door creaked open on darkness.

* * *

Miss Margaret was a tall, stoop-shouldered woman with bony hands and a bony face. She stood in the shadows, at right angles to the door, so that Marra could only make out her profile.

"May I . . . may I help you?" she asked. Her voice sounded as if she was forcing words out around a lump in her throat.

"We need somewhere to stay," said Agnes cheerfully, holding up the chick. "And you're safe. Well, supposed to be safe. The chicken said—"

"Do you have rooms to let?" asked Marra, hastily trying to stem the flow of words.

Miss Margaret looked at her sideways, like a bird. "Yes," she rasped. "Two."

"How much?"

She named a price so low that for a moment Marra thought that she must mean for each of them individually. She stopped herself just before she said *That's all?* and said, "May we look at the rooms?" instead.

The woman nodded again, stepping back down the hall to let them inside the door. Then she shuddered and turned to face them full-on.

Marra's first thought was that there was some kind of animal on her shoulder—a weasel, perhaps, or a particularly long-bodied cat. Then she got a clearer look and she put a hand to her mouth. Even Fenris took a step back.

Him. Of course.

He was a wooden puppet. Some kind of marionette, Marra thought, the kind that traveling performers used to entertain very young children. He had the carved hands and the clacking jaw, the articulated arms and legs. But the only string on him was a black cord that looped Miss Margaret's throat, and the puppet held it in one hand.

He moved as they watched. It was a slow, considered movement, like a tortoise turning its head in the sun, and it set Marra's nerves crawling.

"Oh, *interesting*," said Agnes in a tone of professional curiosity. "That's a curse-child, isn't it?"

The puppet scowled. Bits of wood dragged down across his face. He yanked tightly on the string. The woman nodded, her eyes large and alarmed and clearly begging her visitors not to say more.

"Oh dear! I'm sorry," said Agnes. "No offense meant. That was insensitive of me, wasn't it?" She smiled gently at the woman, as if having a horrible piece of living wood on your shoulder was a perfectly normal sort of thing.

The puppet grudgingly loosened the string. Miss Margaret's throat worked as she swallowed.

"Don't worry," said Agnes. "These things happen. I won'ttttt . . ."

Marra was close enough to see the color suddenly drain out of her face, as if she were a bottle that had been upended. Agnes blinked several times, looking very surprised. Then she said, eyes straight ahead, "Please take the chick, Marra. If I fall on it, I might hurt it."

Marra snatched the handful of fluff out of Agnes's hands, alarmed by the mortal calm in the godmother's voice.

"Good," said Agnes, and fainted.

She collapsed against the wall, rattling the boards, and then slid down into a neat heap. Fenris let out an oath and tried to grab her, but between Marra and Miss Margaret, there was no room in the hallway for another person, let alone one of his size. The chick peeped. Miss Margaret's eyes were enormous.

"What did you do?!" cried Marra. "What did that thing do to her?"

"Nothing . . . nothing . . . I can't . . . he can't . . ." said the land-lady, and then the cord at her throat was yanked tight and she choked.

"It's not the curse-child," said the dust-wife. "All of you, get out of the way! It's the magic. She poured it right out to keep the bless-ing going and pushed herself right to fainting, the little fool."

She looked up at Miss Margaret, ignoring the puppet entirely. "Take us to the rooms. She needs rest and tea and quiet."

Miss Margaret nodded. The puppet's eyes were fixed on the brown hen, whose red comb brushed the ceiling atop the staff. The hen glared down at the puppet and snapped her beak.

Their landlady turned slowly. The puppet shifted, keeping his balance. She led them up the stairs, the dust-wife following, Fenris behind her with Agnes in his arms, Bonedog at his heels, while Marra carried the chick and waited for the puppet to launch himself at someone's face.

He didn't. They climbed the stairs to a whitewashed hallway lined with doors. Miss Margaret stopped in front of one and gestured in-side, eyes downcast. They crowded in.

"The next one, too," rasped the landlady, opening another door. "There is one meal . . . one m-meal—" The puppet yanked on the cord. She stopped, putting a hand to her throat, and gave Marra a pleading look.

"One meal included?" asked Marra. *Listen to how normal I sound. I am having a normal conversation with a woman being strangled by a wooden puppet and we are all acting as if the important thing is meals being included with the price of the room.*

The landlady nodded and fled. Marra inched farther into the room and closed the door. Fenris had arranged Agnes on one of the beds and stepped back out of the way. The dust-wife sat on the other bed, managing to look both annoyed and concerned.

"We can't stay here!" hissed Marra. "That puppet thing—you can't tell me it won't do something awful!"

"It's done something awful to the landlady, certainly," said the dust-wife. "But it won't do anything to the rest of us. It can't. It's just a curse-child."

"Just?" Marra had a hard time imagining that clacking puppet as *just* anything.

"Probably a sad story," said the dust-wife. "They usually are. Somebody gives a lonely child a toy and they pour all their hopes and fears and problems into it. Do it long enough and intensely enough, and then it just needs a stray bit of bad luck and the toy wakes up. Of course, it knows that the only reason it's alive is because of the child. A tiny personal god with one worshipper. It latches on and . . . well." She clucked her tongue. "Normally you get them pried off and burned long before adolescence. Impressive that it lasted this long."

"We can burn it," said Marra. "Burning is fine. I'll get the kindling."

"Not without her permission. You don't go tearing off an adult woman's god and setting it on fire." The dust-wife gave her a sharp look, as if she were suggesting something rude.

"It was choking her!"

"It's her neck, not yours. We can ask before we leave, if you like."

"But it could be wandering the halls at night!"

"No, it would stay attached to her. They really don't have power over anyone else. I suppose it could tell her to murder us in our beds, but any innkeeper could decide to do that, too, so I wouldn't worry about it. It won't risk losing its worshipper if we fight back."

Marra opened and closed her mouth several times, completely unable to form words. How could the dust-wife be so calm?

"This works very much in our favor," said the dust-wife. "She can't tell anyone who or what we are. Nobody trusts a curse-child, and it'll choke her if it thinks she's paying too much attention to something else." She nodded down to Agnes. "Her magic worked. Unorthodox and somewhat inefficient, but it worked."

"Is the chick all right?" asked Agnes from the bed. Her voice was very weak.

Marra looked down at her hands. The chick's fluff was a bit damp from the sweat on her palms, but it seemed fine. "Yes?"

"Oh good . . . I was afraid I'd . . ." Agnes closed her eyes. She was still very pale, almost shockingly white against the pillow. "I'm sorry to be so much trouble."

"You drained yourself down to nothing on that bird," said the dust-wife.

"Did I?" Agnes sounded bemused. "It's never happened before . . . Normally the magic just takes or it doesn't. But I kept redoing it in my head to make it stick . . ."

"Yes, and knocked yourself out in the process." The dust-wife's voice thawed a bit, and she patted Agnes's pillow. "It's fine. It worked. We're here now. Now, you get some rest."

"Wait!" said Marra as the dust-wife began to shoo her out the door. "What about—"

"We're staying," said the dust-wife. "This place is safe. Cheap, too."

"No, I meant the chick."

"What?"

"I don't know how to take care of a chicken."

The dust-wife's angular face drew into tight triangles. "It's a *chicken*. Didn't they teach you at the convent?"

"No! Chickens were someone else's problem. I knit bandages and helped deliver babies." She wedged her foot in the door to keep from being left in the hall in care of the chick.

"Babies happen occasionally. Chickens happen all the time." The dust-wife plucked the chick out of Marra's fingers, shaking her head. As the door was closing in her face, Marra heard, "I know you aren't broody, demon, but you're going to make an exception or so help me . . ."

The door shut with a click.

Chapter 14

The other room had two narrow beds with a small table and basin between them and a shuttered window. Marra collapsed onto one with a groan and put her head in her hands.

"Are you all right?" asked Fenris.

"Horrible puppet," she said, "demon chicken, fairy godmother."

"And it's a fool's errand and we're all going to die," said Fenris. He patted her shoulder. "Still, I have to admit I didn't see the chicken or the puppet coming."

"Nothing's ever easy," said Marra, too tired to yell at him for taking her fatalism to heart. She remembered suddenly that she had cried in front of everyone earlier in the day and felt herself flush with embarrassment. To hide it, she turned away, pulling back a corner of the blanket and investigating the mattress.

It was stuffed with horsehair and the blankets were coarse but clean. The room itself was shabby but painfully neat, much like the rest of the house. She did not see fleas jumping anywhere. "Well, it's not a bad room." It reminded her of her room in the convent.

"I've slept in far worse," agreed Fenris. The small bed looked even smaller when he sat on it. Marra was fairly certain that his feet were going to hang over the edges. He gave her an apologetic look. "I, uh . . . realize it's awkward that you have to share a room with me. If there were a stable, I'd offer, but there isn't one. And honestly, I'd rather be close at hand, in case . . ."

He trailed off, but Marra knew that he was thinking about the curse-child. "I'd prefer you were close, too," she said. "It's fine. No worse than the road."

Fenris made a noncommittal noise. Marra knew perfectly well

what he meant. Once you added walls and a door, things became . . . complicated.

It's not complicated. It doesn't have to be. He's your friend and you're here to kill a prince and that's all you need to know or think about. She forced a smile. "I suppose beds like this aren't quite what you're used to."

Fenris shrugged. "I'm not really used to anything. I slept in barracks for a long time. When I was traveling, I'd sleep on the ground. Sometimes I'd go from sleeping on dirt to sleeping in the best guest chamber in the castle."

"And sometimes in fairy forts," she added.

His face changed. She felt as if a shutter had closed in his eyes. *You fool, why did you say that?* "I'm— I'm sorry," she said, stammering a little. "I'm sorry, I shouldn't have joked about it—"

"It's all right." He reached out and took her hands in his. The room was so small that he could do so easily. "Marra . . . *Princess* Marra . . ."

She winced. "Don't. I'm not. I mean, I am, but I'm really a nun, except I'm barely even that."

"You are the princess of the Harbor Kingdom," he said. "I learned that at the first inn we stopped at in your homeland. Your sister Kania is married to Vorling of the Northern Kingdom."

Of course he'd learn that. You should have guessed. It's not like it was much of a secret. She told herself this firmly, trying to ignore the sudden clawing in her chest that screamed that he would tell Vorling, he would betray them all, he knew too much and it would all be used against them . . .

No. This is Fenris. He is a friend, and he has never been anything but decent. She stared down at their joined hands, trying not to feel trapped, wondering what price she would have to pay for his silence.

"People love to gossip about the royal family," he said. His voice was very gentle. "They told me why you were sent to the nunnery. A few people thought there had been some scandal, but most of them said that you would be Vorling's third wife if your sister died. You were being held in reserve, they said."

no no my mother said that I was out of the game I was set free I was sent away because I did not have to stay at court because I hated it and I was free

She looked at her own thoughts and they seemed to belong to a much younger Marra, one who had never been to the goblin market, one who had never built a dog out of bones. One who could afford to be innocent and ignorant. *I can no longer afford to be that person.*

"It's probably true," Marra said, marveling at how steady her voice was. "My mother never said as much, but Vorling is obsessed with having his own blood sitting on my father's throne. And, of course, our harbor was worth controlling anyway. A good, deep harbor is a kingdom's wealth. I could never have been allowed to marry anyone else and produce a son that might challenge that. And there was always the chance that my sister might die, like our older sister did, and that I would need to be pulled out of the convent and sent to the altar."

Fenris nodded. His hands were warm. He turned them gently and caught both of her hands between his palms. "I suspected as much. So do many of your people. They know that Vorling is ambitious." He paused, as if weighing his words, and then said, almost hesitantly, "They still remember your sister Damia fondly."

"She was so beautiful," said Marra. "And so kind."

He squeezed her hands tightly. She took a deep breath, wondering if she was going to cry again. No, it seemed not. The pain had softened over the years, the edges worn down by time. She gazed dry-eyed at their hands. Her left hand had never quite recovered from spinning the nettle thread. One of the knuckles was more swollen than the others, and there was a numb band along the side of her little finger.

"After the second or third inn, I felt like I knew too much," Fenris said. "You know hardly anything about me, and I had heard so much about you and your family." He took a deep breath. "So. Yes. I slept in a fairy fort. There was a battle, you see. One clan overthrew another. It happens, though the Fathers try to keep it from coming to that. The clan that was destroyed had been fostering a young lad as a squire, and the lady of the conquering clan said that her people would not make war on children, so he was spared by her command. He was handed over to us, who served the Fathers. He could not have been more than thirteen, and a young thirteen at that. His voice was as high as a novice nun's."

"Fenris," said Marra, looking up at him, "you don't have to tell me this."

"I know. I want to. Then we'll be even and . . ." He smiled down at her, with an edge of pain that cut her heart. "And I find that it's important to me that we be even." Marra bowed her head. The edge of one of his thumbnails had a nick in it. She could feel the heat of his skin across hers, crossing the numb band of skin, heat and then vague pressure and then heat again.

"So. This squire was afraid to go home. Afraid that his father would think that he had failed by being captured alive. By not dying like a hero." Fenris's lip curled. "I spent a week convincing him that his father would be so glad that his son was alive that there would be no talk of failure. I could see myself in him. I had been his age once and terrified of failing to live up to my father's example. And I saw myself so clearly that I did not see him at all."

She had a sense of the story to come and she did not want to hear it, as if not hearing the words could erase them. "Fenris . . ."

"You brought me out of the goblin market, and I fear this tale is a part of me. It follows wherever I go." Marra was not certain if that was bitterness or duty speaking, or perhaps both. *Duty and love and hate are complicated . . .*

"I thought there was something odd when we delivered him to his father. 'Hiding behind a woman's skirts?' the lord said. It was odd, and the manner he said it was odd. But I had duties and I went about them and left the son with the father. But it nagged at me."

"And?" said Marra, who knew her duty as the listener.

"And a week later, I returned. I could not get the way that the father had spoken out of my head, or the look in his eye. It wasn't right for a father. I don't have children, so far as I know, but that look . . ." He shook his head. "I went back. But I waited too long, fool that I am."

"He was dead," said Marra. She wondered if the Sister Apothecary felt this way when someone told her of an ailment that she had diagnosed from the first word.

"Flogged to death. His father had branded him a traitor and a coward. He was hanging by his wrists from a pole in the courtyard. I cut him down myself." His voice was flat and utterly emotionless. Marra was reminded of Kania prepared to marry her prince, the same flatness. *This is happening and I am part of it but that is all.* "He had taken at least a day to die."

"I'm sorry," said Marra, feeling the inadequacy of the words. She turned her hands to squeeze his, and he looked down at them, seeming almost puzzled.

"And that is why I could not kill myself, after I had killed his father and his guards. I would not shame that young man's memory any further."

"You were right to kill his father," said Marra fiercely. "That wasn't wrong."

"Everything else I did was wrong," said Fenris, "from first to last." He sighed. "I failed to listen and failed to understand, and a child died a tortured death of my failures. Because my father was a good man, and I was so full of my own foolishness that I could not see why this boy was frightened."

"My father is a good man, too," said Marra. "That's probably why it took me so long to see what was happening to Kania. I knew something was wrong but I suspected all the wrong things. I knew she was pregnant too often, but I never knew why." She tugged at her hands and he released her immediately. "And my mother was my mother, and I knew she loved me, so it took me a long time to realize that she would also move me as a game piece to save the kingdom."

Fenris nodded. "Sometimes that was my job as a servant of the Fathers," he said. "To move people and alliances like pieces on a board. It would have been much harder if I had loved them."

Marra exhaled. Had it been hard for her mother? She wanted to believe that it had been. Life would be easier. But that was her sorrow and Fenris had his own. "You're stronger than I am," she said. "You did it all yourself. I couldn't stop Vorling. I had to go find someone powerful who could. I'm scared all the time and don't tell me that courage is going forward when you're scared because it's not like that. I was scared of the carriages and the people at the inns. The only thing I did right was find the dust-wife."

"Ah, Lady Fox." He shook his head. "I think finding her makes up for anything else you did wrong."

"Maybe, but you . . . you did what you could to make it right." She didn't know how to say what was in her head, that Fenris was a good man and maybe the weakness of being good was that evil didn't occur to you. That never in a thousand years would she have dreamed that Vorling was intentionally hurting her sister. It had never even crossed her mind. "And then you did your best to make sure no one else suffered."

He snorted. "By jumping into a fairy fort. Not the best idea I've ever had."

Marra clasped her hands together. They seemed much colder now that Fenris had released them. "Well, if you hadn't, we never would have met."

"No, we wouldn't have." His eyes held hers for just a moment too long, and in the end, Marra's dropped first.

* * *

"So you *do* curse things," said the dust-wife.

Marra woke, startled. It sounded as if the dust-wife were talking directly to her. *A curse? What was a curse?*

"I don't," said Agnes. "I'm not like that."

"You couldn't bless any of those chicks, could you? Until you gave up and cursed the last one."

Marra propped herself up on her elbows and realized that the walls were so thin that she could hear the conversation.

"Fine." Agnes sounded defeated. "A small curse. Only a small one."

"Not so small. The only reason the magic took was because you cursed the chick, wasn't it?"

"All right, yes. I've never been much good at blessing people, not really. But I didn't hurt the chick. It was fine."

"What was the curse portion? There had to be something."

Agnes mumbled something.

"What?"

"I *said*, if the chick didn't find us a safe place, it would die."

Marra's eyes widened in the dark.

"But it found it," Agnes continued, "so it worked out all right." She sounded worried, even through the muffling plaster, and Marra could picture her fretful expression.

"You're skilled at cursing. Genuinely skilled. More than that, you've got a talent for it. I saw the way the world slipped sideways in the alley. It wasn't just the one mouse that time, was it? You've done it before."

Another mumble.

"Who was your mother, really? Or what? Not just a random maiden with hooved feet, was she?"

Marra glanced across the room. Could Fenris hear this? No, he was asleep, hands folded neatly next to his head, breathing slow and even.

"You're a poor liar, Agnes. Tell me the truth."

Marra had been feeling a slight pang of guilt over eavesdropping, which immediately vanished. She wedged her ear against the wall, just in time to hear Agnes say, "What good is it? I'm not going to go around punishing children for being born. That's a terrible thing to do. People really don't like that."

"So you are giving up your power in order to be liked," said the dust-wife heavily.

"*No.*" That was loud enough that Marra winced. "I am giving up my power in order to be *decent*. If warriors are allowed to stop killing people and bang their swords into plowshares, I ought to be allowed to keep chickens and give children good health and not curse them."

The dust-wife said something else, too low to hear.

"The world can go *hang*," said Agnes, sounding perilously close to tears, and as long as Marra listened, she heard no more from the next room.

Chapter 15

I was thinking," said Agnes the next morning. "Maybe I should go talk to this godmother."

"Eh?" said Marra.

"Eh?" said the dust-wife.

"Is that wise?" said Fenris.

Peep, said the chick.

They were all sitting around a table in a little whitewashed room. The surface of the table was scarred from years of use, but everything was very clean. Miss Margaret's breakfasts were very plain—coarse bread, cooked eggs, and little fish dried whole—but she was not stingy on the portions, which was good because Fenris ate as much as the other three humans put together.

"Well, we don't know exactly what the blessing is, do we?" said Agnes. "We know what the words are. But maybe there's a loophole. It's not always words. You figure that she had to make a good speech to the court, but she might have said something simpler to the baby."

"And you think she'll tell you?" asked Marra.

"She might. Professional courtesy, you know."

Marra nodded, though she had trouble picturing that grim figure with the stained-glass skull extending any professional courtesy to anyone.

Surprisingly, Fenris agreed. "She might," he said. "Very unlikely people, you know, will share confidences with each other if they think the other person understands. A prisoner who won't tell a guard anything will thaw immediately if he's put in a cell with another man in for the same crime. And doctors who would bite off their tongues before showing indecision to a patient will tell another doctor about how little they know and how frightened they are. I've seen it happen many times. It's how spies work."

"There is something to what you say," said the dust-wife. "But if the prince turns up dead, then I would assume that this godmother would be suspicious."

"Why?" asked Agnes. "I'm a godmother. I can't do anything to an adult. And I've got a perfectly good reason to be here. The queen's about to bear another child. As the godmother for the royal family, I've got an interest."

"I'll go with you," said Marra. She could just imagine sweet, cheerful Agnes running into the prince's godmother, in much the same way that Bonedog might run headlong into an unexpected wall. *I wouldn't go see her by myself, either. Maybe the dust-wife could hold her own, but the rest of us mortals . . .*

"She's seen you before," said the dust-wife.

"Not really." Marra shrugged. "I was a long way off and there was a king and a queen and a prince in the room. I wasn't on the dais. I don't think she even glanced in my direction."

"So that's settled," said Agnes. "Will you look after Finder?"

"Finder," said the dust-wife in a tone that did not invite further comment.

"The chick. I named him Finder."

The dust-wife looked at her, then at the little black chick, then back at Agnes. "Finder," she said again.

"Because that was the blessing. That he'd help us find somewhere safe."

"You named the chicken."

"Well, of course! Doesn't your chicken have a name?"

The dust-wife looked at the brown hen, who glared back. "First of all, no, and second of all, she's got a demon in her, so I would be naming the demon, which already has a true name. I am not going to go around naming demons. It gives them ideas."

"I name all my chickens," said Agnes. "Specky and Buff and Milady and Jonquil and Shadow. Don't you name any of your chickens?"

"No. They're chickens. They don't come when they're called."

"Well, no, but it's easier if you're going to talk about them to other people. You can't always be saying 'the big tan one with the feathered feet' and whatnot."

"I do not talk about my chickens to other people," said the dust-wife with an air of finality.

"I've heard you talk about other people to your chicken, though," put in Fenris. Agnes giggled.

"For the first time," said the dust-wife, mostly to the ceiling, "I am beginning to question the sense of this entire enterprise."

"I've been questioning it since day one," said Marra.

"I have not," said Fenris. "I have faith in all of you."

"You *would*," muttered the dust-wife. "Fine. I'll watch . . . Finder."

Agnes beamed at her. "Be a good chick," she instructed Finder, and handed him over to the dust-wife. Finder peeped. The brown hen made a low, reptilian noise of disdain.

Agnes dusted off her hands. "Let's go," she said. "I can't wait to meet another godmother."

* * *

Finding where the prince's godmother lived was easier than it should have been. Agnes simply asked the landlady.

"I don't know," she rasped, while the puppet glared at them and tapped his wooden nails together. "But someone like that will live rich, and the houses get richer as you climb the spiral. Go up the spiral road and ask again."

"Right, then!" said Agnes happily, and off they went, Marra in her drabbest robes with no medal, a servant or a poor relation.

"Won't she live in the palace?" asked Marra.

"Would she?" asked Agnes. "I don't."

"Yes, but . . ." Marra identified a conversational pit trap and carefully stepped around it. *Yes, but you're you. Yes, but in the Northern*

Kingdom, the godmother is terrifying and respected, not a poor relation. Yes, but . . .

And an hour later, *Yes, but you were right.*

The godmother did not live in the palace. She lived in the temple district, among the tall, narrow houses of the gods and saints, as if she were a priest.

"Near the top of the city, of course," said Agnes. While the city was arranged in a spiral of roads, steps had been cut as short cuts. They worked. They were also extremely steep. "Why do gods always want you to walk to them? You'd think they'd do more good if they were near where most of the people live."

"I suppose it depends on what people want in a god," said Marra. "But the abbess always said that most people want gods to be close enough to get them if you want them, but not have them breathing down your neck all the time."

Agnes grunted, waving for a halt. They sat down on a bench halfway up the steep flight of stairs. Both of them were panting.

"So," said Agnes.

"Unnnh?"

"Fenris?"

"Fenris what?"

Agnes nudged her in the ribs. "*Fenris,*" she said, lifting her eyebrows.

"Oh gods," said Marra. She rested her elbows on her knees and dropped her head. *Please do not make me have this conversation with my great-aunt. Please.*

"Eh? Eh?" Another nudge. "Handsome lad, isn't he?"

"He's not a lad; he's nearly forty. And I haven't been thinking about it, Aunt Agnes. I've had other things on my mind."

"You watched him chop firewood the other day."

"What does that . . . ?" Marra had to pause. Yes, she had. He'd taken off his shirt. There had been a lot of muscle on display. Even the dust-wife had paused for a look. Her hen had cackled so loudly it had set off the others in the nearby barnyard. "Oh. That. All right. I'm not *dead.*"

An elderly woman, older than Agnes, went by. She was bent double under the weight of a basket and she went up the stairs twice as fast as either of them. Marra didn't know if that was inspiring or depressing.

"So you *have* noticed," said Agnes, pleased. "And he's quite a gentleman, too."

"He's wanted for murder in his home country."

If she'd been expecting that would stop Agnes, she was sadly disappointed.

"I'm sure he had his reasons."

"Well, yes."

"Good with chickens, too. Finder likes him."

Marra put her face in her hands. *Lady of Grackles, if you would like to open the earth and let it swallow me whole, now would be an excellent time.* "Aunt Agnes, we have—" No, she couldn't very well say that they had an assassination to plan, could she? Not where people might be listening. Blast. "—a lot going on right now."

"All right, all right. I'll stop. Just, you know, keep it in mind. Not every day a man like that comes along, eh?"

"I am very suspicious of men right now," muttered Marra through her fingers.

"A little moth told me he's what you need."

"He's *not*—" Marra dropped her hands, realized the exact words that Agnes had used, and glared at her great-aunt. Agnes looked smug.

"Besides, I'm sure he doesn't think that about me," said Marra. "So it's all moot anyway."

"You're sure about that, are you?"

Fenris's hand on hers, absently stroking her palm. Fenris's wry smile. His solid presence against her back. The mutual awkwardness of finding themselves in a bedroom together. The way he had held her hands, then let her go the moment she pulled away. "Completely sure," grated Marra. "Now, come on. We're supposed to be meeting a terrifying godmother, or have you forgotten?"

"Yes, yes." Agnes got to her feet. "More stairs. Joy."

"Humph."

Both of them were red-faced and gasping by the time they reached the temple district. A tall woman with close-cropped hair, wearing the medals of the Unconquered Sun, gave them directions. "For all the good it will do," she said. "She sees no visitors."

"Oh, it's all right," said Agnes cheerfully. "She'll see me. Probably."

Marra expected a cynical look, but the woman's eyes softened as she looked down at Agnes. "Then good luck to you, grandmother."

The godmother's house looked like a temple. It shared walls with the buildings on either side, one a priest's home and one a shrine to the Saint of Dust. There was a guard standing outside the door, armed and armored, holding a halberd before him.

"Hello," said Agnes, walking up. "I'd like to see the godmother, please."

The guard tilted his head almost imperceptibly. "She does not see any visitors."

"It's important," said Agnes.

"You waste your time. She does not bless anyone but the royal family."

"Oh, that's all right." Agnes reached out and patted his arm as if he were a small child. "I don't need a blessing. I'm a godmother."

Marra braced herself to grab Agnes and roll out of the way if the guard took offense to being touched, but he only looked bemused. "Another godmother?"

"Yes. Can you go tell her I'm here?"

"Is she expecting you?"

Agnes shrugged. "Well, I don't really know, do I? If she's an extremely powerful godmother, she might be able to see the future, in which case yes. But if she's like the rest of us, then probably not. Or she might be very powerful, but not good at seeing the future, which happens, too. Futures are very muddy. You can't really get much out of them, you know."

He was beginning to get the look that most people dealing with Agnes got. Marra wondered if that was something a person could learn, or if you were born with it. *Or perhaps it only works if you're obviously older and seem a bit silly and so obviously devoid of malice . . .*

"How do I know you're a godmother?"

Agnes searched his face. Little strands of white hair had escaped from the pins and gave her a wispy halo. "You . . . did not have a godmother," she said slowly, "but your mother did, and the blessing was . . . was . . . Oh dear, I'm afraid I can't tell exactly. That her children be born strong or born healthy, one of the two." She patted at the air with her hands. "It was a good blessing," she said. "I think it worked."

The guard's eyes widened. He looked over his shoulder at the door, as if expecting to find someone looking at him.

"Wait here," he said, pulling the door open, and stepped inside.

"You could really see that blessing?" whispered Marra.

"Oh yes. Normally you can't go too far back, but the ones about what kind of children you have leave marks on the child. They have to or they wouldn't work. It doesn't last forever, though. I tried with mice." She shook her head. "By the third or fourth generation, even if you wish that all their descendants be healthy, it's just too faint. Magic spreads itself thin after a while. It has to, I think. To keep itself going past that, it'd be constantly drawing on the person who cast the spell, and that's no good. One litter of mice isn't much, but a hundred or so, having litter after litter? You saw what happened making the magic stick to Finder. I don't want to find out how many healthy baby mice it takes to make me drop dead of exhaustion."

The guard opened the door again. "The royal godmother will see you," he said, his face impassive once more.

"Thank you," said Agnes, beaming at him. Marra gave him a wry look as she passed, aware of the effect that dealing with magic could have on ordinary souls. She thought that she caught the trace of a smile around his eyes, but perhaps that was only her imagination.

The godmother's dwelling was also a temple.

It was strange to see. Marra had expected doors, apartments, the trappings of normal living. Instead it was a long, narrow hall, hung with tapestries. The godmother sat on a dais at the far end, her robe forming a triangle with her pale skull at the apex. Bowl candles with a dozen wicks flickered, casting deep shadows on the ceiling, and the room smelled of scented wax.

Does she sit here all day? Marra wondered. *Is this how she receives visitors, or does she simply sit here and wait to be called to the palace?*

It was somehow easy to believe the latter. There was an immobility to the godmother in this pose, as if she had been crafted from leather and layered fabric, a doll that had never been made to move. She looked like the god of the temple, not like a person in her own home.

When she moved, it was a visceral shock. Marra took a step back as if she'd suffered a blow. It seemed as if that ancient skin should crack apart instead of stretching.

"Come closer," said the godmother in a voice like an echo from the bottom of the bone pit.

"Hello!" said Agnes. "I'm a godmother, too."

"Yessss . . ." The sibilants drew out and faded away. The godmother's eyes flicked over Marra, dismissed her, and settled on Agnes. Marra wondered if, having said that, the godmother was about to throw them out again.

And then the godmother smiled, her almost lipless mouth pulling tight across bone. "Come in and have some tea."

* * *

Marra's hands ached, and the little numb patch of skin had flared as if brushed with the ghosts of nettles. Nothing bad had happened, though. Had it? The godmother had made tea. Hadn't she? Marra couldn't quite summon the memory of the water boiling, only the long, withered hands on a black iron teapot, pouring it into little lacquer cups.

Marra concentrated on breathing in and out. The room was not spinning or anything so dramatic, but something was happening inside her ears, a queasy, dizzy feeling. She felt as if she were standing just behind her own shoulder, watching herself breathe.

The godmothers seemed very far away. She could hear them

talking and understand the words, but only if she concentrated. It was as if they spoke in a language that she was not fluent in, and had to focus on every word.

". . . a curse? Heh. Yes, of course there is a curse . . ."

Is there something in the tea? Or the candles? No, Agnes was obviously unbothered, and Marra had barely drunk the tea.

She stood up. Neither Agnes nor the godmother seemed to notice. When Marra glanced over at them, she was struck by how similar they looked, which made no sense. The godmother was very tall, wasn't she? But Agnes was as well, somehow. Had she been wearing black? Marra couldn't remember. *Of course she must have been. It's not like she could have changed clothes without you noticing.*

". . . that's very clever. I couldn't have done that . . ."

The godmothers did not seem very interesting. The hangings, though—the hangings were very strange. *Tapestry weave,* Marra thought absently, *but what on earth was the weaver doing?* It seemed as if they were switching back and forth between styles with no sense of pattern or structure.

She drifted over to one of them while Agnes and the godmother continued talking. Up close, it was even more complicated and less aesthetic. Blocks of color interlocked or failed utterly to do so. Marra had never been much of a weaver, preferring embroidery. Tapestry weaving required a great deal of advance planning, and she could never get her head around it well. Still, even her worst efforts were neater and more regular than these.

This bit is a weft lock . . . and this is split weaving here . . . but why? Weft locks interwove two threads; split weaves left a small but perceptible gap between them. Neither was terribly unusual, but weavers usually picked a style and stuck to it. This followed no discernable pattern. Six splits would be close together, followed by a run of weft locks and then straight runs of a single color. The effect was disorientating. At the bottom right corner, for no apparent reason, the weaver had used golden embroidery thread to make a kind of knot, as if tying off the tapestry, except that was certainly not how you did it—you'd need to tie off the warp ends and this looked more like a child had stabbed thread into the weaving, over and over, leaving ugly loops. *Is this a signature?*

Agnes laughed, and her voice sounded deeper and somehow older. Marra glanced up, but they were only two women sitting together, cloaked in darkness. What mattered was the tapestry, the strange irregular weavings . . .

"Are you a weaver?" asked the godmother.

Marra had been leaning so close to the tapestry that she hadn't registered that conversation had stopped. "No," she said, pulling back. "I mean . . . I have. I'm not good at it. I embroider, mostly."

"I have been working on these for many years," said the godmother in that strange, flat voice that seemed to echo in some other space. "You might find them of interest."

"Ah . . . yes, of course," said Marra. She schooled her face into a polite smile. You did not tell anyone that they had produced a muddled lump of ugliness. She would not have insulted a novice that way, let alone an undying creature of terrible power.

She went to the next tapestry and found that the bottom third was identical to the first one she had looked at, but then it wandered off into other colors, other patterns, other erratic joinings of warp and weft. The next one also shared the same bottom third as the others, and the next.

Is this supposed to look like something? Regardless of how she squinted or turned her head, she could not make it resolve into anything. There was a blob of red that might have been a sword, but it might also have been a lizard or the head of a rabbit with particularly stiff ears.

She was sufficiently engrossed that she only half heard the two godmothers finishing their pleasantries. "A moment before you leave," said the godmother. "I will give you something."

Marra's pulse leapt, as if the offer of a gift was a threat. *Which possibly it is . . .*

The godmother rose to her feet. Marra took a step back, ready to flee.

Agnes gave her a sharp look and offered the godmother her arm. Marra half expected the woman to shun the offer, but the godmother leaned heavily on her colleague, then picked up her cane.

"As I said," she said, moving slowly to the second tapestry, "I have worked on these for some time." She stood before it, but her eyes were on Marra. "Do you know what they represent?"

"No?" said Marra. The blocks of color did not look like anything. They were not even enough to be a map or a floor plan, not varied enough to be writing.

The godmother nodded. "Then I may give it to you." She reached into her sleeves. Metal flashed and Marra thought, *Oh god it's a knife she's going to stab Agnes*, and then, *Why am I so frightened? She has never offered us so much as an unkind word.*

She knew why, of course. Vorling feared the godmother and Marra feared Vorling, links in a chain from predator to prey. *I am a worm and Vorling is a starling. The worm has nothing to fear from the hawk, but I cannot quite convince myself of that . . .*

Shears. They were shears that the godmother carried. She caught hold of the tapestry and closed the blades over a spot not quite half-way up. Marra cried out in surprise. Even as ugly as the weavings were, they represented hours and days of work.

The godmother was ruthless. She chopped off the bottom of the weaving and held it out to Marra. Her hands shook and the stray threads, unraveling from the top, swayed back and forth. Marra was suddenly reminded of the silk threads of the cocoon in the goblin market, the moth that had taken days of her life away, and what would this strange, violent gift take away from her?

"Take it," said the godmother. "You may find it useful. Or you may not." Her eyes bored into Marra as she spoke.

The worm has nothing to fear from the hawk. She took the piece of tapestry and their hands touched for an instant. The godmother's skin should have been cold, but it was the same temperature as the air, as if she had no heat of her own.

Marra noticed that her hands were shaking as badly as the god-mother's. She stared down at the ragged-edged bit of weaving. "I . . .

I . . . Thank you," she said finally, as if she were a small child and her nursemaid was prompting her to remember her manners.

The godmother made a noise somewhere between a hiss and a grunt. She nodded to Agnes, and then Agnes took Marra's arm and led her out of the strange little temple.

The light outside was shockingly bright. Her eyes watered. She blinked, looking down at the strange, butchered weaving in her hands.

Wait . . . wait—what just happened? Did I really leave Agnes talking to the godmother and go wander around the room?

"Agnes?" she said, surprised at the volume of her own voice. "Agnes, did something just happen? I was sitting with you, and I was paying attention, but then I wasn't . . ."

Agnes chuckled softly. "She's good," she said. "As powerful as the dust-wife and ten times as old."

"Was there something in the tea?"

"No, not at all. She just wanted to talk without anyone listening. Including you." Agnes patted her arm. "It'll wear off in a minute. It wasn't anything harmful, just misdirection."

The dust-wife is going to have my head. I went along to keep Agnes safe, and instead I get caught by a spell. "Do you think she knew who I was?"

"I don't think she cared," said Agnes. "I don't think she cares about very much anymore." She chewed on her lower lip. "It seems like it would be lonely, to be that old and not care, but maybe she doesn't care about being lonely, either."

Her step was light as they went down the stairs, almost dancing. Marra's head throbbed and everything seemed very bright. She tried not to be curt. "Did we learn anything?"

"Oh yes, a great deal," said Agnes. "For one thing, she's not blessing those babies. She's cursing them. And has been for centuries now."

Chapter 16

"A curse?" asked the dust-wife, sitting in the little parlor room in Miss Margaret's house. The innkeeper brought them a pot of tea and the curse-child stared balefully over her shoulder. "A protection from malign magic. How is it a curse?"

"Because we're listening to the wrong part," said Agnes. She waited until landlady and puppet had left the room and dolloped honey into her tea. "We all were obsessing about the foreign magic and enemies taking the throne. That bit's mostly theater. But the actual curse is that she will serve them as she served the family, her life bound to theirs, as long the godmother still draws breath." She beamed at the other three people at the table.

". . . I don't get it," said Fenris. Underneath the table, Bonedog gnawed happily on a soup bone, which felt vaguely like cannibalism to Marra.

"She'll serve them as she served the rest of their family, and she bound their life to hers. How do we know that's a good thing?"

The dust-wife sat back, suddenly thoughtful. Marra frowned. "Do you mean she's hurting them?"

"The royal family of the Northern Kingdom has been dying young for centuries, haven't they?" Agnes tapped the tabletop. "It's not even gossip anymore. Everybody just knows."

"A maid told me there was a curse on the kingdom and the kings burned out from it," said Marra slowly. "And it was the godmother who protected them from it."

"It's the godmother who's doing it," said Agnes. "She got immortality from somewhere, and that's how. Their life is bound to hers. She's pulling it out of them to keep herself alive." She paused.

"You know, I don't think she likes it at all. One of the kings—the very old kings, way back when, the one who built the first palace, I think—bound her to the royal family. She has to serve them. It's not something she chose to do. But she has to stay alive to serve them, so she's draining the life out of them. It's awful for everybody, when you think about it."

A terrible thought struck Marra. "Is that why my niece died? Did the godmother kill her?" Fenris inhaled sharply.

"No, no." Agnes waved her hands. "Probably not. Not when she's got Vorling, and the king was still alive to work on then, too. But she's also keeping any magic from helping them. That means that if I went in and tried to give a baby a blessing of health, it'd fall right off. The royal family can't so much as get a wart removed by a witch. Magic can't touch them. Which means magic can't break the spell, either."

The dust-wife grunted. After a moment she said, "But that doesn't help us, does it? It's the same as it ever was. We can't enchant Vorling."

"Not while the godmother draws breath," said Agnes. "That's the other half." She looked up at the trio of puzzled faces. "Oh dear. Look, it's like Finder, right?"

Marra rubbed her forehead. The chick was currently snuggled under the brown hen's body. The hen didn't look terribly happy about it. "What about Finder?"

"The spell—" Agnes caught the dust-wife's eyes. "Fine, the *curse* on Finder was that he'd find us a safe place to stay or . . . well, it'd be bad," said Agnes. "Most curses are like that. They come in two halves. This curse is that the royal family is bound to her, isn't touched by any other magic as long as they live, *and as long as the godmother draws breath.*"

"That's not promising," said Fenris. "Do we have to kill her?"

Agnes's eyes went round. "I don't think we could. I mean, she might want to let us, but if she could die that easily, she would have just done it already. I don't think she can be killed in the normal sense."

"This is getting worse and worse," muttered Marra. Agnes had seemed so excited earlier, but when she tried to explain things, they sounded terrible to Marra. What happened to the next of Kania's children? She was probably due to give birth soon—she'd already been round at the funeral . . . What if they did kill Vorling somehow and the child grew up and was drained of life to fuel a curse?

"But she's only doing this because she has to!"

"Does she resent them?" asked Fenris.

Agnes gnawed on her lower lip. "I don't think so," she said. "I think maybe she would have, a long time ago. I'm sure she hated them once. But now she just doesn't care. She's been alive too long. She outlived any real feelings. She can't die. She just goes and curses a child and then she goes away and sits in her temple and just . . . exists."

"What a dreadful fate," said Fenris.

"She should at least keep chickens," said the dust-wife. "Or take up gardening. Immortality is wretched, but you can always make the best of it."

"Do you think she'll help us?" asked Marra.

Agnes gave her a worried look. "I don't think the spell would let her. I think she already did as much as she could."

Marra took out the butchered chunk of tapestry. Another few strands had come loose. It was agonizing to look at, like an open wound. "She said she could give me this, because I didn't know what it was."

The dust-wife looked it over but shook her head. "It doesn't mean anything to me. It isn't any kind of magic, or if it is, I can't sense it. I don't know why she gave it to you, but presumably she had a reason."

Marra stared at it, trying to make sense of the pattern. Nothing came to her. She leaned her head back against the wall. Fenris had sat down opposite her, trying to minimize the amount of space he took up in the tiny room. Bonedog was half under the table, his illusionary tongue hanging out. Finder the chick had wandered down to sit between his paws, apparently napping.

Bonedog freed from the pit of bones. Fenris freed from the goblin market. Finder freed from a pen in the market. *Everywhere we go, we set things free, and we're trying to free Kania from Vorling . . .*

"Could we free her?" asked Marra. "The godmother?"

"The king who bound her is long dead," said Agnes. "I don't—"

She stopped. Her eyes went round. She looked at Marra and Marra felt the same idea strike her all at once, a shared moment of realization. *The king is dead.*

Slowly, holding the thought in her head as delicately as an egg, Marra turned to the dust-wife. "The dead kings live in a palace of dust below the living palace," she said. She remembered the billow of tapestries, and the maid telling her about the maze beneath the palace. She'd seen it herself, however briefly, hadn't she? She remembered the stone underfoot and staring at the back of Kania's dress, trying not to get lost in the dark. "They're all there. Can you find the king who bound the godmother? Find him and make him let her go?"

The dust-wife drummed her fingers on her knee. "I don't know," she said. "Let's find out."

* * *

"Three sets of iron doors and a portcullis, each of which requires teams of draft horses to move," said Fenris grimly. "That's leaving aside the honor guard and the fact that it's on the main square opposite the living palace, where anybody can see us trying to get in."

Fenris had spent two days lurking outside the palace, scouting the main entrance to the palace of dust, occasionally with help from Agnes and the dust-wife, sans chicken. Marra couldn't go in case she was recognized, but she remembered the place well enough. When members of the royal family were interred, the horses wore black caparisons and were blessed by the priests of seven temples. Marra remembered the solemn pacing of the great beasts as her niece's coffin was carried through the iron doors, the thudding of drums.

"There must be a way in that doesn't require horses," said Marra. "People have to go in first to prep the tomb. You couldn't get a bunch of horses in every single time."

"It's theater," said Agnes.

Fenris looked puzzled, but Marra nodded. "Yes, exactly. A royal funeral is like a wedding. And the christening is the same way. You need set dressing and staging and schedules. Horses don't just show up spontaneously in the right outfits and march."

Fenris considered this. "I suppose you're correct. Though it is not work I had considered. The coronations I have overseen mostly involved getting someone to a point of being crowned. Actually setting up the feasts and the clothes and the priests was someone else's problem."

Marra thought privately that it was probably mostly a woman's problem, but at least Fenris was acknowledging it was work.

"So there must be a way to get in and out of the tomb," said Agnes. "Without all the horses."

"It might be inside the palace, though," said Marra. While she was reasonably confident that no one would recognize her in the city, going into the palace itself seemed like tempting fate.

"It's a tomb," said the dust-wife. "There are always entrances. If they are hollowing out new areas, or building new rooms, there must be an entrance for masons that does not involve tracking brick dust through the palace."

"Do the dead know?" asked Fenris.

The dust-wife rolled her eyes. "The dead are already there. They don't worry about how to get in and out. They're corpses, not cat burglars."

Fenris leaned back, tapping his thumb against his lower lip. "Bricks. Hmm. Could there be a quarry? Or an entrance from a quarry? How can we find out?"

"Put out that you want work as a stonemason," said Agnes.

"A stonemason?" He raised his eyebrows. "I don't know the first thing about stone."

"Take off your shirt," said the dust-wife, poking Fenris with her staff, "and I suspect you won't have nearly as much trouble as you think."

*　*　*

In the end, Fenris did not have to take off his shirt. Apparently he was sufficiently well muscled that no one questioned a history of chiseling stones into shape. (Marra tried not to act disappointed. Agnes didn't even bother to try.) He came back from his first day, drenched in sweat and covered in white dust, and went immediately to the well to dump water over his head. ("Almost as good," said Agnes, elbowing Marra. The dust-wife's chicken cackled.)

"It's not terrible," he said. "I'm the low man on staff, so nobody's handing me a chisel. I'm just moving things around and trying to memorize the jargon. I don't know how long I can keep it up before they realize I'm a complete novice, though. They may fire me tomorrow."

"Hopefully it won't matter," said Marra. A knot of excitement was forming in her chest. *This is it. We're on the way. We're actually doing something.* "You just have to last long enough to find the way in."

Fenris was a quick learner, and apparently he picked up the specialized speech of the trade at a good enough pace that he wasn't sacked the next day, or the day after that. But there were also a number of connected quarries and no way to know which one might lead to the palace of the dead unless the dust-wife went along and asked the dead, and so for about five days, she and Fenris wandered through the quarries at night, dodging guards and talking to spirits, while Agnes made friends with the neighbors and Marra bit her nails down to the quick.

This was exactly what she had always feared. They would get to the city and then no one would know what to do and they would talk and talk and talk and nothing would get done and whatever they tried would fail and eventually they would run out of money and Fenris would probably get a job cutting firewood and Agnes would want to go home and check on her chickens and Kania would take a mysterious fall just as Damia had and eventually Vorling would die of old age and all of Marra's efforts would have come to nothing. Except now that she knew that if Kania had a living child, that child would also be cursed and grow old before its time.

She sat in the tiny, dilapidated courtyard of the boarding house and tried not to scream. *I did three impossible tasks—well, two—and went to the goblin market and now I am just sitting here while my friends break into quarries. Oh, Lady of Grackles, this is hard.*

Maybe skipping the third task was where I went wrong. Maybe that was the one that makes you a hero. The first two were just gritting my teeth and beating up my hands. She rubbed her thumb over the numb line of skin along her little finger.

She wondered if all the old stories of heroes slaying monsters and maidens locked in towers had involved long, tedious stretches of trying to find the monsters or build the towers in the first place. *Probably. No, almost* certainly. *Who wants to hear the dull practical bits?*

Me. I do. It would make me feel less like I am failing.

She sighed and sat back on the bench. It was midafternoon, just barely warm enough to sit outside. The view in the courtyard wasn't much. One bench, three walls, one door. A half dozen pots that had probably held flowers once but now held sticks. There was a climbing rose that had died back for winter and shed curled greenish-brown leaves across the bricks. It looked like it had seen better days and was only holding on out of habit. Marra found herself identifying a little too much with the rosebush.

Agnes had befriended a woman next door and was doing laundry with her. Marra could hear her laugh drifting over the wall from time to time. *And did the great heroes do laundry? I don't remember hearing about it. You'd think after slaying a hundred men, they'd need a good wash.*

Bonedog watched a bird hopping through the dead rosebush, his illusory ears twitching. Marra started to stand up and then Agnes burst through the door and gasped on one breath, "*Thequeenhasgivenbirthtoaboy.*"

* * *

"She can't have," said Marra blankly. "It can't have been that long. Surely."

Agnes shrugged. Her face was pink with exertion. Finder was tucked into her generous cleavage, presumably dreaming the dreams of small warm chickens. "It's all anyone is talking about. There are criers in the marketplace, announcing that Vorling's heir has been born."

Early? thought Marra. And then she remembered Kania kneeling uncomfortably, her belly on her knees, and it had been months after that that she left the convent and another month before she came back to the Northern Kingdom. *It could easily have been nine months. You never asked how far along she was.*

"Kania?" she croaked. "Have they said anything about Kania?" She snatched up her cloak and grabbed Bonedog's leash. *It's not as if they'd send out criers if they weren't sure. The babe must be expected to live. But Kania—how is Kania? How is my sister?*

They were halfway down the corridor when the innkeeper stepped in front of Marra. She gestured to the outside and rasped, "Have you heard? The queen . . . the queen—" Her eyes were wide with delight. The puppet on her shoulder chattered its jaw and glared. "A boy, they say. A b—" The puppet decided that this was enough words and yanked the cord. Miss Margaret hung her head, but her eyes still danced.

"We heard," said Marra. "Going to get more details."

"It's so exciting!" bubbled Agnes. "A royal baby!"

Miss Margaret got her finger under the puppet's leash and pulled a little slack. "And after . . . after the last . . ." She beamed.

Marra considered screaming but settled for turning sideways to pass the innkeeper and her rider.

"Relax," said Agnes, as they emerged into the alley. "It's normal. Gossip about the royal family is the only real benefit to having one. You have to let people enjoy it."

"They're gossiping about my sister," grated Marra. "And my niece. My *dead* niece."

"Who is also my great-great-niece," said Agnes calmly. "But it doesn't feel that way to them. And if you go around listening to this news with a face like thunder, people will think you're not happy, and that will seem suspicious."

Marra took a deep breath. That much, at least, was true. She schooled her expression to one of polite interest and followed Agnes through the alley, Bonedog tugging on the leash.

"This is hopeless," said Marra, after ten minutes and as many stories. The queen was dead. The queen was alive but dying. The queen had died and her dying wish was that the prince take religious orders. The queen was alive but the baby was drinking her blood mixed with breast milk and would not survive. The queen was fine but tired. The baby was alive. The baby was dead. There were two babies. There was one baby. The queen had given birth to a school of fish.

At last, they found a crier in the market, surrounded by a crowd. The crier wore the livery of the palace and shouted, "Rejoice! Rejoice for the heir is born! The queen has borne an heir to the throne!"

"And the queen?" called Marra, jostling through the crowd. "How does the queen fare?"

"She has borne an heir," bellowed the crier. "A son to take the Northern throne!" Scattered cheers erupted from the crowd.

"But is she alive? Is she well?" The crowd surged and Marra could not be certain that the crier had even heard her. He didn't answer. She looked around at the crowd and saw only mouths, opening and closing, as if they were biting off pieces of her sister's story and devouring it.

You have to let people enjoy it, Agnes had said. This did not feel like enjoyment. This felt wicked and terrible and strange.

She started to push forward again, but Agnes took her arm. "Let it lie," the godmother said. "We'll find out soon enough. There's nothing we can do either way."

"I can fret," snapped Marra. "And I intend to!"

"And I won't stop you." Agnes patted her arm. "A good fret is balm for the soul. Just don't overdo it."

Marra ground her teeth. *If I go to the palace and demand to see the* queen . . . *No, no, I can't. My mother might be here, and if she's here, she'll see me. And this is all far too much to explain.* She took a deep breath and let it out again. She walked back to the boardinghouse, with the woman who had a puppet at her throat and the girl sitting on the steps who missed more meals than she ate and who was crowing about babies that weren't quite right.

You have to let people enjoy it.

This is not right. This is not fair.

And what is fair? Marra snarled to herself. *How is it fair that you grew up and ate meat at every meal and were never expected to shovel a stable because your mother married a king? How is it fair that Vorling cannot be brought to justice? How is it fair that some women wear themselves out in bearing and others cannot have a child? How is it fair that Fenris can never go home again because he killed a terrible man? How is it fair that gods punish starving people in the blistered land?*

Nothing is fair. Nothing is right.

She took a deep breath and stared at the wall, dry-eyed. Agnes touched her arm, concerned.

Nothing is fair, except that we try to make it so. That's the point of humans, maybe, to fix things the gods haven't managed.

The front door opened. The brown hen squawked.

"We know how to get in," said Fenris.

Chapter 17

There's always a haunted quarry," the dust-wife explained. "People moving giant blocks of stone around like they do there, someone's bound to get crushed sooner or later." She waved her hand dismissively. "I don't know how long it's been abandoned, but there's definitely an opening to the catacombs there. There are a couple of curses and some bars on the entrance. The ghost who told me said that the bars have been there as long as he could remember, and he's been dead longer than he was ever alive." She sniffed. "Nice fellow. Chief stonemason once upon a time, one of those people who has to keep checking up on everything. That sort never lets death stop them."

"What sort of curses?" asked Marra.

"Oh, they're all ostentatious ones. Very impressive looking but nothing that will stick." She scowled. "Once we're inside, there may be real ones."

"Do you think we can get to the old king's tomb from there? The one who bound the godmother?"

"It's as good a chance as any."

"We have to go soon," said Agnes. "Tomorrow night at the latest. They'll be holding the christening in a few days, as soon as they're sure the child will live. Three days is usual. She has to be unbound before that. Then I can go and . . . well, I have an idea."

Marra barely heard her. A christening. A few days. It was happening. It was happening *right now.* All the talking and fretting and standing around and everything was suddenly falling together.

"How will we get into the palace itself?" asked Fenris. "The christening will be full of nobles and nobles come with guards. Are they just going to let us walk in, because we've got the queen's sister with us?"

"Maybe," said Marra. She looked over the other three, wondering if a princess, even a princess who was sister to the queen, would be able to sweep inside with a large dog and a woman with a chicken on her staff. *After they treated us as poor relations the last time . . . No, it might not be that easy.*

Agnes cleared her throat.

"I can get in," she said.

"What?"

"How?"

"I'm a godmother," said Agnes.

All three of them looked at her blankly.

"I know I wasn't invited," said Agnes. "That's the point."

"Eh?"

She smiled gently, that tiny, frazzled woman. "There's only one story about godmothers that's always true. Bad things happen if you don't invite us to the christening."

* * *

"Try to sleep," said the dust-wife. "I don't know what's going to happen, but I suspect we'll be glad to be well rested for it. We'll go tomorrow night."

"What about Miss Margaret?" asked Marra. "Don't we have to . . . ?" She trailed off, gesturing at her throat.

"Oh, that. Yes. We'll offer before we go."

Marra tried to sleep that night and couldn't. She tossed and turned, her mind roiling. Agnes thought that she could do . . . something . . . at the christening. The dust-wife seemed to agree. Marra would have been much happier if she knew what, but Agnes had waved her hands and said that if it didn't work, it would be better if nobody worried, and the dust-wife just folded her arms and said that Marra had come to her for help, not an education in magic.

"Free the godmother and the protections go away," she said. "That's all you need to know. And once the protections are gone, there are a thousand magics that can . . . rectify . . . the situation."

"You can't tell me more?"

"The less you know, the less you can spill when you talk to your sister about getting us into the palace. You're a terrible liar, Marra. You look as if you're afraid the universe is ashamed of you."

Marra didn't want to accept this, but the dust-wife locked the door to the bedroom and left her to toss in bed and fail to sleep. Her sister had given birth. They were going to the palace of the dead. Her sister had given birth to a boy. Kania's life was in terrible danger and if she died, she would be buried in one of the tombs underground, next to Vorling's tomb, and she would have to stand next to him for eternity. Could ghosts torment one another? Would Vorling's bones creep from his sarcophagus and hammer on the lid of Kania's coffin?

Oh gods and saints, she thought, rolling over and burying her face in the pillow. *Oh. Let them only be empty bones.*

"I never could sleep the night before a battle," said Fenris.

Marra turned to face him, even though she couldn't see. "Is this going to be a battle?"

"I don't have the slightest idea what to expect. It might be. Or maybe we'll just wander around in the dark for a while and the dust-wife will wave her hands and it will all be over."

Marra shook her head, forgetting he couldn't see her in the dark. "I doubt it. Whenever I go anywhere with her, something terrible and magical happens and then I wish it hadn't."

"I had noticed something of the sort, yes."

"I suppose that's still better than a battle."

"Mm." She could picture his expression, the way his lips would be twisting at one corner as he considered this. "Battles are terrible, but they're also comprehensible. You know what you're doing. Well . . . all right, that's not entirely true. You know what you're *supposed* to be doing. There's a lot of yelling and hitting things and then you look up and it's over. But once you've been through a few of them, you know more or less how things go. Magic, though . . . I don't know how it's supposed to work or why."

Fenris paused for so long that Marra wondered if he had fallen asleep. Then he said, "I was never so frightened as when we were leaving the goblin market. If you had not led me out, I would still be hiding in a corner there, hoping that everything would go away."

Marra blinked up at the darkness. "I didn't lead you out. We went together. I leaned on you for half of it."

He chuckled softly. "That's not how I remember it. I remember you holding my arm. You were very calm and very brave, even though you'd just had someone yank your tooth out."

The Toothdancer. Marra shuddered. "I didn't feel calm *or* brave."

"You hid it well."

It was easier to talk in the dark, somehow. Marra took a deep breath. "I don't feel brave now. I feel frustrated. I want to run in and drag Kania away from that monster, but I can't. If you hadn't found the way into the tombs tonight, I would probably have done something foolish."

"So long as you take me with you."

"I'd rather you didn't get killed for my foolishness."

"I have been resigned to dying for a long time."

"Fenris . . ."

"No, no, don't sound stricken. What else am I good for now? You gave me something useful to do with my death. I will be grateful forever."

"No dying," said Marra angrily. "I don't want you to die! I want you to live to a ripe, old age so that I can say, 'Hey, Fenris, remember the time we went into a horrible catacomb and the dust-wife said something cryptic and Agnes waved a baby chicken at us,' and you say, 'Of course I remember,' and I don't have to try to explain to someone who wasn't there."

The silence from the other side of the room was suddenly deeper and more textured. Marra bit her lip. "Besides," she said, after a moment, "someone has to chop all my firewood. I've gotten spoiled."

"Hmm."

She rolled over again. She could not seem to get comfortable.

If I ask, he'll think I'm propositioning him.

. . . Am I?

No. Definitely not. Not while all this is going on. It'll just make things terrible and complicated, and they're already terrible and complicated enough.

I might never get another chance.

But if I do and it's awkward and weird, then we'll probably die with things being awkward and weird and I cannot handle that.

Marra thumped the pillow and then gave up. "Fenris?"

"Yes?"

"I don't know how to ask this without giving you completely the wrong idea."

"All right?"

"Do you remember on the road, when we slept back-to-back?"

He did not answer, but she heard the bed creak, and then the indignant snuffle of Bonedog being nudged out of the way. Her own bed sagged as Fenris sat on the edge of it. Marra scooted up against the wall to give him room.

His back was as solid and warm as she remembered. She sighed and felt something unclench, although whether it was in her jaw or her gut or her soul, she couldn't say.

"You're a saint," she mumbled, tugging the blanket up around her shoulder.

"You have no idea," muttered Fenris.

* * *

They slept as late as they could, and then got up and stared at the walls. They ate. Marra threw the nettle cloak over her clothes, watching the owlcloth break up the outlines. Fenris went out for an hour and came back with his pack full of food. "God knows how long it'll take us down there," he said. "I'd rather we didn't starve."

Marra had been doing frantic math in her head. If the child had been born before midnight, they had two days to the christening. If the child had been born after midnight, they had three days. Neither of these options were good.

The only kindness was that darkness fell early. The moment the shadows began to stretch, she was up and pacing.

"For the love of the gods," said the dust-wife. "Let's go. I'd rather fight with the dead than watch Marra wear holes in the floor."

"Will we have to fight the dead?"

"Anything's possible."

Marra paused. "There are stories about graverobbers having their souls ripped out and haunting the catacombs."

"These things happen." The dust-wife stood up, held out her staff, and let the chicken settle herself. Agnes tucked Finder under her scarf.

They made their way down the stairs in a grand procession, only to encounter the innkeeper in the hallway.

"Miss Margaret," said the dust-wife. "We thank you for your hospitality." Her words rolled out with the air of a dread pronouncement, as if she were sentencing the innkeeper to be thanked, perhaps for all eternity.

Miss Margaret looked bewildered, then dropped a curtsy. The puppet glared from her shoulder.

Quick as a striking snake, the dust-wife reached out and grabbed the puppet's head. As soon as her fingers locked around it, it went limp. The cord at the woman's throat went slack and she gasped, clutching at her neck. Raw furrows had been etched against the sides of her throat, the skin abraded so many times that it had left patches as red and scaled as a dragon.

"It cannot hurt you now," said the dust-wife.

"Don't hurt him!" cried Miss Margaret, voice suddenly loud. "Don't!"

"I have not hurt . . . him. If I release him, everything will be exactly as it was. But you have been kind to us, so I offer you a choice." She loomed over the innkeeper, a tall, rattle-bone creature of deserts and dust, shockingly out of place in the little hallway. "Say the word and you can be free. He will be destroyed and never trouble you again."

The choice was so obvious that Marra never doubted, and so the innkeeper's words were doubly shocking.

"*Put him back!*" she shrieked, tugging on the dust-wife's wrist. "Let him go! He never hurt you; he never hurt anybody!"

. . . *What?*

"You are certain?" asked the dust-wife, implacable as death.

"Let him go! Don't hurt him!"

"Very well." The dust-wife released the puppet and stepped back.

The gnarled wooden face gave her a savage glare, and then the innkeeper gathered the puppet to her like a child, holding him against her breast. "It's all right," she crooned. "It's all right." And to the dust-wife, furious, "You'd better go."

"Very well," said the dust-wife again, and the four of them walked out of the boardinghouse forever, with Bonedog hushed and silent at their heels.

* * *

"What just happened?" hissed Marra. "What— Why didn't she— Was it still controlling her?"

The dust-wife shrugged. "She didn't want to lose it. People get to choose."

"But she's choosing *wrong*! I don't understand! And . . . and . . ." Marra ran out of words and waved her hands.

"I know," said the dust-wife. "I know."

"She can't have realized—she must not have understood!"

"She understood."

"Was she scared? Did she not believe us?"

"Maybe," said the dust-wife. "But more likely she simply did not want him destroyed."

"You cannot help people who do not want help," rumbled Fenris. "You can't force someone to do what you think is best for them." He paused, then added, somewhat reluctantly, "Well, you can. But they don't appreciate it and most of the time it turns out that you were wrong."

"But—"

"We can only save people who want to be saved," said the dust-wife. "If it's still bothering you, we'll come back afterward, assuming any of us are alive to do so. But we are out of time."

Marra clutched Bonedog's collar and shut up.

It was a long way to the quarry. The shadows got longer and then pooled together, deep blue on the white walls of the city. Marra kept looking up, to the palace, where her sister and her newborn nephew waited.

She bore an heir. After the christening, Kania's life will mean nothing to the prince.

No, no, surely not. Children die too easily; he'll wait until he has another one, won't he? Surely? It would be the sensible thing to do.

Why do you expect a man who tortures his wife to be sensible?

Marra gripped her temples. Concerned, Fenris reached over and took Bonedog's leash. "Are you all right?"

"No, but I'll manage."

It was dark when they left the city. No guards stopped them. This was the poorest quarter, where you lived because you could not afford better. No one cared who went in or out. Rats and alley cats watched them, and children with eyes like alley cats, but no one else.

For a moment, looking down into the quarry, Marra thought that she was looking back into the bone pit in the blistered land. The white stone was the color of moonlit bones and the chunks of abandoned rock looked unpleasantly like skulls. Her brain sang that it had all been a long, impossible dream and now she was back at the beginning with everything still to do again. Her foot slipped on the edge of the slope and Fenris reached out to steady her.

"I'm fine," she muttered. "It's nothing." Her head was still full of Miss Margaret clinging to the puppet and probably it was no wonder that she was a bit vague right now. *Also you're about to enter the cursed palace of the dead. That tends to have an impact on your nerves.*

She wondered what Mordecai had thought, standing at the swamps at last, and whether the poison worm had been right there in front of him or if he'd had to go wandering through the swamp trying to locate it. They still didn't have a map. She had the ruined fragment of the godmother's tapestry, but unless it started glowing or talking, it didn't seem like it was going to do any good. Another of life's little intelligence tests, and as usual, Marra had failed to even learn the question.

The entry to the palace was halfway down the slope, but a good road had been built to it once. Even though it was long abandoned and had corrugated with neglect, it was still stable underfoot. They approached the entryway three abreast, while Fenris walked behind with his hand on Bonedog's leash.

The paleness of the stone continued inside the passage, which meant that the iron bars stood out like bands of shadow. Marra wondered how they were supposed to break them down. There were no keys or gates. No one had expected this way to come into use again.

The dust-wife tapped her nail against each of the bars in turn, then grunted. She muttered a few words under her breath, lifted her staff, and cracked the end across the iron, which promptly shattered.

Marra gasped. The dust-wife cackled. So did the hen. She smacked the next bar and the next, and each one shattered like a black icicle.

"Is that magic?" breathed Marra. "Can you do that to the guards' swords?"

"Of a sort," said the dust-wife. "And I suppose I could, if you can get me the swords at least a day beforehand."

"She did something to them last night," murmured Fenris. "Rubbed them with grit and then poured a little vial over them." Marra stifled a sigh. Magic never seemed to be much use at doing the things you wanted done in a reasonable time frame.

They stepped over the broken teeth of the bars and into the passageway. Fenris wrapped Bonedog's leash around his wrist and took a candle from his pack. The dust-wife pulled something from her many pockets, said two sharp words, and moonlight blossomed under her hands.

"Is that the moon in a jar?" asked Marra, feeling a pang of recognition.

"Only a little of it. It won't mind. The moon loves things like this." She hung the little vial of moonlight from her staff. The brown hen cast a molten shadow on the ceiling, crowned with horns.

"So that bird really is a demon," said Fenris, eyeing the shadow.

"Of course she is. Why would I lie about something that ridiculous?"

The light revealed carved words overhead. Marra pointed upward. "What do those say?"

"Curses against graverobbers. Threats to tear your soul out and sentence you to wander for all eternity—that sort of thing."

"Should we be worried?"

"No, it's the usual grandstanding." The dust-wife sniffed. "Although I wouldn't rob any graves, just in case."

They set out. The passageway was rough, the kind of tunnel built for service instead of ceremony. Bits of broken stone littered the ground. Bonedog snuffled but clearly didn't smell anything of interest.

"Do we know where we're going?" asked Agnes. "We want the first king, the one who bound the godmother."

"Was it the first king, then?" asked the dust-wife.

"Oh yes. It was the godmother's power that let him keep his dynasty going. Before that, all these little Northern witch-kings were cursing each other constantly, knocking down any clan that looked like they were getting too powerful. The godmother tipped the balance. Imagine, a godmother changing everything like that!" Agnes beamed with pride, the way she did when Finder did something clever.

"The tombs are laid out by family," said Marra. "So presumably we'd need to just go back and back until we find the oldest one." Her voice echoed down the passageway and sent back words: ". . . one . . . one . . . one . . ."

"Easier said than done," muttered the dust-wife. Her chicken flapped its wings, leaving demon shadows on the wall.

The passage opened up into a larger room, littered with broken pick handles and old logs that had probably been used as rollers. Bonedog was very interested in the smells and had to poke them all.

There were three corridors leading off from the room. Marra looked from one to the next in dismay. "We need the oldest one," she muttered. "But which one is that?"

For lack of any better ideas, they took the smallest. The ceiling was low enough that Fenris had to duck his head and the dust-wife had to hold her staff at an angle, much to the brown hen's annoyance.

The roughness underfoot gave way suddenly to a smooth floor, and the hallway flared out. The dust-wife paused, looking around. "I believe we are entering the tomb proper," she said.

Marra stepped out behind her and said, "Whoa." She had seen the carved and vaulted room where her niece had been laid to rest but had not really considered the implications for the rest of the catacombs.

This was truly a palace of the dead. The ceilings vanished into darkness. The entire boardinghouse where they had spent the last week could have fit within the walls. Carvings circled the room, an endless procession of warriors and great beasts chasing each other for eternity. Racks of weapons stood against the walls, pole arms bristling like wheat, swords still gleaming dully after who knew how many years.

The center of the room held a single slab of stone, and on it, inlaid with metal, a sarcophagus. The slab had been worked into the shape of a great bear, holding the coffin on its back, its teeth buried in the belly of some unfortunate animal.

Fenris whistled softly, and the sound woke echoes like a flight of birds in the far reaches of the ceiling.

"Ostentatious," muttered the dust-wife. She laid her hands on the sarcophagus and scowled. Marra was struck by the incongruity of it, the thin woman with her robes full of packets and string, presuming to command the sort of person that could be laid to rest in such a room as this.

"Nothing." The dust-wife stepped back. "This ghost is long gone."

Marra bit her lip. "What if the king we're after is gone?"

"If he was gone, he couldn't still compel the godmother. No, he's around. Probably mad as hell, too."

"That was comforting," said Fenris. "I am comforted." He shared a bemused look with Marra, who smiled in spite of herself.

Two doorways led in opposite directions. Fenris and Marra took one side and the dust-wife and Agnes took the other. Bonedog trotted between them, bored by the lack of new smells or motion.

"Oh," said Marra softly, taking in the next room. "Oh, I see." The room was much smaller, the walls holding touches of red paint. There were neither weapons nor carved warriors, only small jars ornamented with gold. The death mask on the sarcophagus was of a woman younger than Marra. Perhaps it was only the shadows, but she thought the woman's eyes looked sad.

"His wife," said Fenris. There were two more rooms branching off, barely more than niches. He stepped forward and looked into each one, then turned back, shaking his head to Marra. "I don't think what we're looking for is in there."

"It's her children, isn't it?"

"Yes." He took her hand. Marra could picture the small coffins and wondered if they were more or less ornate than her niece's. She was glad of the hand in hers. He was very much alive—him and Bonedog, who wasn't alive but didn't know it.

"Over here," called Agnes. "We've got a hallway."

The hallway was as broad as the wife's room had been. It vanished in both directions, with branchings off on the same side as the tomb they stood in. "Lady Fox?" said Fenris. "I think you likely have more experience here than the rest of us. Which way?"

"Huh!" She lifted the light on her staff. "My dead were all sensible people in the ground. Not these great frozen tombs. Your ghost would rattle around like a pea in a dish in here. I've no idea."

Bonedog solved the problem by straining at his leash in toward one of the branchings, although it turned out that he only wanted to pee against a wall, which he did, meditatively, while everyone else pretended to be interested in the bas-reliefs on the walls.

The branching, newly anointed, led to another room like the last one, but with no hallways leading away from it. "Unmarried?" hazarded Marra. "So there are no other rooms for his bloodline?"

"Makes sense." Fenris nodded to the grave mask, which was young but bore the lines of pain. There were fewer weapons here. They backed out of that room, and the next. At the end of the hall was an ornate threshold with carvings that stretched out five feet from the doorway itself—screaming faces, reaching hands, broken swords.

"That's a little disturbing," said Marra, poking the toe of her boot at one of the carvings.

"Enemies defeated in battle?" asked Agnes.

"Or sinners cast into hell."

"Do they believe in hell, up here?"

"They do," Marra said. "You freeze in eternal cold." She shook her head. The concept had seemed foreign to her when she heard it. The Harbor Kingdom, sensibly, believed that the dead went into the sea, and the good were reborn from it, while the damned sank to the bottom and were devoured by crabs. Still, she couldn't blame the Northern Kingdom for their confusion. There probably weren't very many crabs up here.

"I hate to walk on them," she muttered.

"They're only stone," said the dust-wife. "They were never alive." She walked across the screaming carvings, the hem of her robes brushing over their faces. One by one, the others followed.

This tomb was as large and ostentatious as the wife's tomb had been plain. The walls were ribbed with statues, each one of a stern-faced Northern god, and yet despite their faces, the impression was of a great throat waiting to swallow the unwary.

There were shadowy figures flanking the sarcophagus. Marra paused in the threshold, trying to make sense of the number of legs, the shapes . . .

"Oh," she said softly. "Oh, I see."

The cold air of the palace of dust had preserved the dead horses far better than she would ever have guessed. They had sagged and withered, but they were still identifiable. Poles thrust up into the bodies held them in place, standing at attention around their dead master. The proud arch of their necks had sunken in, but Marra could still recognize the marks of breeding and the richness of the golden bridles.

"A wealthy man," said Fenris. "To be buried with his warhorses like this."

"The father?" muttered the dust-wife, gazing up at the sarcophagus. "Or the son? Are we going forward or back?"

"If we go long enough in one direction, the weaponry should change," offered Fenris, studying the carvings on the walls. "These saddles have stirrups. If we find a tomb without them . . ."

"If I could find a damn ghost, I could just ask," said the dust-wife, annoyed. She smacked the sarcophagus lid and a hollow ringing filled the crypt, then died away. "But these are too quiet and too long dead. We need younger corpses. Or at least angrier ones."

Marra did not have much time to worry about that, because the next corpse they found was positively furious.

Chapter 18

It was a small tomb off the grand one. A concubine's room, perhaps. The materials were costly and exquisite, gold and jade and rosewood, and the death mask was beautiful and painted with lapis. Despite the materials, though, it seemed . . . hasty. As if everything had been slapped together swiftly and in fear. Jade tiles crunched under their feet, having fallen from the coffin, and there were no carvings, only faded paintings. The threshold was plain and uncarved and the doorway was hidden in the shadow of one of the scowling statues.

"This one," said the dust-wife, with professional satisfaction. "This one here. This one is old, but she has *grudges*."

She pulled something out of a pocket—Marra got a glimpse of orange red, like cinnabar—and dusted it over her hands, then knocked on the coffin lid as if it were a door.

Marra expected it to take a few minutes, as the drowned boy had, a slow swelling of horror as the ghost manifested itself, but she barely had time to brace herself before the room erupted.

Dust exploded up from the coffin. Broken tiles flew around the room. Fenris flung himself over Agnes and Marra, while Bonedog yapped silently, trying to catch one in his mouth. Only the dust-wife was unmoved, standing in the center of the chaos, with the light of the moon and her familiar's shadow falling over her like a shield.

"Calm yourself," she said. "Or I'll lay you back down and find another spirit to work with. Your rage does not impress me."

The entire sarcophagus twisted as it came alive, bouncing on the slab, and then it rolled to one side so that the death mask faced them.

The beautiful face was still and calm but the eyes were alive and smoldering with fury.

you wake me!

The voice was made of echoes, of small green tiles falling from the badly mortared sarcophagus, of golden ornaments rattling together like metal cobwebs.

you dare to wake me!

peasant! commoner! you come into the tomb of the great . . . the great . . . the consort of kings, the great . . .

"Forgotten your name, have you?" asked the dust-wife. "Well, it happens, kings and commoners alike." She thumped her staff on the floor of the tomb. "So what kept you furious all this time?"

replaced replaced replaced! The wind went around the room again. *set aside! how dare they, how dare they. do they not know who I am? the great . . . the great . . .* Again the stirring wind, the sense of a shriek somewhere beyond human hearing, like bats hunting overhead.

"Poor thing," murmured Agnes, having freed herself from Fenris's attempt to protect her. "Set aside, were you? Were you the king's mistress?"

mistress! I was his wife of seven years! but I bore him no child so he took another and when her brats were murdered with a scarlet cord, they put the blame on me! me!

"Did you murder them?" asked the dust-wife, sounding interested rather than horrified.

no.

I wish I had.

if they would blame me and send me home to my parents to die, at least I might have done the crime.

I did not love them.

but no.

Marra was starting to think that Vorling had come by his wickedness honestly, at least.

"It seems we've stumbled on an ancient scandal," said Agnes. "A daughter of the king sent home in disgrace."

disgrace.

oh yes.

they could not kill me, you know, so they locked me up in here.

I was buried alive to hide their shame.

Fenris inhaled sharply.

does that shock you, peasant?

it shocked me down here in the dark.

I screamed and no one came and eventually I died and still no one came.

"So they buried you alive . . ." The dust-wife frowned. "Do you know the layout of the catacombs?"

no.

why would I?

I am a queen, not a crawler of tombs.

The dust-wife narrowed her eyes. "What did you see when they brought you here to bury you? They must have already begun your father's tomb, but what did your grandfather's tomb look like?"

The death mask rolled its painted eyes.

I don't care.

he is long dead and he was dull.

I am a queen and the consort of kings. I am the great . . .

The dust-wife slapped her red-tinted palm against the sarcophagus and the spirit yelped as if it had been struck.

aah!

how dare you, peasant.

do you not know who I am?

"No, and at the moment, neither do you."

The spirit went raging around the room, tiles flying. The dust-wife lifted her hand again and it quieted. When it spoke next, the voice was sullen, the distant keening of resentful birds.

he was buried with his boat.

he always talked of it until I wanted to scream.

the raids up the rivers when he was young.

dull dull dull.

"Thank you," said the dust-wife gravely. "That is very helpful."

I do not care about helping you.

you are also dull.

the thief-wheel will catch you soon enough and you will go wailing through the dark forever.

do not think that I will acknowledge you, peasant.

"Thief-wheel?" said the dust-wife, but the ghost only laughed. One last, weak sweep around the crypt, stirring the broken jade fragments to knee height, and then the death mask closed its eyes and the sarcophagus was only a coffin knocked off its plinth, and the gold ornaments fell silent.

"Is she gone?" asked Marra.

The dust-wife shrugged. "More or less. She's still in there, but she doesn't want to come out, and it would take more power than I'm willing to spend to compel her."

"Imagine being here all this time," murmured Agnes, "and still being so angry."

"Injustice and the desire for revenge age the body, but they keep the soul going halfway to forever," said the dust-wife practically. "And being buried alive for a crime you didn't commit will certainly keep you going for a while. I doubt she was a particularly nice person to begin with, but we don't bury people alive for being snobs."

"What do you think a thief-wheel is?" asked Marra.

"No idea."

"I have visited countries where they break criminals on cart wheels," said Fenris slowly. "They strap them across the wheel and lay them out to die of exposure. It's ugly business."

"They don't do that here," said Marra, "at least, not that I've ever heard of." She frowned. "Of course, in this ghost's time, maybe things were different."

"At least we know to look for a boat," said Agnes practically.

They found the boat about twenty minutes later, after a few hallways leading to minor royals and their various family members. The dust-wife reported no ghosts, or if there were, they were sleeping soundly.

"Well, that's a boat, all right," said Agnes.

It was about twenty feet long, with a prow carved in the shape of a snarling beast. Oars stuck out like centipede feet and the sarcophagus sat in the center of the longboat in a place of honor. The carvings all around the tomb were of waves and sea monsters and naval battles, and the mast of the ship still bore a sail, preserved by the cold dry air. Marra could look up at it and make out blue and white stripes on the fabric.

She rather wished that they had time for her to go up and look and see what it was made of. *No. Focus. We have to find the old king before the christening.*

"Which way from here?" asked Fenris.

"If we assume that one of the earliest kings bound the godmother," said Marra, "then we head toward his father, and then his father, and so forth."

"This direction, then," said the dust-wife. They crossed the tomb with its ancient ship and into the hallway beyond.

There were five openings off this hallway, but they ignored them all. The tomb at the end was less grand than the ones that came after, though the carvings were more realistic. Marra could have done without the image of the beast with its mouth full of entrails, each curl and twist lovingly detailed, crouched over the entryway.

The tomb was a crossroad, four openings on four walls. They looked at each other helplessly and went forward. Another three openings, another cross . . .

Marra began to feel an itch at the back of her brain, as if she'd seen something like this before.

Was there a map somewhere in the palace? Something about this seems familiar.

She did not have time to dwell on it. The next tomb had been robbed.

"Saint's teeth," muttered Agnes. The sarcophagus lid was smashed. The rows of weapons had clearly been plundered. A broken pike lay discarded on the floor where it had been used unsuccessfully as a lever. Someone had chiseled the gems from the plinth, leaving beasts with broken sockets for eyes.

"They didn't finish raiding it," said the dust-wife thoughtfully.

"How can you tell?"

"In my line of work, you get a feel for it. They may have been interrupted, or were too nervous to finish the job." She laid her hand on the sarcophagus and tilted her head. After a moment she said, "Whatever's in there, it's lost most of its personality. It's probably annoyed that it's been robbed, but there's just not enough left to work with."

Something whistled nearby. Everyone jumped. Bonedog jerked upright, straining against the leash. Fenris was holding him now, and the dog pulled so hard that he nearly jerked the warrior off his feet.

"The ghost?" asked Fenris, trying to hold Bonedog.

"Not this one," said the dust-wife. "Another one wandering the halls, perhaps." She turned in her tracks. "I can't quite find it . . ."

Bonedog subsided slowly, his illusionary hackles lowering. The whistle was not repeated.

Two tombs later, they heard it again. Bonedog actually bayed this time, his ghostly voice waking echoes like sibilant birds. "I don't like that," said Agnes to no one in particular.

"I can't get a grip on it," said the dust-wife. "It should have some attachment to a body somewhere, but there isn't one. The bodiless dead are much harder to grab. But they also can't hurt you, usually."

"Usually?"

"Never say never."

The last syllable of *never* echoed for much too long, *er . . . er . . . er . . .* And then Marra realized it wasn't an echo at all. She took a step back from the mouth of the hallway behind her.

. . . un . . . un . . . un . . . run . . . run . . . !

"Did an echo just tell us to run?" asked Agnes, adjusting Finder and looking rather calmer than Marra felt.

"Do ghostly echoes have our best interests at heart?" asked Fenris, also remarkably calm.

"Rarely," said the dust-wife.

Marra thought, *I'm surrounded by lunatics, and I love them all, but maybe we should be running anyway.* She took another step back.

*. . . run . . . running . . . coming . . . coming . . . coming for you . . .
run . . .*

Erk, said the brown hen, with deep distrust.

Whistles erupted from the hallway they had just come down. The echoes sped up until they tripped over each other—*Run! Coming! Hide! Robbers! Run! Run!*

Bonedog went berserk. Fenris stopped trying to hold his leash and just picked him up bodily, hands slipping through the illusion to clutch at his spine. The dust-wife slammed the butt of her staff on the ground. The hen crowed.

The thief-wheel filled the passageway and came spilling out into the room.

* * *

At one point, it might indeed have been a wheel. When it was smaller, perhaps, when there were only five or ten souls jammed together, rolling over each other, ghostly faces screaming before being ground into the floor to move the bulk of the creature along. Now there were dozens of faces and the wheel had become a thick slug, elongating through the passageways, ten feet high and the gods only knew how long.

Run!

Hide!

It's coming!

Run, robbers, run!

It filled the doorway, heaving with screams as if breathing. The echoes rang through the room. Some of the faces had hands beside them, waving frantically, and Marra realized that the graverobbers trapped inside were trying to warn the living humans away. *They aren't threatening us. They're trying to tell us to get away before it gets us, too.*

The dust-wife never faltered. She stepped forward, directly into the thief-wheel's path. "Bodiless dead," she said. "We are not graverobbers. You have no power over us."

She was so calm and so confident that Marra believed her. Of course the dust-wife could fix it. She was the master of the dead. She could raise ghosts and lay them. Why had she ever doubted?

The thief-wheel screamed a warning from fifty mouths and ran the dust-wife down.

The moonlight vanished. The room went pitch-black.

Marra blundered away from the thief-wheel, staggering through the dark. She pitched over something and went down hard, skinning her palms on the ground. She could hear shrieks and shouting, the wails of the dead, and over it all, the furious clucking of the demon hen.

Something grabbed her. It didn't feel like a human. It felt like a great wall of glue that engulfed half her body. Marra screamed and slapped at it, which was a mistake. Her arm went in and got stuck. She retained enough presence of mind to throw her head back to try and keep her mouth free.

"Marra!" shouted Fenris.

Then the thief-wheel was moving with a sickening forward slide. She bashed the back of her head against the wall and saw pinpricks of white against the blackness.

Run!

Run!

Run! piped the faces around her in the dark. And then one, next to her ear, *I'm sorry, I'm sorry, I can't make it stop, it just keeps going . . .*

Were they going through another corridor? Stone scraped her back. She was being carried forward but also sliding inexorably toward the back of the thief-wheel in a queasy, seasick motion. *Oh god,* she thought very clearly. *I will be devoured and stay as a ghost forever under the palace.*

This seemed uniquely horrible. Not that she would die, but that she would be trapped here, in the palace, which she was beginning to hate with a fine and enduring passion. Her back scraped against more stone and she tried to lean closer into the thief-wheel but she couldn't, not without putting her face in it, and she'd rather not have any skin on her back at all than do that.

I'm so sorry I can't stop it, sobbed the voice next to her ear. *I keep trying but it won't stop . . .*

"It's all right," she said automatically. She was going to be ill and she was being dragged backward along the length of a creature made of lost souls and glue and still she was trying to reassure someone. Of course she was. That was how she was going to die, telling someone it was all right for stabbing her, really, she didn't mind . . .

The thief-wheel dropped her. Perhaps she had worked her way to the end. She struck the floor of the corridor and then, mercifully, she fainted.

Chapter 19

When Marra came to, she was freezing. She had curled up under the nettle cloak but had no idea how much time had passed. Long enough for the stone floor to leach all the warmth out of her, at least. She listened for the sound of the thief-wheel but could hear nothing. "Fenris?" she called. "Agnes? Dust-wife?"

Her voice echoed but brought no response. There was no spark of light anywhere.

She got to her feet and spread her arms wide, feeling for walls. A corridor. She yelled for her friends again to no avail.

"When you're lost in the woods, stay put," Marra muttered. "That way people can find you. But this isn't the woods, and I don't think we've got enough time . . ."

Which direction had the thief-wheel dragged her? How far had she gone? She had no idea.

She took a deep breath and pulled the nettle cloak tightly around her. "All right," she murmured. "All right." She picked a direction and began to walk.

Doorways to tombs opened under her fingers. She ignored them. The big tombs were always at the ends of the corridors. She walked forward until she reached some kind of threshold and then felt her way forward in the dark. The echoes sounded like a large room.

Smooth metal. Carved stone. Tiny square edges. Something that felt familiar, and then Marra realized she was touching a death mask. She jerked away and blundered toward the wall, only to realize that she had lost track of where her entryway was. How would she know if she was going in the right direction?

She fetched up against a wall and felt like weeping.

I'm lost. I'm lost in the dark and I will die down here. The dust-wife might already be dead. Oh, Lady of Grackles, help me, help me. I tried to help myself, but I don't think I can help this bit . . .

Silence. Cold. Dust.

And then, in the great darkness under the palace, Marra saw a light.

It was only a spark at first, more golden than torchlight. She thought perhaps it was not really there, because it looked like the gold sparks that came when she rubbed her eyelids. But it strengthened and came closer and closer still, illuminating the walls with their carvings of cold, dead kings.

It was a woman. Where she walked, she kicked up clouds of light, like dust.

Marra lifted her eyes and saw that the woman held a severed hand in her right hand and that her left wrist ended in a stump.

It was the saint from the goblin market.

A long time later, it would occur to Marra to wonder why the saint had been there, in the palace of dead kings. At the time, it did not. She was a saint. Saints walked where they would.

The saint lifted her severed hand so that the first finger lay across her lips in a gesture for silence. Marra crouched at her feet, gazing up, and nodded.

The saint beckoned, and Marra followed.

They went slowly but sure-footedly. The light of the saint's passage glittered off carvings of men and gods and stranger things. Marra watched whole histories unfold, as carved generals defeated armies of beasts misshapen and beautiful and strange.

Then, step by step, she began to fade.

Marra wanted to cry out, to beg her not to leave, but she bit her lower lip. The gods had intervened on her behalf. Surely they would not take her only halfway.

Wait. Wait and see. The world is not always cruel.

She followed the fading footsteps of the saint. It seemed to take a long time, shifting slowly from gold to silver, and finally Marra realized that the saint was gone and the silver light came from farther ahead, from a vial filled with moonlight trapped in a jar.

She broke into a run, not caring if the thief-wheel heard her now, half sobbing. "Fenris! Agnes! Dust-wife!"

"Marra?"

She broke into the room and before she could even focus, Fenris had thrown his arms around her and had his face pressed against her hair. "You're alive," he said. "I thought I'd lost you. You're alive."

"You're alive, too!" she said. She wanted to stop and think about what *I thought I'd lost you* might mean, but it didn't quite seem like the time. And he was very warm and she was very cold and it was very pleasant to be held in such a fashion. "You're alive."

"Yes, yes," said the dust-wife testily. "We're all alive. Please don't cry on me about it, though."

Fenris finally released her, although not without reluctance. Bonedog immediately leapt up on her, washing her face with his tongue.

"What happened to you?" asked Marra. "I got picked up by the thief-wheel . . ."

"So did I," said Agnes. "Didn't realize it got you, too."

"Bonedog ran after you," said Fenris. "Dragged me with him, and I thought he might have the best chance of following you. When he finally lost track, we were totally lost."

"How did you get back?" asked Marra.

"Oh, I had Finder do it," said Agnes. She patted her chest, where the exhausted chick was sleeping. "Asked him to take me somewhere safe. Then the dust-wife turned up."

"Bonedog found them," said Fenris. "I was going to suggest we start looking for you, but then you turned up. How did you find us?"

"A saint led me," said Marra. "The one from the goblin market."

All three of them stared at her.

"Huh," said the dust-wife.

"How fascinating!" said Agnes.

"A few months ago, I would have thought you were mad or lying," said Fenris. "Now I suppose I'm just surprised she didn't stay for tea."

"But how did you get away?" asked Marra. "The thief-wheel fell on you. I saw it."

The dust-wife sniffed haughtily. "It was nothing."

"It squashed you!"

"Fine, it was something." She looked annoyed. Marra noticed that her coat was rumpled and there were a few stains where the contents of the pockets had broken. The brown hen was missing a couple of tail feathers. "They were very disobedient dead."

"Bad dead. No treat," said Fenris, not quite under his breath.

Marra choked and spluttered and began, helplessly, to laugh. So did Agnes. The dust-wife folded her arms and the hen went *errrk* indignantly, which only made Marra laugh harder.

"I'm glad you're all amused," said the dust-wife when they had giggled themselves out.

"What *was* it, though?" asked Marra, torn between hilarity and renewed shudders.

"A tangle. A mangle. Graverobbers and a few unfortunate souls, probably lost builders. The curse ripped their spirits out and wadded them all up together, to roam the catacombs and find more. But it wasn't terribly well designed. They never put an upper limit on the souls, so it collected too many over the centuries and got muddled. That was the problem giving it orders. Nothing's in charge anymore; it's just blundering around in confusion." She grimaced. "I slapped it and it ran away. And you didn't steal anything, so it couldn't eat your souls, it just dragged you around. It's still out there, but it won't come anywhere near me again."

"Can you unmake it?" asked Fenris. "Set them free?"

"I could if we had a few days to spare. But we don't, so I sent it away." She looked down her nose, the lines drawing tight around her mouth. "We're running out of time."

"Are we?" asked Marra.

"What?" said Agnes.

"I fainted for a bit," Marra admitted. "How long has it been?"

Fenris's face was suddenly grave. "Almost a full day," he said. "We have to hurry. We're going to be late to the christening."

*   *   *

Four corridors and an intersection. Two intersections and three more corridors. Marra's mind tugged again at the sensation that she knew this pattern, that she had seen something like it, but it wouldn't surface. Perhaps it didn't matter.

They had found the tomb of the first king.

It was small. Marra had expected something huge and grand, vast archways framed by carved warriors, gold and jade and glory. Instead it was a little stone room with wooden beams holding up the ceiling. There was a single sword, tossed almost casually across the stone coffin lid. The king's death mask was very simple and had cracked across the forehead like a scar.

The walls were the most impressive part. Red and black paint glimmered in the captive moonlight. The murals were stark and strong and age had tinted the white pigment of the Northern faces to blue, so it seemed that an army of stylized blue-skinned warriors swept across the walls of the tomb. In the center, a blue king sat upon a throne, holding a sword across his knees.

The dust-wife laid her hands on the sarcophagus and gave a short, sharp little laugh, like a fox's bark. "Oh yes," she said. "Yes, he's in there."

"You can tell?"

"Gods, yes. Like having a sleeping bear in the room." She closed her eyes and leaned her weight on her palms. "Wake up, dead man. We have business with you."

Marra, insomuch as she expected anything, thought that perhaps the death mask might begin to speak, as it had for the daughter who had been buried alive. Instead the sword rattled on the lid, and on the wall, the painted king lifted his head and stared with pigmented eyes at the dust-wife.

Why have you come here?

The words had no sound, but the echoes rang through the room.

Marra felt as if they were being pounded into her skull with a metal hammer. There was weight to them and a mind like steel and stone. Bonedog yipped and tried to hide behind Fenris's knees.

Why do you intrude upon my grave?

"You must release the godmother from her service," said the dust-wife. "She has been held far too long and it is harming your descendants."

Godmother? What godmother do you speak of?

"The woman who blesses your children and who serves the royal line."

Oh. The witchskin. The contempt tasted like tin inside Marra's head. *I won; she lost. I could have slain her on the spot, but I gave her immortality. She should be grateful.*

The dust-wife's fingers curled into fists against the sarcophagus lid. "Eternal slavery is no gift."

The painted king narrowed his eyes. Behind the throne, the painted warriors moved and rippled, lifting their shields. An archer drew the charcoal line of his bowstring taut. *Who are you?*

"One who can talk to the dead."

What is the witchskin to you?

"Nothing. We've never even met. But I do not allow the living to serve the dead forever. Release her, and I will leave you to your rest."

Beg me, then. Perhaps I'll release her if you beg.

The dust-wife raised her eyebrows. "Do you think I wouldn't beg for another person's life? I will, if it would sway you."

The painted king looked away, the blue paint moving around the sour black slash of mouth. *It would amuse me.*

"Amusement is not enough. You must free her."

I will not.

The dust-wife took one hand off the sarcophagus and took up her staff, which had been leaning against it. The brown hen flapped her wings. "Then I will fight you," she said.

You? You who have lived a puny mortal lifetime would fight me for a witch who should have died a thousand years ago? The king began to laugh. It was a deep, roaring laugh, even more like a hammer on metal than his voice, and Marra started to feel like her skull was on the anvil. *Go away, little deadspeaker. I am older and greater than you.*

The dust-wife ran her fingertip across the crack in the death mask and the laughter in Marra's head stopped abruptly.

"There," said the dust-wife as calmly as if they were discussing where to place a stitch. "There, I think. Yes." She reached up to the brown hen, who stepped onto her hand. Marra had held goshawks on the wrist that did not look so proud as the demon hen in that moment. The dust-wife set her down on the sarcophagus and the hen stabbed her beak down into the crack in the mask.

The king's scream sounded like a sheet of iron being ripped in half, a long metallic shriek that made Marra's teeth rattle in her jaw. Her head pounded. Bonedog barked, not an alarm bark but the high, rapid bark of a dog in trouble and desperately calling his pack for backup. It was barely audible, but it hung in the air around them.

What are you doing, witch?!

"Fighting," said the dust-wife as if it should have been obvious. The hen began to hammer at the crack, occasionally pausing to lift her head and rake her claws across the death mask.

"There's something else happening," whispered Fenris. "Isn't there?" He slumped against the wall next to Marra, holding his temples. "It's not just a chicken and a mask. She's doing . . . something . . ."

"Oh yes," said Agnes. Alone of all of them, she seemed to be enjoying herself. Her eyes were bright with interest. "You can see it—oh dear, I suppose you can't see it! But it's very good. His magic is all laid out like swords on a rack and she's . . . no, that's a terrible analogy; it's not like that at all. But it's good, though!"

"Good?" said Marra weakly, her skull still ringing with the dead king's scream.

"Let go," said the dust-wife. "You tried to protect your descendants and instead you shortened their lives for generations. Their souls are feeding the spell that keeps the godmother alive. I can see it. Can't you?"

Her voice was so confident that Marra found herself looking at the air over the sarcophagus as if there might be something that mortal eyes could see. There was only dust and the brown hen busily cracking open the death mask.

The spell works. It has worked for a thousand years. My descendants are strong and they have endured. I will not allow you to break it.

"You are dead," said the dust-wife coldly. "Your time to control your family is done." The demon hen cackled as chips flew from the broken mask. "They cannot live in your shadow any longer."

The king gathered himself. It felt as if the tomb were breathing in. The painted warriors lifted their swords and the archers let fly their arrows, aimed at the dust-wife. They were trapped in the wall and it should not have been possible for them to reach her, and yet for a moment, it seemed as if she would be drawn into the wall, as if the arrows must reach her . . .

Moonlight flashed as she held up her staff and the painted arrows fell apart into scattered pigment across the floor.

I will not bend! hissed the dead king, rising from his throne.

"Then you will break," said the dust-wife, and slammed her staff across the painted wall.

It sounded like a thunderclap in that small room. The moonlight went out. Something metallic hit the floor. For a second time, Marra stood in complete and utter darkness. She heard Bonedog's ghostly whimper and then Fenris fumbling with his tinderbox. "Candle . . ." he muttered next to her. "Candle, candle. Where is the— Aha!"

Light flared. The dust-wife was lying half-sprawled across the sarcophagus, her hair wild around her shoulders. She pushed herself up, looking annoyed. The brown hen stood on the death mask, which had split in two, looking as serene as only a chicken can look. As Marra watched, the hen lifted her tail, voided her bowels on the king's broken face, and then strolled to the dust-wife's shoulder with a satisfied cluck.

Fenris lifted the candle. The sword had fallen to the floor. On the wall, the king was back in his throne, the archers back in their original positions, but there was a long, jagged mark across the paint, like a lightning bolt, that cut across the king's face and broke the shield of the guard beside him.

"Is it over?" asked Marra. The air seemed very still and the room somehow smaller. "Is he gone?"

"Gone, no," said the dust-wife. "People like that hang about for ages. I pried his fingers loose from the world for a bit, though, and that should be enough for the godmother to slip her bonds."

"Just like that?" asked Marra wonderingly. "That's all it took?"

"That's all," said the dust-wife, striding confidently forward, and promptly crashed to the floor in a semiconscious heap.

Chapter 20

W ell, it was a little bit more than it looked," said Agnes, when they had rescued the indignant hen and made certain that no bones were broken. The dust-wife protested weakly as they propped her against the wall and poured water down her throat. "You don't just knock out a dead sorcerer-king and then go for breakfast after."

"I'm fine," grumbled the dust-wife. She tried to push herself to her feet and failed spectacularly.

"You poured yourself into the magic and knocked yourself to fainting, little fool," said Agnes in a remarkably good imitation of the dust-wife herself. "Isn't that what you said to me?"

The hen cackled. The dust-wife glared up at Agnes and snatched the leather bottle of water out of her fingers. "Fine. Possibly I deserved that. Possibly."

"Definitely."

"Can you walk?" asked Fenris. "I can carry you on my back if need be."

"I can walk," she growled. "Give me my staff. And give me a minute."

"I do not know how many more minutes we have," he said. "My sense of time is not working well, but I think that we are very close to running out of it."

"I might be able to still enchant the babe," said Agnes a bit doubtfully. "Even if we miss the christening. But it doesn't take as well, not with humans. You lay a name on them and suddenly their whole future is rolled out like dough in front of you, but it doesn't last. Life starts to bake it pretty quick."

"That," said the dust-wife witheringly, "was a *terrible* analogy. Someone give me my staff so that I can beat her about the head and shoulders." Agnes giggled.

Fenris went to pick up the staff and paused. The sword lay on the ground beneath it. "The sword fell," he said.

"Take it," said the dust-wife. "Mine by right of conquest. But I'll let you have it. You might need a sword, and not even the thief-wheel could think that was grave robbery." She took the staff from him and this time managed to get upright, with the help of Fenris under one arm and the questionable assistance of Bonedog bouncing around her feet.

"What happens now?" asked Marra. "Is the godmother dead?"

"I imagine so," said the dust-wife. "I wouldn't stick around if I were her." She took another limping step forward. "I'm most curious about all the other spells that people have cast over the years. If any of them are active, now that the godmother's gone, they might come home to roost."

They all shuffled to the door of the tomb and then stopped. The hallway stretched out before them. Three openings on one side, two on the other.

"Now what?" asked Agnes. "I got turned around when that screaming thing dragged me along."

"Going back to the source was one thing," said Fenris, holding up the candle. "We could follow so many dead ends . . . Can Finder help?"

Agnes frowned. "I don't think so. We're much safer here than we are in the palace, aren't we? Maybe once we run out of food and water, but Finder will just keep moving us around the tombs to avoid the wheel thingy."

Three openings on one side . . . two on the other . . . six openings on one side . . . five openings . . .

Do you know what they represent? . . . Then I may give it to you.

"I've got it," she said. She laughed incredulously. "We've had it this whole time—the tapestry."

She unrolled the frayed bit of tapestry in her pack, running her fingers along the weave. Three lines of thread. The middle one a single continuous line, the two flanking a combination of split weaves and weft locks. Six split weaves in a row. At the time she'd thought it was absurd, ugly, fiddly stuff, but it wasn't. It was marking the openings on the walls of the tombs. Six corridors, and then a weft lock to mark . . . *to mark the place where you go through? Yes! That's it!*

She laughed again. Fenris looked over her shoulder. "Is it a map? It doesn't look right."

"No, no, it's not a map. It's *directions*. The godmother couldn't help us, not really, because of the spell on her, so she couldn't have given me directions if I knew what they were. But I thought it was just an ugly tapestry, so she could." Possibly this was not the clearest explanation. Fenris looked baffled. She tried to explain about split weaves and weft locks and Fenris held up his hands. "Can you read it?"

"Yes."

"Then that's good enough for me. Lead the way."

"I have to figure out where we are," she said. "The gold knot . . . Is that the king or . . . No, no, the weave doesn't match. I think that's the way out. The palace, maybe, or another exit. I just have to find where we are on the tapestry." She ran her fingers over the thick threads, letting touch work where eyesight failed. Three split weaves on one side, two on the other, and a weft lock in the middle of the center row, indicating that you'd reached your destination—there it was, yes!

Marra flipped the ragged cloth around and walked forward. Fenris held the candle aloft. Bonedog bounced around Agnes, and the dust-wife grimly brought up the rear, her footsteps uneven on the stone.

"Weft lock . . ." she muttered to herself. "Split weave, split weave . . . weft lock here." She took the indicated turn, then the next.

"This is the way we came," said Fenris. "So far so good."

Suddenly confident, Marra hurried onward. The tapestry came alive under her fingertips and she knew where she was going. She did not realize that she was practically running until Fenris called ahead to her. "Wait a moment, Marra."

"Right." She stopped, letting the dust-wife and Agnes catch up. "Right. I'm sorry. I just . . ." She waved aimlessly overhead. *What time is it up there? It can't have started yet, surely? We must be close.* Time suddenly seemed physically present, rushing past her like air through the tunnels. *What happens now that the godmother's gone? Old spells? Agnes thinks she can use her powers if we get to the christening, or maybe the dust-wife was going to cast a spell on Vorling, or raise up the dead, but she can't do that now . . .* Could she get to her sister before the christening and warn her that something was going to happen? Was there time? Or would spells laid centuries ago, biding their time, already be exploding like fireworks over the palace?

They followed the tapestry path for another half dozen familiar turns, and then it diverged. Fenris looked up. "I think this is not the way we came," he said. "But I trust your directions."

"Don't mind us," called Agnes. "We're coming."

Marra took a deep breath and led them forward into the dark.

* * *

It was a much shorter route than the one from in the quarry, or perhaps that route had seemed longer because they had gotten turned around and gone so slowly and down so many dead ends. Once they reached a tomb that seemed to have no exits and Marra began to wonder if she had misread, until Bonedog ran snuffling to a tapestry that moved in an unseen breeze. Behind it, half-hidden, was the next door. And then, practically before she had time to comprehend it, there was a bright outline at the end of the hall and Fenris pushed open the door and stepped through, sword at the ready . . . into the godmother's temple.

It was a small room, but Marra could see the main hall through a carved screen. Perhaps priests had once prepared for their sermons here. The godmother sat on a little raised platform, still in that perfect dark triangle of skull and robe and shoulders. She did not move her head when she spoke. "Stay your sword, warrior," she said. "I suspect that I will die very soon in any event."

"I wasn't going to . . ." Fenris lowered his sword and looked abashed. "Forgive me, madam."

She laughed. "There is nothing to forgive. You did not free me, though. Nor did you." Her eyes moved to the door as Agnes came through. "And you are powerful, for all you try to hide it, but not in a way that could compel the dead. So it must be . . . ah. Of course. It must have been you."

The dust-wife inclined her head.

"I could have died when the spell broke," said the godmother. "I thought about it. But I was curious as to who had finally set me free." She searched the dust-wife's face, took in the coat full of pockets and the brown hen hunkered down on the staff. "Why? I have never done you a kindness. And we are a long, long way from your own beloved dead."

"A friend asked me to," said the dust-wife.

"Ah." The godmother smiled then, and cracks ran across her skin from the motion, like a plaster wall falling apart. As Marra watched in horror, a chip of skin fell from her cheekbone. There was no blood under it, nothing but cool, brown bone. "Yes. Agnes, will you pass me my teacup? It seems that I am about to die, and I would like a little more tea."

Agnes rushed forward and poured the tea with trembling hands. She tried to press it into the godmother's hands, but they were only bone, folded politely in a pile of dust. "Oh no," she said softly. "Oh dear." She knelt, held the teacup to the ancient lips and tipped it up.

"Thank you," said the godmother against the rim of the teacup, and then she fell apart. Marra took a step back but there was something oddly peaceful about it, about bones sinking down into the robes and the dust pattering down around them. There had been very little flesh left to the godmother, only skin and skeleton and iron will. Her robes stayed in their perfect triangle, stiff with gold brocade.

Agnes wiped her eyes. "Dammit," she whispered. "I have to go be impressive. I have to go be the wicked godmother. I can't cry."

"She's at peace now," said Fenris.

Agnes gave him an ironic glance. "She's been at peace for centuries, I think. I still get to cry about it."

She rose and wiped her hands on her dress. She looked small and bedraggled in her shapeless dress, scarf around her neck with a sleeping chicken in it. Her hair was in flyaway wisps and there were lines around her eyes from worried smiling.

And then she took a deep breath and shook herself and her eyes flickered green as poison. "All right," she said. "Let's go."

* * *

The front door of the godmother's temple was locked from the inside, but Marra could hear frantic pounding. *The guard. Yes, of course there was a guard.* A merely human guard seemed so banal now. The metal door rang like a gong, and when Fenris opened it, the guard was so shocked that he fell back a step, his mouth hanging open. "The godmother," he said. "They've summoned the godmother and she was supposed to come and she always does but she didn't. Where is she? She's going to be *late!*" His voice cracked on the word *late,* panic rendering him much younger than his years.

Agnes patted his hand kindly. Marra stayed well back in the shadow of the door, wondering if they were going to have to hit the guard over the head, but Agnes said, "She's coming. Don't worry."

"Yes," said the dust-wife. "We apologize. We were consulting her on a matter of wizardly importance."

The guard blinked at her, then at the staff and the chicken. "Oh. Uh. I . . . Is she ready?"

"Yes. You should go in. She's very tired, though."

He bolted past them, not even glancing in Marra's direction. They closed the door behind them and the dust wife took out a little jar from her pocket and dabbed something on her finger. She smeared it down the seam of the door and the metal knit together from either side, as high as she could reach, soft and malleable as clay.

"What is that?" asked Fenris.

"Slip from the potter's wheel of a great saint. He preached to statues and they came to life to praise the gods." She shrugged. "He's dead now, of course."

"He is?"

"You can't keep bringing statues to life for religion. Sooner or later they figure out they don't have souls, and then things go very badly for everyone." She tried to turn, then sat down heavily on the steps. "Oh hell."

"Lady Fox!"

"No, no," the dust-wife said. The hen clucked warily. "I'm done. Go on. I'll make sure our friend here doesn't bother anyone."

"Are you going to kill him?" asked Agnes, not sounding particularly appalled.

"No, losing his memory for a few days should be plenty. Hopefully he hasn't accepted any surprise offers of marriage or anything." She made shooing gestures. "Go, go. You heard him. The christening is about to start."

* * *

Marra had very little memory of the panicked rush through the streets. Bonedog galloped beside her. Just before they reached the palace gates, Fenris caught the dog's leash and Agnes waved Marra forward. "Go," she said. "I'll make my grand entrance just behind you."

She had no time to question. She ran to the guards. "My sister," she gasped. "My sister. The queen. I'm her sister. The nun." She lifted her necklace with the grackle feather. She was gasping for breath, but hopefully that made her story more plausible. She waved frantically toward the lower city. "My carriage. Horse. Threw a shoe. Please. My mother's already there. I have to be there!"

She didn't expect it to work. It probably shouldn't have worked. But the guards blinked at her and then at each other and she moved between them. Both of them clearly waited for the other one to say something but neither one did and by the time they had realized it, she had pushed past them.

Thank the Lady of Grackles, there was a footman that she recognized just beyond the guards. "Please!" she gasped to him. "Please, I'm late, I'm so late. Where is the christening?"

"Princess Marra?"

"Yes! My carriage— The horse—" She couldn't remember if she'd said the wheel broke or the horse threw a shoe, so she just waved her hands.

"You know her?" asked one of the guards. "She's the princess?"

"Yes, of course. But where is the godmother?" He peered over her shoulder. "She always comes." He sounded a bit lost.

"Didn't see her," said Marra. "Take me to my sister. I'm sure she'll show up."

The footman led her away through the hall, still occasionally turning to look behind them, which footmen never did. Marra's skin crawled. Was Agnes coming? Was Fenris? Had they gotten past the guards? Surely they could, but she would have felt much better if the dust-wife were with them.

I can do this, she thought grimly. *I can do this. I did two impossible tasks and found the way out of the palace of dust. I can finish this. I just have to find Kania.*

They reached the room full of courtiers. All eyes turned as the great doors opened and the room held its breath. "The godm— The princess Marra!" announced the majordomo at the door.

The silence broke. The courtiers looked away and began murmuring among themselves as Marra entered the room. They knew Princess Marra, and they knew that she was of no consequence.

"Marra?" said her mother, and did not ask *Where have you been?* or *How did you get here?* though her eyes were full of questions.

"Where is the godmother?" said Vorling. He, too, sounded lost and Marra hated him for it, the way that she had not hated the footman or the guard. *How dare you?* she thought. *How dare you pin the royal bloodline on a woman held captive so long that she turned to living dust? How dare you?* Which was unfair, and she knew it was unfair, but she did not feel any need to be just to the man who left bruises on her sister's arms.

"Marra?" said Kania. She stood back from the cradle, her eyes huge. "Marra, is that you?"

"I'm sorry I'm late . . ." Marra babbled, rushing across the vast room. She could feel eyes on her, but they were contemptuous and dismissive and that was good, that was all good—no one cared about her here, no one knew to be afraid of what storm might follow in her wake. She fetched up at Kania's side and clutched her sleeve. "Kania. Kania, I have to tell you— Kania—"

"Tell me what?"

Marra opened her mouth and realized she had no idea what to say next. She had always planned to speak to her alone, to warn her that there would be a different godmother, that something strange was probably going to happen, but Vorling was only a dozen feet away and her mother was right there. "It's . . . it's . . . I'm late . . ." she heard herself say.

"Where is the godmother?" said Vorling, turning toward her. He did not sound lost any longer. He sounded angry. "Was she behind you? Why am I being made a fool of in my own palace?"

Kania's hand crept to Marra's and squeezed in sudden fear.

Marra lifted her chin and met Vorling's eyes. *You are not so big. You are only a living king. I saw an old woman defeat a dead one. You cannot hurt me any worse than spinning thread of nettle wool, and you cannot confuse me any more than the palace of dust. Even your cruelty is small compared to the blistered land.*

Perhaps he saw some of that defiance in her. Men like him always had a sense for it, did they not? He took a step forward and his hands clenched at his sides.

"Everyone's asking about her," said Marra in a clear voice. "No one at the gates has seen her. They're saying she's dead."

"*What?*"

He took another step toward her and Kania took a step back. Marra pushed herself between them, wondering if decorum would hold him, knowing in her bones that if a king decided to beat his wife and her sister in front of the court, the court would stand there and watch. *Please, Lady of Grackles. Please.*

"I will stand as the child's godmother," cried Agnes from the doorway.

Chapter 21

gnes, tall. Agnes with her eyes flashing green like beast eyes reflected in a fire. Agnes, a wicked godmother.

Vorling wheeled around and this time he was the one who took a step back.

She did not look like a tiny, fluttery woman who lived with chickens and a garden that had gotten out of control. She looked like a creature of magic and terror, the dark mirror of a saint, more at home in the goblin market than the throne room.

Despite everything, Marra's first instinct was to lunge for the cradle and throw herself over her nephew to protect him. Instead she grabbed Kania tighter.

Her sister tried to move forward. Marra clutched her arm. "Don't," she whispered. "Don't! It's our old godmother, the godmother's gone, the curse . . ." She was making no sense and she knew that she was making no sense, but it didn't matter. She didn't have to make sense. She just had to hold Kania until Agnes reached the cradle, and then it would be over quickly.

"The godmother of the Northern Kingdom has died at last," said Agnes, her voice ringing like steel in that great stone room. "The curse is broken. And so to this child, I give a new gift for a new age."

Marra looked at Vorling, surrounded by his little triangle of guards, and saw his lips moving. *Dead?* He looked astonished, as if this was not something he had ever considered, as if the sun had risen in the west and then fallen from the sky.

Agnes leaned down and laid her fingertips across the infant's skull. Kania tried to move again but Marra had her arm in a death grip.

"This gift I give you," said Agnes. "You shall grow up fatherless."

And then, in a voice much more like the old Agnes, she added, "And healthy."

For the length of a half dozen heartbeats, the room was absolutely still. Then everyone seemed to breathe in at once. Vorling shouted, "Stop her!" and the courtiers leapt forward or stepped back, depending on their nature, and the guards rushed Agnes, drawing their swords, and Agnes hiked up her skirts and ran for the door, no longer a towering figure of darkness but a little round woman with a flushed face and a half-grown chicken tucked into her scarf.

"Stop her!" shouted Vorling again. "This is an attack! Cut her down! Bring me her head! Find the real godmother!"

The two guards flanking the doorway stepped forward, halberds at the ready. Marra stuffed the side of her hand in her mouth. Agnes was going to get cut down and there was no way to save her. Pretending to be a nun wouldn't work—couldn't work—

A ghostly growl filled the hallway. Bonedog took the guard on the left from behind, his teeth sinking into the silks of the dress uniform and tearing out a great gash of thigh. The man screamed, his leg buckling, and he went down.

Bonedog snapped and snarled soundlessly at the second guard and Agnes got past him into the hallway. "Go, go!" yelled Vorling to the men surrounding him, "Go! Kill her familiar and bring me her head!"

They charged across the room. Vorling stood alone and then there were four of them going after Bonedog and he couldn't get all of them. *Oh, Bonedog, no, no, run—Fenris, where are you? You have to save him, Fenris!*

Fleeing had never been in Bonedog's nature. Marra dragged in one long breath and held it, and Bonedog's jaws closed on a man's knee. Then the halberd came down and the ghost of a yelp filled the room.

Bones exploded in every direction, no longer held together by wire. The tiny joints of paw and tail rattled across the floor like unstrung beads. Marra moaned and the only mercy was that the courtiers were gasping and shrieking in surprise so that no one noticed except her sister.

"Foul magic!" cried one of the courtiers, a big man with a fox-colored beard. "Sorcery!"

"Stop h—" Vorling shouted again, and then the last word went soft and wet and startled. Marra wrenched her eyes away from Bonedog, back to Vorling.

Fenris had his hand on the king's shoulder, almost a friendly gesture, except for the foot of steel protruding from Vorling's chest. Vorling stared down at the blade, his expression just as puzzled as before, and then Fenris pulled the sword out and blood came from the king's mouth and he died.

"He did it," said Marra in a very small voice. "He did it." *He must have been working his way along the wall while everyone was staring at Agnes and Bonedog. That was the right thing to do. That was why we came. Wasn't it?*

She would have traded victory in a heartbeat to have Bonedog whole again.

Kania turned her head. Her eyes swept over her dead husband and then to her living sister, and Marra could see everything snapping into place. But then, unlike Marra, Kania had never been a fool.

The guards who were trying to chase Agnes skidded to a halt. They ran back toward Fenris. There were five of them, four with swords, one with a halberd. Fenris had no armor and only the old iron sword stained with the king's blood.

He looked across the room and his eyes met hers. It was the same look he always had, the one that said, *Can you believe two sensible people like us are caught up in this?* And then he turned to meet the guards and Marra saw on his face the moment that he decided to die.

They circled him. He raised his sword. She was trapped in one of those nightmares where no matter how fast she ran or how loudly she yelled, she would be too slow, the air was like glue, and so she stood with her throat closed and her feet nailed to the floor, unable to look away.

Swords rose. They had only to attack him, all together, and it would be over. He could not defend from all directions, and all of them were young.

Into that terrible moment of waiting, the queen of the Northern Kingdom shouted, "*Hold!*"

* * *

The guards obeyed. It seemed impossible, but they all took a step back, widening the circle around Fenris. Their eyes flicked to Kania and then back to Fenris.

Kania spoke as clear and crackling cold as ice. "This man was sent by our enemies to kill our king. I want to know everything he knows before he dies." She walked forward and somehow the guards were listening and the courtiers were watching her as if she was truly the queen and not merely the king's beaten wife. She stood over the cradle. "My son has been cursed," she said, still in that cold, clear voice. "My husband is dead. I will know who did this. You will take him alive."

Another long, terrible waiting moment, but somehow the balance had shifted. The pivot point was no longer the blades of the guards but the queen standing over the cradle. The man with the fox-colored beard moved forward to stand a little behind her, as if lending her his presence, and all the courtiers saw it and Marra saw it register on many faces, although she did not know what it meant.

Please, thought Marra. *Please, Fenris, please.* She begged him with her eyes to surrender. If he lived, she could get him out of this. Probably. Or at least the dust-wife could, or Agnes, or someone.

Fenris laid down his sword.

The guards rushed him and they were not gentle. He went to his knees and they dragged his arms behind him. "Put him in a cell," said Kania. "He will be alive when I see him again, or all of your lives will be forfeit. Do I make myself clear?"

"Yes, my queen," said the guard with the halberd, and they dragged Fenris away.

Kania did not watch. She turned to Marra, and Marra recognized the look in her eyes. It was the look that she had as a child, when she had been doing something she should not have done. It said, *Don't you dare tell on me, or I will end you.*

It settled Marra's nerves as hardly anything else could. Suddenly they were both children, both in this together, and the awareness of her sister's hate, the one that had been under her breastbone since she was a child, fell away. She took a step forward.

"You tried to warn us, Sister," said Kania. Throwing her the lie, waiting for her to catch it.

"I did," she said in her best nun's voice. "I'm sorry. I was late and the . . . the false godmother was behind me. I could tell something was wrong. I only wish I'd realized what she had planned."

Kania nodded. "Your warning might have spared us much worse. This was a cunning trap, well laid," she said, and somehow, because she said it like a queen, it became true. All the courtiers had seen Agnes run away and Fenris was just one man with a sword, and yet Marra could practically hear the story shift inside their heads.

"My son is the rightful king," said Kania. "But he is not a week old and already he has been cursed by this kingdom's enemies." Her gaze swept the room. "I will stand as his regent, but I will not stand alone. I will require loyal advisors to stand with me, men who will put the kingdom first, above power or personal gain." She turned to the fox-bearded man. "Lord Marlin, I would have you be first among those. Will you accept?"

Lord Marlin inclined his head gravely. Marra suspected that he had begun planning the moment that the king had died, but he let the silence draw out, to give the question appropriate gravity. "Yes, my queen," he said. "For the young king."

"And General Takise," said Kania, sweeping in the other direction. "You were his grandfather's closest confidant. Will you stand with the young king, also?"

General Takise had iron hair and an iron bearing. He put his fist over his heart. "For the young king," he said gruffly.

"Then we are agreed," said Kania. She reached into the cradle and lifted her son. "We three shall serve as regents, until my son reaches his majority. And now . . ." For the first time, her voice filled with emotion, with sorrow so finely feigned that Marra marveled at it. "Now I must mourn my husband and make arrangements for his funeral. And his murderer. I beg you, my fellow regents, to bring me proposals for my son's safety. It seems that we are at war with someone, and we must learn who. And quickly."

And she swept out of the room, her head held high, carrying her son, while the courtiers erupted into amazement behind her.

* * *

"That was astoundingly well done," said Marra's mother, less than an hour later. "You got the two biggest rivals to the throne backing you."

"They had to back me, or risk the other one gaining ascendancy. Takise is a good sort, anyway. Marlin you can't trust any farther than you can throw him, but he is at least predictably power hungry." Kania held her son to her breast, gazing at him with a kind of baffled astonishment. "Mother . . . what the hell do I do now?"

"Exactly what you've been doing. You seized control at the moment when it was all up in the air. If one of the others had acted like they were in charge first, you would have lost everything, but you moved first and that matters."

Marra shook her head. She was beyond exhausted and she could hardly think. "Fenris . . ." she began.

Kania looked around. She had dismissed the servants and they were all in the tiny chapel again, ostensibly praying for the soul of Vorling. "I'll do what I can," she said, half in a whisper. "But I don't know if I can spare his life. He murdered the king in front of everyone. I don't know."

Marra's stomach clenched. She rested her forehead on the rail that separated mourners from coffins. There was no coffin yet. Would there be a coffin for Fenris?

I thought we had a better plan. I thought it was going to make more sense. I thought that Agnes would give the curse and then magic would make Vorling trip on the stairs or choke on a fish bone or something. I didn't realized Fenris would just . . . just . . .

But of course he had. He was a man who got things done. He had been willing to die and he had seen a way to end the matter. Agnes had gotten away. Kania was free. A tyrant was dead. Fenris would have thought it was a fair trade, his life for Vorling's death, but all Marra could think was that it was not fair, it was one more cruelty, as if Vorling had reached out from the grave and struck a final blow.

"We'll figure something out," Kania said. Marra lifted her head.

Her mother looked unconvinced. "Sometimes there are sacrifices that have to be made," she said. "It may not be possible without risking everything you have gained. Your position is not secure, not yet. It is only the lack of clear rules of succession that let you step into the regency as you have."

"Bless the paranoia of these Northern kings," muttered Kania. "None of them allow anyone with power to oppose him to flourish." She rubbed her forearm, and Marra wondered what bruises lay concealed beneath the sleeve.

"True. Nevertheless, if you are seen as soft on your husband's killer . . ."

Kania stared down at her son. It occurred to Marra that she did not even know the child's name. They had arrived too late to the christening for such niceties.

"I hated him so much," she said softly. "So much, and for so long. I thought if he died, it would feel like a great weight off my shoulders, and yet I am just as weighed down as I was. Is he really dead? Is this truly happening?"

"It is," said her mother.

Kania gave a single dry sob, startling the infant king, who began to cry.

"You did so good," said Marra. "You did. All that with the lords and the generals and you even convinced people I wasn't part of it. I couldn't believe it."

The sob had a laugh at the bottom this time. "Oh yes," Kania said. "Oh yes, *that* part I knew. I've been running it through in my head for years, what I'd do if he miraculously died. I had every possible scenario memorized. It's only now that I don't know what I'm doing."

"I'm sorry I couldn't do it sooner," said Marra helplessly. "I'm sorry. Everything took so long to do and . . . and . . ."

She tried to explain. She got as far as Bonedog and began to cry and Kania also began to cry and their mother put an arm around each of them and held her daughters as if they were all much younger.

"I'll help you," her mother said. "I'll help as much as I can. I can't stay for terribly long, but grandmothers are allowed some time to dote on their grandchildren, and we'll go through all the details while I'm here. There may be angles that you can find to keep the rest of the courtiers from seizing power."

Kania wiped her eyes. "I wish Damia were here," she said. "I wish she could have known that it got fixed. That there was justice."

Marra gulped. Her eyes and nose were streaming and she wiped them on her sleeve. Justice seemed so little, so late. Kania had suffered for long years and the godmother for long centuries. The Northern kings had left scars on time. Even the thief-wheel still roaming the halls, even the furious ghost daughter . . .

I was buried alive to hide their shame.

She looked up. An idea had come to her, as terrible in its way as the very first idea had been, the one that had set her on the road to kill a prince and curse a kingdom.

"I know how to save Fenris."

Chapter 22

The funeral of King Vorling was small by the Northern Kingdom's standards. He had reigned for less than half a year and
barely any preparations had been made on his tomb. His wife,
the new queen regent, said that her husband would have preferred
the wealth be spent on strengthening the kingdom's defenses, as they
were clearly targets of an enemy who might strike again, whatever
ridiculous tale the Hardishman assassin had spun about a dust-wife
and a goblin market and a geas. Diplomats had been dispatched to
Hardack to demand answers, but no one was optimistic. There was
sorcery afoot.

Perhaps the nobles might have been worried, with a foreign
woman on the throne, but Queen Kania had already proven herself
as ruthless as the kings of old. For at the foot of Vorling's sarcophagus,
under a screaming death mask, the assassin had been interred alive, to
die of thirst in the halls of the dead. The queen had stood at the head
of the procession and watched the lid come down. "For what you
did to my husband," she said, "for what you did to me." And then
darkness had covered the face of the Hardishman and the procession had left the tomb behind, deep in the dark and the dust.

It was fourteen hours later that Marra and the dust-wife flung
themselves at the stone lid, scrabbling with all their strength. For
a horrible moment, she thought that it would not be enough, that
they would have to come back with levers, but it began, inch by agonizing inch, to slide. They got it perhaps six inches and had to stop,
panting.

Fingers slid out of the gap and caught the edge. Marra nearly wept
with relief. Fenris shoved the lid aside and sat up, gasping for air.

"You're really here," he said, bending over so that his forehead touched his drawn-up knees. "I kept imagining voices, but you're really here this time."

"We're here," said Marra, the words *this time* jabbing her like pins.

He took a half dozen sobbing breaths. "It is very close in there," he said, "even with the holes." His face was slick, with sweat or tears, Marra did not know. "Close and cold."

"I'm sorry," said Marra. "I'm sorry. It was the only way I could think of." She pulled him out of the coffin, or he climbed out and she helped, and he wrapped his arms around her and they stood together, shaking.

"It worked," he said. "I would not want to do it again. How many days has it been?"

"A little over half a day," said the dust-wife.

"Only that? It seemed so much longer."

They slid the lid back in place and crept out of the tomb, through the tomb that had been cut for Kania, through the small, sad room where Marra's niece lay in her bed of stone. She had to help hold Fenris up. His muscles had cramped and knotted and he staggered as he walked. "Why are there no guards?" he whispered.

"Because of the queen," said the dust-wife.

"She could not pull the guards from the entrance without it looking peculiar," said Marra, "but she called on the others to escort her. She had gone to Vorling's mother's tomb. She said that no one thought of the mothers in this time and she wanted to commune with the shade who had lost a child and— Oh, it was amazing. It really was. She's so good at this. At being queen. Everyone was very impressed."

"I was certainly impressed," he said a bit dryly. "When she looked down on me in that stone box, I thought that she was going to let me die a slow death in the dark." One corner of his mouth crooked up. "And I found that I did not want to die. Not like that."

"I'm sorry," said Marra again.

"Don't be. I had faith. I thought if I could just hold out long enough . . . well, you and Lady Fox here would come for me."

The dust-wife snorted. "I would have," she said. "You might not have been alive at the time, though. Dead men are much less trouble."

He staggered again. Marra winced. "Did they torture you?"

"Very little, considering. General Takise is a good man, but more importantly, a good soldier, and he knows how little torture is worth for extracting usable information. I made up a tale that had truth scattered through it, and he decided that I was likely mad, but with the magic we had seen, he could not be sure. Torture only tells you what the victim thinks will save him, and they knew that. So they beat me a little, and when my story did not change to anything they could use, they stopped."

"Where are we going now?" asked Fenris.

"Away." The dust-wife glanced over her shoulder. "Agnes arranged for a cart."

"Agnes is walking around freely?"

Marra laughed. "Everyone remembers her as very tall," she said, "with bright green eyes. It's the damnedest thing."

"She was, though," said Fenris. He had to stop and lean against the wall for a moment, stretching his legs and bending his knee to work the kinks out. "When I saw her. Wasn't she? Was it an illusion, like the one on Bonedog?"

"It's not an illusion," said the dust-wife. "Not exactly. Your mind knows what certain things ought to look like, and when your eyes are wrong, your mind wins. Agnes's magic thinks she ought to be six feet tall with eyes like a starving wolf. That Agnes's body didn't comply is just an oversight, so far as the magic is concerned."

"She's a very wicked godmother, isn't she?" asked Marra.

"Evil magic could flow through her like a river in full flood. Fortunately for the rest of us, there's a lot of Agnes in the way. Whether that makes her wicked, I'll leave to philosophers. This turning here, I think."

They emerged into the gritty light that precedes dawn. Marra barely took note of their surroundings. Another quarry, it looked like. She was too busy helping to shore up Fenris. One step after another, one step, one step more, and then there was a wagon in front of them and Agnes was falling off the driver's seat and threw her arms around them. "You're alive!" she said. "But of course you are; I didn't think you were dead— I mean, Fenris, I thought there was a chance you were dead, I didn't know, but of course Marra wasn't dead—not to disparage the dead, obviously they serve their purposes and we'll all be dead eventually anyway, so you probably shouldn't speak ill of them, although I can't say that I'm sorry to see Vorling go—"

"How is Finder?" asked Fenris, stemming the flow of words.

Agnes rummaged around in her scarf and produced Finder, who was half asleep and clearly indignant at being awoken.

"You need to train him to sit somewhere else," said the dust-wife disapprovingly. "Otherwise you'll have a rooster who thinks he should dive headfirst into your cleavage when he wants to roost."

"It's been a while since any man wanted to dive into my cleavage," said Agnes. "It might be a nice change."

"Not when the spurs grow in."

"Oh, well, probably not."

They got Fenris into the wagon and Marra handed up the bag slung across her back. It rattled as he took it. "What's in here?"

"A friend."

His eyebrows went up. Marra climbed up beside him and she and the dust-wife arranged empty feed sacks to conceal him. He sneezed a few times but did not argue.

"I see you have much to tell me," he said. "Ah . . . not over the face unless it looks like we'll be stopped. I was in that box too long, and having things on my face . . ." He smiled up at her, but it was a thin layer over deeper horror. Marra found his hand under the layers of burlap and squeezed. *Another wound for Vorling's tally. But if we get away, then it is done. It is all done, at last.*

"No talking now," said the dust-wife. The wagon wheels creaked as they left the quarry, going away from the city. Marra pulled the nettle cloak tight around her shoulders, chilly in the predawn cold. Fenris's fingers were warm in hers.

By the time the sun had risen, the white city was behind them. She could still see it, like a canine tooth in the earth's jaw, but it was far away and had no more power to bite.

And I will never go back.

When she had taken leave of her sister for the last time, they had both known it. Kania had said as much. "I do not know how long I can keep you out of this. I can try, but . . ."

"I know," said Marra. "I know. Someone will remember seeing me. Someone will make a connection. As long as I'm here, there's the risk. It's better if I go."

"It's not quite that," said her sister. "Although that is certainly true. You are now the sister of the queen regent of the Northern Kingdom, and you are no longer staying unwed to appease Vorling's paranoia. Mother will begin thinking where to put you."

For a moment, Marra was too astonished to be appalled. "But I'm . . . I'm not a virgin and not a princess. I'm almost a nun!"

"*Almost* is the key," said Kania a bit dryly. "You could rush home and try to take orders, and I will bet you the finest horse in the kingdom that the abbess won't accept them."

Marra inhaled sharply. To be wed for politics. To be shipped off to a strange man's bed, while Fenris lay in a box in the palace of dust, waiting for rescue . . .

"She doesn't mean to be cruel," said Kania. "She isn't. She stopped a war by marrying our family into Vorling's. The Northern Kingdom would have rolled over us like a tide and our people would all be feeding the crabs by now. She had to choose the people over us, and use our bodies to seal the deal." She rubbed absently at her forearm, where the bruises were yellow and faded. "She saved thousands of lives."

"I know," said Marra. "I know."

Kania had given her two gifts before she left. One was a pouch full of money and one was a sack full of bones.

"They gathered them all up," her sister said. "Every one, down to the smallest claw. They were terrified that if they left any, it would give evil magic a way into the room. I told them that they needed to be disposed of properly and that my sister would take them to Our Lady of Grackles for the nuns to sanctify before they were burned."

Marra could not see through sudden tears, but Kania wrapped her arm around her sister's shoulder. "Go," she whispered in Marra's ear. "Run and be free. They cannot use what they cannot find."

And Marra hugged her back and went out through the god-mother's palace door with her hood over her head, then slipped away into the city to meet the dust-wife and save her friends.

* * *

They meandered south, day by day. The wagon was drawn by an exceedingly patient mule who tolerated the brown hen standing on his back. Marra sat in the back of the wagon and worked as well as she could with everything moving and rattling under her. At night, by the fire, she made much better progress, but then the light was bad and she jabbed her fingers bloody again. Agnes tutted and salved her fingertips. The dust-wife watched her, her long face ex-pressionless.

"Will it work?" asked Marra, wrapping wires.

The dust-wife stood looking down at her and her skirt full of bones. "It would never work on a human," she said. "Humans know when they're dead. It might work on a dog. Dogs are simpler."

She slept back-to-back with Fenris at night. No one commented. Sometimes he moved and she knew that he was also awake in the darkness, but neither of them quite had the nerve to act on it, not with Agnes and the dust-wife there. *I could roll over. I could put my arm around his waist. I could . . .*

"I'm going home," said the dust-wife one morning. "Agnes, you should probably come with me. They'll sort out the godmother thing one of these days, and you'll be left trying to fend off the enemy with a chicken."

"I know," said Agnes. "I always expected I'd go with you."

"Oh?"

"Yes, of course." Agnes tapped Finder's beak. The young cock-erel was growing in his adult feathers, though he was still half the size of the brown hen and had no wattles to speak of. "Finder, find me the safest place for me to be."

Finder cocked his head to one side, then turned and walked to the dust-wife's feet, where he began scratching in the dirt after an interesting worm.

"Ah," said the dust-wife.

"But we have to stop by my cottage. I want my good medicine chest and I'm not leaving all my chickens. And I want seeds of all my good plants. And . . ."

"Yes, yes." The dust-wife turned back to Fenris and Marra. "You two will be better off making your own way. By which I mean that all this poorly suppressed longing is giving me hives."

Fenris coughed. Marra put her hands over her face.

"Come see us," said Agnes. "Please. I'll want someone to talk to who isn't grumpy."

"I'm not grumpy."

"You are an absolute grump and so is your chicken." The two old women climbed into the wagon and drove away, still bickering. Marra felt a pang in her heart and a surge of relief, all at once.

They spent the day where they had made camp the night before, in a little shepherd's hut on a hillside, out of the wind. Fenris kept the fire up, and Marra threaded wire through bits of bone, rubbing her fingers across the broad, faithful skull and the long cage of ribs, the narrow whip of tail.

He sat beside her and handed her bones and wire as she asked, but he did not press her.

At sunset, just as the light from the fire became brighter than the light from the doorway, she finished. The skeleton lay across her lap, complete, claws wired to paws, vertebrae strung like beads.

"Wake," she whispered, while the light faded outside the door. "Wake. *Please.*"

The bones lay motionless in her lap. She bowed her head. *Please. Please, Bonedog. I'm never going to see my sister again, or my mother. I'm not going to see the Sister Apothecary or the abbess. I need one more friend. Please.*

It was too much like the first time. The second impossible task was also the third. She had always known that she had gotten off too lightly, being handed the moon in a jar.

Fenris took her free hand, careful of her sore fingertips, and held it between his palms, waiting with her.

"Please," she said again, and a single tear ran hotly down her cheek and splashed on the white expanse of skull.

Bonedog yawned and stretched and woke.

Marra let out a sob of relief and buried her head in Fenris's neck. He held her in the crook of his arm while Bonedog stood up and bounced and cavorted around the hut.

"We'll have to get him enchanted again," said Fenris, watching the dog trying to lick parts that had vanished along with the glamour.

"We'll figure something out."

"Mm. And what happens now? Are you going back to your convent?"

Marra thought about sitting up, but it was very warm against his side. "You said once that you couldn't go back," she said. "You said that homesickness wasn't worth a clan war."

Fenris nodded. "It's still true."

"If I go home now, I don't know what will happen. Maybe nothing. But they'll probably marry me off and I'll be back in that world and I . . . I'm not good at it. I'm so very bad at it. And there's always a chance that someone figures out what we did." Marra took a deep breath. "I think it's more trouble than it's worth."

"Very likely." He was looking at her with that grave, thoughtful look again, but there was a hint of humor in his eyes, which was encouraging or maddening or both together.

"And I already agreed to help you ransom the other humans in the goblin market."

"You did."

"So. Maybe you and I could . . . not go home together?"

The words hung in the air between them, as fine as spun glass and just as fragile. Marra waited for him to say something, to catch the words or shatter them, whichever he chose.

"I think I'd like that," said Fenris.

Marra sagged with relief.

She had been so focused on what he might say that she hadn't quite expected what he might do. So it came as a surprise when he wrapped both arms around her and put his lips against her hair. "I think I would like that very much," he murmured.

"Oh good," said Marra against his neck. And then she would have kissed him or he would have kissed her, but Bonedog decided that they were wrestling and jumped up and barked soundlessly at them both.

Black dog, white dog,
Live dog, dead dog,
Yellow dog, run!

Author's Note

This book started in a grocery store parking lot, with the line "with the dog made of bone at your side." I don't know why, but that line showed up in my head and started hammering away like a tuneless earworm.

It's always neat when something drops in your lap like that, but you generally spend the first hour trying to figure out if you thought of it or if it's a fragment of something you read once. Authors have minds like packrats and a lot of stuff gets squirreled away, some of which belongs to other people. Nevertheless, the line was insistent and didn't seem familiar.

By the time I reached the grocery store, it had grown to "You came to me in your cloak of nettles with the dog made of bone at your side." At the checkout line, I had most of a very short story called "Godmother." It had a lot of imagery in common with the book you just read, though the plot, such as it was, was very different. I put it on the internet and then in an anthology and then went on about my life.

Still, the images nagged at me. Why did she build her own dog out of bones? Why were her hands stained with a prince's blood? What does building your own dog feel like? Who was the godmother narrating the story? Judging by some of my reader mail, it nagged at them too. People wanted to know about the woman with the bone dog.

At the same time and unrelated, in my other life as a children's book author, an editor asked me if I could do a fairy tale retelling of "The Princess and the Pea," and I couldn't do it. I have always found that story . . . well . . . squicky. Why does a prince want a bride with skin that sensitive? If a pea under a dozen mattresses is enough to leave bruises, what would a human touch do? Why would you *want* that? What does it say about the prince? None of my thoughts were the sort of thing you want in an upbeat romp aimed at seven-year-olds. We compromised on "Little Red Riding Hood" and I took my squick elsewhere.

Somewhere between the bone dog and the prince obsessed with tender skin, I wound up with the opening chapters. It included someone called a "dust-wife" about which I knew nothing, and the blistered land and Kania and Damia being married off. And then, as often happens, the story sat fallow for a half dozen years, occasionally getting dusted off and poked and prodded, and then one day I sent about ten thousand words off to my editor with my usual note: "Hey, I got this thing, you want it?" (I have heard some authors write cover letters and synopses and so forth. Someday I will have to try that.)

Well, she did want the thing, as it turned out, and that meant that I had to come up with a lot more book, in relatively short order. What's a dust-wife? What do they do? Where's the godmother? Why are godmothers involved at all? Why is my deadline only two months away? What am I doing? Why did I not become a medical test subject, like Mom always wanted? Do I really need both these kidneys, when the black market for organs is so lucrative?

This is a standard part of the authorial process, and of course the questions got answered and the book got written eventually. I suspect that I would probably still be stuck in the grocery store parking lot if not for the aid of a couple of people, though. First, my fabulous editor, Lindsey Hall, who would get excited about certain bits and thus make me realize I had to actually do something with those bits instead of just leaving them dangling in the wind; my agent, Helen, who has made peace with my "you want this thing?" style of cover letter and makes sure that I actually remember to sign forms and get money for the thing; my beta reader, Shepherd, who explained patiently about spinning and drop spindles and weft locks and tapestries, and even demonstrated how a drop spindle worked, despite my refusal to add more sheep to the book; and my beloved husband, Kevin, who is endlessly supportive and also keeps chickens, several of which found their way into the story in one form or another.

I could probably write books without all these people, but they would be significantly worse books and I would be far more frazzled and possibly short a kidney. Any particularly good bits are probably their fault, and any errors were almost certainly mine, made despite their best efforts to stop me.

I hope your dogs are all loyal and goofy and good-natured and that your chickens remain free of demons.

T. Kingfisher
North Carolina
May 2020

Turn the page for a sneak peek at
T. Kingfisher's bestselling horror novella

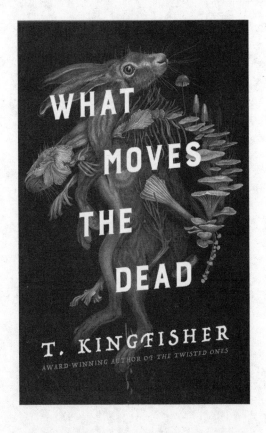

Available now from Tor Nightfire

CHAPTER 1

The mushroom's gills were the deep-red color of severed muscle, the almost-violet shade that contrasts so dreadfully with the pale pink of viscera. I had seen it any number of times in dead deer and dying soldiers, but it startled me to see it here.

Perhaps it would not have been so unsettling if the mushrooms had not looked so much like flesh. The caps were clammy, swollen beige, puffed up against the dark-red gills. They grew out of the gaps in the stones of the tarn like tumors growing from diseased skin. I had a strong urge to step back from them, and an even stronger urge to poke them with a stick.

I felt vaguely guilty about pausing in my trip to dismount and look at mushrooms, but I was tired. More importantly, my horse was tired. Madeline's letter had taken over a week to reach me, and no matter how urgently worded it had been, five minutes more or less would not matter.

Hob, my horse, was grateful for the rest, but seemed

annoyed by the surroundings. He looked at the grass and then up at me, indicating that this was not the quality to which he was accustomed.

"You could have a drink," I said. "A small one, perhaps."

We both looked into the water of the tarn. It lay dark and very still, reflecting the grotesque mushrooms and the limp gray sedges along the edge of the shore. It could have been five feet deep or fifty-five.

"Perhaps not," I said. I found that I didn't have much urge to drink the water either.

Hob sighed in the manner of horses who find the world not to their liking and gazed off into the distance.

I looked across the tarn to the house and sighed myself.

It was not a promising sight. It was an old gloomy manor house in the old gloomy style, a stone monstrosity that the richest man in Europe would be hard-pressed to keep up. One wing had collapsed into a pile of stone and jutting rafters. Madeline lived there with her twin brother, Roderick Usher, who was nothing like the richest man in Europe. Even by Ruravia's small, rather backward standards, the Ushers were genteelly impoverished. By the standards of the rest of Europe's nobility, they were as poor as church mice, and the house showed it.

There were no gardens that I could see. I could smell a faint sweetness in the air, probably from something flowering in the grass, but it wasn't enough to dispel the sense of gloom.

"I shouldn't touch that if I were you," called a voice behind me.

I turned. Hob lifted his head, found the visitor as disappointing as the grass and the tarn, and dropped it again.

She was, as my mother would say, "a woman of a certain

age." In this case, that age was about sixty. She was wearing men's boots and a tweed riding habit that may have predated the manor.

She was tall and broad and had a gigantic hat that made her even taller and broader. She was carrying a notebook and a large leather knapsack.

"Pardon?" I said.

"The mushroom," she said, stopping in front of me. Her accent was British but not London—somewhere off in the countryside, perhaps. "The mushroom, young . . ." Her gaze swept down, touched the military pins on my jacket collar, and I saw a flash of recognition across her face: *Aha!*

No, *recognition* is the wrong term. *Classification,* rather. I waited to see if she would cut the conversation short or carry on.

"I shouldn't touch it if I were you, officer," she said again, pointing to the mushroom.

I looked down at the stick in my hand, as if it belonged to someone else. "Ah—no? Are they poisonous?"

She had a rubbery, mobile face. Her lips pursed together dramatically. "They're stinking redgills. *A. foetida,* not to be confused with *A. foetidissima*—but that's not likely in this part of the world, is it?"

"No?" I guessed.

"No. The *foetidissima* are found in Africa. This one is endemic to this part of Europe. They aren't poisonous, exactly, but—well—"

She put out her hand. I set my stick in it, bemused. Clearly a naturalist. The feeling of being classified made more sense now. I had been categorized, placed into the correct clade, and the proper courtesies could now be deployed, while we went on to more critical matters like mushroom taxonomy.

"I suggest you hold your horse," she said. "And perhaps your nose." Reaching into her knapsack, she fished out a handkerchief, held it to her nose, and then flicked the stinking redgill mushroom with the very end of the stick.

It was a very light tap indeed, but the mushroom's cap immediately bruised the same visceral red-violet as the gills. A moment later, we were struck by an indescribable smell—rotting flesh with a tongue-coating glaze of spoiled milk and, rather horribly, an undertone of fresh-baked bread. It wiped out any sweetness to the air and made my stomach lurch.

Hob snorted and yanked at his reins. I didn't blame him. "Gahh!"

"That was a little one," said the woman of a certain age. "And not fully ripe yet, thank heavens. The big ones will knock your socks off and curl your hair." She set the stick down, keeping the handkerchief over her mouth with her free hand. "Hence the 'stinking' part of the common name. The 'redgill,' I trust, is self-explanatory."

"Vile!" I said, holding my arm over my face. "Are you a mycologist, then?"

I could not see her mouth through the handkerchief, but her eyebrows were wry. "An amateur only, I fear, as supposedly befits my sex."

She bit off each word, and we shared a look of wary understanding. England has no sworn soldiers, I am told, and even if it had, she might have chosen a different way. It was none of my business, as I was none of hers. We all make our own way in the world, or don't. Still, I could guess at the shape of some of the obstacles she had faced.

"Professionally, I am an illustrator," she said crisply. "But the study of fungi has intrigued me all my life."

"And it brought you here?"

"Ah!" She gestured with the handkerchief. "I do not know what you know of fungi, but this place is extraordinary! So many unusual forms! I have found boletes that previously were unknown outside of Italy, and one *Amanita* that appears to be entirely new. When I have finished my drawings, amateur or no, the Mycology Society will have no choice but to recognize it."

"And what will you call it?" I asked. I am delighted by obscure passions, no matter how unusual. During the war, I was once holed up in a shepherd's cottage, listening for the enemy to come up the hillside, when the shepherd launched into an impassioned diatribe on the finer points of sheep breeding that rivaled any sermon I have ever heard in my life. By the end, I was nodding along and willing to launch a crusade against all weak, overbred flocks, prone to scours and fly-strike, crowding out the honest sheep of the world.

"Maggots!" he'd said, shaking his finger at me. "Maggots 'n piss in t' flaps o' they hides!"

I think of him often.

"I shall call it *A. potteri*," said my new acquaintance, who fortunately did not know where my thoughts were trending. "I am Eugenia Potter, and I shall have my name writ in the books of the Mycology Society one way or another."

"I believe that you shall," I said gravely. "I am Alex Easton." I bowed.

She nodded. A lesser spirit might have been embarrassed to have blurted her passions aloud in such a fashion, but clearly Miss Potter was beyond such weaknesses—or perhaps she simply assumed that anyone would recognize the importance of leaving one's mark in the annals of mycology.

"These stinking redgills," I said, "they are not new to science?"

She shook her head. "Described years ago," she said. "From this very stretch of countryside, I believe, or one near to it. The Ushers were great supporters of the arts long ago, and one commissioned a botanical work. Mostly of *flowers*"—her contempt was a glorious thing to hear—"but a few mushrooms as well. And even a botanist could not overlook *A. foetida.* I fear that I cannot tell you its common name in Gallacian, though."

"It may not have one." If you have never met a Gallacian, the first thing you must know is that Gallacia is home to a stubborn, proud, fierce people who are also absolutely piss-poor warriors. My ancestors roamed Europe, picking fights and having the tar beaten out of them by virtually every other people they ran across. They finally settled in Gallacia, which is near Moldavia and even smaller. Presumably they settled there because nobody else wanted it. The Ottoman Empire didn't even bother to make us a vassal state, if that tells you anything. It's cold and poor and if you don't die from falling in a hole or starving to death, a wolf eats you. The one thing going for it is that we aren't invaded often, or at least we weren't, until the previous war.

In the course of all that wandering around losing fights, we developed our own language, Gallacian. I am told it is worse than Finnish, which is impressive. Every time we lost a fight, we made off with a few more loan words from our enemies. The upshot of all of this is that the Gallacian language is intensely idiosyncratic. (We have seven sets of pronouns, for example, one of which is for inanimate objects and one of which is used only for God. It's probably a miracle that we don't have one just for mushrooms.)

Miss Potter nodded. "That is the Usher house on the other side of the tarn, if you were curious."

"Indeed," I said, "it is where I am headed. Madeline Usher was a friend of my youth."

"Oh," said Miss Potter, sounding hesitant for the first time. She looked away. "I have heard she is very ill. I am sorry."

"It has been a number of years," I said, instinctively touching the pocket with Madeline's letter tucked into it.

"Perhaps it is not so bad as they say," she said, in what was undoubtedly meant to be a jollying tone. "You know how bad news grows in villages. Sneeze at noon and by sundown the gravedigger will be taking your measurements."

"We can but hope." I looked down again into the tarn. A faint wind stirred up ripples, which lapped at the edges. As we watched, a stone dropped from somewhere on the house and plummeted into the water. Even the splash seemed muted.

Eugenia Potter shook herself. "Well, I have sketching to do. Good luck to you, Officer Easton."

"And to you, Miss Potter. I shall look forward to word of your *Amanitas.*"

Her lips twitched. "If not the *Amanitas,* I have great hopes for some of these boletes." She waved to me and strode out across the field, leaving silver boot prints in the damp grass.

I led Hob back to the road, which skirted the edge of the lake. It was a joyless scene, even with the end of the journey in sight. There were more of the pale sedges and a few dead trees, too gray and decayed for me to identify. (Miss Potter presumably knew what they were, although I would never ask her to lower herself to identifying mere vegetation.) Mosses coated the edges of the stones and more of the stinking redgills pushed up in obscene little lumps. The house squatted over it like the largest mushroom of them all.

My tinnitus chose that moment to strike, a high-pitched

whine ringing through my ears and drowning out even the soft lapping of the tarn. I stopped and waited for it to pass. It's not dangerous, but sometimes my balance becomes a trifle questionable, and I had no desire to stumble into the lake. Hob is used to this and waited with the stoic air of a martyr undergoing torture.

Sadly, while my ears sorted themselves out, I had nothing to look at but the building. God, but it was a depressing scene.

It is a cliché to say that a building's windows look like eyes because humans will find faces in anything and of course the windows would be the eyes. The house of Usher had dozens of eyes, so either it was a great many faces lined up together or it was the face of some creature belonging to a different order of life—a spider, perhaps, with rows of eyes along its head.

I'm not, for the most part, an imaginative soul. Put me in the most haunted house in Europe for a night, and I shall sleep soundly and wake in the morning with a good appetite. I lack any psychic sensitivities whatsoever. Animals like me, but I occasionally think they must find me frustrating, as they stare and twitch at unknown spirits and I say inane things like "Who's a good fellow, then?" and "Does kitty want a treat?" (Look, if you don't make a fool of yourself over animals, at least in private, you aren't to be trusted. That was one of my father's maxims, and it's never failed me yet.)

Given that lack of imagination, perhaps you will forgive me when I say that the whole place felt like a hangover.

What was it about the house and the tarn that was so depressing? Battlefields are grim, of course, but no one questions why. This was just another gloomy lake, with a gloomy house and some gloomy plants. It shouldn't have affected my spirits so strongly.

Granted, the plants all looked dead or dying. Granted, the windows of the house stared down like eye sockets in a row of skulls, yes, but so what? Actual rows of skulls wouldn't affect me so strongly. I knew a collector in Paris . . . well, never mind the details. He was the gentlest of souls, though he did collect rather odd things. But he used to put festive hats on his skulls depending on the season, and they all looked rather jolly.

Usher's house was going to require more than festive hats. I mounted Hob and urged him into a trot, the sooner to get to the house and put the scene behind me.

About the Author

JR Blackwell

T. KINGFISHER writes fantasy, horror, and occasional oddities, most recently including *What Moves the Dead* and *A House With Good Bones*. Under a pen name, she also writes bestselling children's books. She lives in North Carolina with her husband, dogs, and chickens who may or may not be possessed.

Look out for T. Kingfisher's
next novel from Tor Publishing Group

Available Spring 2023 from Tor Nightfire